"I'm sorry."

Lars's apology for the kiss only made Nikki angrier. Hadn't he felt what she had—that spark between them? She'd never felt anything like it before. But maybe she'd only imagined it.

"Why the hell did you do that?" she asked.

He shrugged.

"Well, don't do it again."

"Or what?" he challenged her, and he leaned a little closer as if he intended to do it again.

Her pulse leaped, and she nearly licked her lips. But she could taste him already—or still—on the tip of her tongue.

"Will you tell your brother on me?" he asked.

"No," she said. "I'll just slap you again."

He touched his fingers to his cheek—not that she actually believed he'd felt her blow. She could have hit him harder. But then she hadn't really wanted to hurt him. She'd only wanted him to stop—to stop making her feel what she didn't want to feel. Attraction. Temptation. Desire.

* * *

Be sure to check out the previous books in the exciting Bachelor Bodyguards miniseries.

* * *

If you're on Twitter, tell us what you think of Harlequin Romantic Suspense! #harlequinromsuspense

Dear Reader,

I hope you've been enjoying my Bachelor Bodyguard series about the Payne Protection Agency. Many readers have asked me when Nikki Payne was finally going to get her story, and I'm thrilled to say right now! Poor Nikki has been waiting for years for her brothers to give her a real bodyguard assignment. When she finally gets one, as the nanny bodyguard, the job is not what she expected, and neither is Lars Ecklund. He's an old friend of her brother Cooper and now works for Cooper with Nikki as a bodyguard. But Lars has ulterior motives for joining his friend's franchise of the Payne Protection Agency. Nikki has vowed to never risk her heart on a man she can't trust, and Lars is keeping secrets. Those secrets might not only cost Nikki her heart but her life, as well.

As always, the Payne family sticks together, so you will see characters from earlier books in the series. And just because Penny found her own happiness doesn't mean she's stopped meddling in the lives of her children. I hope you enjoy Nikki's story, and that it will prove worth the wait!

Happy reading!

Lisa Childs

NANNY
BODYGUARD

Lisa Childs

PAPL
DISCARDED

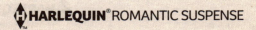

HARLEQUIN® ROMANTIC SUSPENSE

Recycling programs
for this product may
not exist in your area.

ISBN-13: 978-0-373-40202-1

Nanny Bodyguard

Copyright © 2017 by Lisa Childs

Printed in U.S.A.

Ever since **Lisa Childs** read her first romance novel (a Harlequin story, of course) at age eleven, all she wanted was to be a romance writer. With over forty novels published with Harlequin, Lisa is living her dream. She is an award-winning, bestselling romance author. Lisa loves to hear from readers, who can contact her on Facebook, through her website, lisachilds.com, or her snail-mail address, PO Box 139, Marne, MI 49435.

For all the wonderful readers who've been asking me for Nikki's story—here it is! Thank you so much for following the Payne family from Shotgun Weddings to Bachelor Bodyguards!

Prologue

The alarm blared with such intensity the windows rattled. But the door held tight, the lock refusing to budge. Just messing with it had triggered the ultra-sensitive alarm. The sirens screeched so loudly that the noise blasted Lars Ecklund's head, threatening to split his skull. He squinted against the strobe lights flashing in the night and grasped the stubborn doorknob, struggling to turn it.

He was too close to give up without getting inside the three-story brick, glass and wrought iron mansion. But was it a house or a prison? Was his sister in there? He needed to know, needed to get to her. Now. She had been missing too long already.

Strong hands grabbed his arms, dragging him back. He turned toward the other man. The muscular guy was intimidating as hell with an intense dark-eyed stare. Lars couldn't hear what he was saying, but he didn't need to. He knew.

We need to get the hell out of here...

Frustration gripped him. He wanted to refuse, wanted to stay even if the police showed up. But his friend wouldn't leave him. A Marine never left a man behind. And he couldn't risk Dane getting in trouble, too.

Or worse...

Gunfire flashed. With the alarm blaring, he couldn't hear the shots, but he saw them like bursts of light in the darkness. These weren't police officers; they wouldn't have arrived yet.

These were security guards. Hell, they weren't even that or they wouldn't have fired before investigating. They were hired guns. Lars reached for his weapon to return fire.

But Dane dragged him off—to where the truck waited in the driveway. His friend shoved him inside the open passenger's door before slamming it shut on him and rushing around to the driver's side. As Dane shifted the truck into Reverse, Lars peered through the windshield at the dark house.

Was Emilia locked in there? Was that why he hadn't heard from her in months?

"We need to get inside!" he yelled at his friend.

His arm across the back of the seat as he reversed the truck, Dane shook his head. "We'll be lucky if we get out of here."

And as he said that, the gates in the tall brick wall surrounding the estate began to close. The dark-clothed gunmen advanced on the truck, shots pinging off the metal and hitting the glass.

No. They might not get out—alive.

Chapter 1

Cooper Payne had known these guys a long time. He would trust them with his life. Hell, he had. But could he trust them with this chance to prove himself to his older brothers? He stared across his desk, like he'd watched his brother Logan do a hundred times, at the four guys seated across from him. But this was his desk—his office—his franchise of the Payne Protection Agency.

He suppressed the surge of pride that threatened to swell his chest. He hadn't earned a right to that pride—not yet. His office had just opened, and he had only one employee. And that employee was his sister. He needed these guys but he sensed the hesitation in them.

Hell, Lars Ecklund, who was probably his closest friend in his Marine Corps unit, wouldn't even meet his gaze. Usually Lars was so direct, his eerily pale blue

eyes stared through a person—making the Marine even more intimidating than his massive size.

Dane Sutton nudged Lars's shoulder with his. He was a big guy, too—nearly bald his dark hair was so short, with eyes that went from topaz to black depending on his temper.

All four of them were big; that was why Cooper needed them. He wanted the biggest, toughest bodyguards Payne Protection offered to be on *his* team.

"I'm in," Jordan "Manny" Mannes told him. And he extended his hand across Cooper's desk to shake on it. He was dark haired and dark eyed—nearly the direct opposite of Lars's blond hair and light eyes. But he was just as big.

"Me, too," Cole Bentler said. He also shook on it. At just a couple inches over six feet, he was probably the smallest of the four guys, but his grasp was strong. He was blond like Lars but his hair was a much darker shade of it.

"You sure?" Cooper felt compelled to ask him. "River City is a long way from your family."

Cole glanced around at the other guys in the room and shook his head. "No, it's not."

They were family. After everything they'd endured together, they were closer than family. No one understood them like each other.

Dane extended his hand across the desk, too. "Thanks, Cooper, for thinking of us."

He had felt bad—like he'd left them behind when he hadn't reenlisted when they all had. They had just returned from their last deployment whereas he'd been back over a year. He'd gotten married, had a baby and

had never been happier. He wanted that happiness for his friends.

"Always," he told Dane. He'd thought of them the entire time they'd been gone. He'd worried and prayed and hoped they would all return.

Dane nudged Lars, who finally met Cooper's gaze. Was his friend okay? Or had he come back like Gage Huxton—another Payne Protection bodyguard—damaged from everything he'd been through?

Lars's broad shoulders were slumped as if something was weighing on him, and there were dark circles beneath his pale eyes.

What the hell had happened on that last deployment?

"Are you up for this?" Cooper asked, concern and guilt gripping him that he hadn't been with them—that he didn't know what dangers they'd faced. "I know you guys haven't been back long." Just a couple of weeks.

Maybe he should have given them more time. But then he knew downtime was usually the last thing a Marine wanted; it gave him too much time to think. The other guys didn't look like Lars, though. They didn't look rested or relaxed but they also didn't look like he did, like something was haunting him.

Nikki Payne refused to be haunted. She would not let that bitch get to her. She wouldn't see those eyes—with the life slipping from them to leave only hatred—in her sleep. If she could sleep...

But it wasn't like she had time to sleep anyway. She needed to help Cooper get his franchise of Payne Protection up and running. She had set up all the computers, had security systems ready to install, ads ready to be placed in every publication online and in print.

But that wasn't what she really wanted to do; she wanted—she needed—to be out in the field. She needed to actually do protection duty, not desk duty. That was why she'd left her oldest brother Logan's franchise— because he'd been determined to keep her chained to a desk.

But so far Cooper had, too. He claimed it was because they didn't have any assignments yet. But she knew he'd had inquiries. His wife, Tanya, worked as a social worker, and an adoption lawyer she knew had asked her about Payne Protection. Everyone knew about their family security business. They'd had a hell of a couple of years.

So maybe it was no wonder that Nikki lay awake at night, her eyes open so that she wouldn't see the gun- fire and the explosions and the death...

She shuddered as she remembered how close she had come a few times to death herself. The car crashes, the gunfire...

But she had survived every danger. Hadn't that proved to her brothers that she could handle the job? That she could handle anything?

She stared at Cooper's office door. It had been closed since she'd come in, which was strange. His door hadn't been closed since he'd opened the office six weeks ago. Well, unless Tanya stopped by to visit...

Nikki was glad he closed it then. She'd seen too much romance and love the past couple of years, too. It sick- ened her nearly as much as the danger and the death. She would never be so stupid as to risk her heart like her brothers and now even her mother had.

She would much rather risk her life.

If Cooper ever gave her the chance...

The knob rattled just before his door opened. She settled onto the edge of the receptionist desk, for the receptionist they had yet to hire, and turned to the door with a smile. Tanya Chesterfield was Nikki's first sister-in-law and as Cooper's childhood crush and friend, the woman had been a part of their lives nearly as long as Nikki could remember. She loved her like a sister. But it wasn't the beautiful blonde who walked out the door.

It was a mammoth blond. The guy was so big he had to turn a little for his shoulders to fit through the doorway, and he had to duck slightly so he didn't hit his head. When his eyes—an eerily pale blue—focused on Nikki, her pulse quickened. Some other guys filed out with him. They were nearly as big but she barely noticed them or her brother, who stepped out of his office behind them.

"This your secretary, Coop?" the big blond guy asked. "Can't imagine your wife is too happy having a beauty like this working with you."

Despite the backhanded compliment, Nikki's blood heated with anger. "I am not a secretary," she answered for herself. "I'm a bodyguard."

The guy's gaze skimmed down her petite body, and his mouth curved into a slight grin. "Okay..." he remarked, as if humoring her.

"Lars, this is my sister, Nikki." Cooper introduced them.

The guy's face flushed slightly. "Oh, sorry..."

Nikki knew the bro code: guys' sisters were off-limits. Apparently her brother Nick hadn't gotten that memo when he got his best friend's sister pregnant. But he and Gage were good now that Annalise and Nick

had gotten married, and their son—Woodrow Gage Payne—had been born.

Cooper didn't need to worry about any of his friends getting that close to her. She had sworn off relationships; they weren't worth the risk.

Now a fling…

Maybe then she would be able to sleep again. With the dark circles under his eyes, Lars didn't look like he'd been getting much more rest than she was. Not that she would be interested in any of these guys even for a fling. These were macho males like her brothers who would mistake her size for weakness—like Lars apparently already had.

Cooper introduced the others. "Dane Sutton, Cole Bentler, Manny Mannes…"

She shook hands with each of them, who treated her with more respect than Lars had. But then they now knew she was Cooper's sister.

Then Cooper announced, "These guys are part of my old unit with the Corps. And now they're my new team."

They were his team. But what about her? Was there a place for her on it that wasn't behind a desk?

She didn't like this, not at all. And she especially didn't like Lars Ecklund because she was worried that he might be right. Maybe Cooper hadn't hired a receptionist because he wanted her for that position.

Lars had royally pissed off the cute, little brunette. He felt her angry gaze boring a hole in his back as he walked out of the office of the Payne Protection Agency. But minutes later, as he climbed into the pickup beside Dane, he realized she wasn't the only one he'd pissed off.

Dane had already been irritated that his truck was in a shop for repair of the bullet holes and gate scrape and that he'd had to ride with Lars.

"What the hell's the matter with you?" Dane asked from the passenger seat.

"Hey, I didn't know she was Coop's sister," Lars defended himself.

But he was embarrassed. Not that he'd flirted with her but that he'd come across like such a chauvinistic jackass. The way Cooper had been looking at him in the office had made him nervous. His friend had known something was up, so Lars had been struggling to act like his old self. While he hadn't been the playboy of their unit, he had never let a pretty girl pass him without making a compliment. He hadn't complimented Nikki, though; he'd insulted her.

"I wasn't talking about that," Dane said. "We were all together. Why didn't you tell anyone else that Emilia's missing?"

A twinge of pain struck Lars's heart. "I can't."

"You know they would help you," Dane said. "We're all there for each other. It's what we did. It's what we do."

It was who they were. Even though Lars had never had much of one—but for Emilia—he knew their unit was family. And not the kind that bickered and fought like Cole Bentler's but the kind that would do anything for each other. "That's why I can't tell them."

"Because they'll help you?"

He nodded. Then he turned the key in the ignition to start up the truck. They should have used his vehicle the other night, but Dane had worried that the security

guards might have already noticed him casing the estate and following the lawyer.

"You're losing it, Lars," Dane said, shaking his head. They'd been friends so long that he knew when not to argue with Lars. So he said nothing more.

But because they'd been friends so long, Lars owed him an explanation. "I have no proof," he said. "I'm not even sure my sister is still in River City."

He had told her that if she got in trouble and needed help while he was deployed, that she should come to River City—to Cooper. She hadn't met with Cooper, though. In her last letter, she'd told him that she'd come here but she was going to meet with a lawyer instead of his friend.

That lawyer wouldn't even take Lars's calls. Anger tightened his stomach muscles into knots. He had to have something to do with Emilia's disappearance. He had to know where she was.

Because he was a lawyer, he knew his rights. Even if Lars called the police, they wouldn't have enough cause to be granted a search warrant. So Lars wouldn't be able to legally get inside that estate. That was why he and Dane had resorted to illegal methods.

Methods that could have gotten them in prison or a casket. Cooper had too much going for him right now with his new family and his new business. Lars wouldn't let his friend risk his life on his hunch.

The same went for Manny and Cole, too. If he told them, they wouldn't give him a choice—just like Dane hadn't. He shouldn't have told Dane, but his friend had caught him in a weak moment, when the fear for Emilia had been overwhelming him.

Not being able to find her...

Not knowing where she was…

He hated it—hated feeling helpless—just like he'd felt when they'd lost their mom to her disease. He hadn't been able to help her, either, hadn't been able to save her.

He had to save Emilia.

"You don't need proof for your friends," Dane said.

He hadn't needed proof to offer to help. He had trusted Lars's instincts that something was wrong. During their deployments, they'd had to trust each other, or they wouldn't have survived.

"No," Lars agreed. "But I need proof to keep my friends out of trouble. We can't go storming in on a hunch."

Dane grinned. "Again?"

"We barely got out of there alive," Lars reminded him.

The gates had scraped along the sides of the pickup as Dane had backed out, but he had made it onto the street. And they had escaped the gunfire with only the truck getting hit, not them.

This time.

He had no idea what might happen next time. The lawyer had already taken measures to increase security at the estate. Myron Webber was determined to make sure nobody got in.

Or out?

"We need a better plan before we try again," Lars said.

And taking the bodyguard job was the biggest part of that plan. Since he'd been following the lawyer, he knew how the guy intended to increase security. He'd overheard a conversation the guy had had with a pretty blonde woman Lars had recognized from the picture Cooper had carried in his wallet since boot camp. And

now he knew: Myron Webber intended to hire the Payne Protection Agency.

Lars felt a flash of guilt for taking advantage of his friend. That was why Cooper couldn't know. This way he had plausible deniability for whatever Lars had to do in order to find his sister.

And Lars would do whatever was necessary for Emilia. He had promised their dying mother that he would always keep his sister safe, that he wouldn't let anything happen to her. He had to find Emilia; he had to keep that promise.

He didn't care if he wound up in prison or a casket.

Chapter 2

The blow struck Nikki's chin with enough force to snap her neck back. She grunted as her teeth snapped together.

"Sorry," Candace Baker-Kozminski murmured as she lowered her gloves. "You need to protect yourself better."

That wasn't the first time Nikki had been told that and not just from Candace.

"I know," she replied, and she tasted the metallic flavor of blood in her mouth. She lifted her gloves in front of her face and struck out.

Candace easily dodged her blow. Of course all she needed to do was lift her head. She was so much taller than Nikki. Most people were, except for her mother. They were both petite, curly-haired brunettes.

Why couldn't Nikki have inherited the male DNA in her family? Her brothers were tall and muscular like

their dad had been. Not that Nikki remembered him all that well—he'd been dead so long. But she would never forget what he'd done, how he'd hurt her mother.

Candace struck her again—a glancing blow off her shoulder that propelled Nikki back a few steps—in the middle of the dimly lit gym. They were the only ones in the place, thanks to Nikki charming a key from the owner.

"What the hell's wrong?" Candace asked. "You are not protecting yourself at all."

Nikki was. She was protecting herself from the heartache her mother had suffered. "I'm a little distracted."

"A little." Candace snorted.

"Maybe more than a little," Nikki admitted, and as she said it, an image of a light-eyed, blond-haired giant popped into her mind.

Candace lowered her gloves, and her navy blue eyes warmed with concern. "Is it about the shooting at the church?" she asked. "Is it bothering you?"

"That I killed that bitch?" Nikki shook her head and lied, "Not at all."

If she hadn't shot the gunwoman who'd crashed a wedding at the chapel Nikki's mother owned, Andrea Nielsen would have killed her and probably more innocent people. Before Nikki had taken her out, Andrea had shot a good man, the man who would soon be Nikki's stepfather.

"Well, something's bothering you," Candace persisted. "What is it?"

Nikki sighed. Her friend and fellow bodyguard wasn't going to give up until she'd made Nikki talk. So she talked. "Cooper hired some more bodyguards."

"That's great," Candace said. Then she narrowed her eyes as she studied Nikki's face. "Isn't it?"

She shook her head. "No."

"You didn't really think you would be his only employee, did you?" Candace asked with a teasing smile.

"No. But I thought he'd let me be a real bodyguard." Of her three brothers who now ran branches of Payne Protection, she'd thought Cooper would be the most likely to actually let her do protection duty.

"What makes you think that he won't?" Candace asked.

Nikki snorted now. "He's going to send me out in the field over the four former Marines he hired? Not damned likely." She swung now, and this time she struck Candace's arm. The glove bounced off the woman's hard biceps.

No matter how many weights Nikki lifted, she doubted she would ever develop the muscles her idol, Payne Protection's previously only female bodyguard, had.

"Why don't you ask Logan if you can open your own branch?" Nikki asked.

Candace had been with Payne Protection when Logan had first started the agency. She'd left the River City Police Department to work with him. If Candace had her own franchise, she would hire Nikki. And since she'd been working with Nikki, she knew she could handle field work.

Candace's lips curved into a slight smile, and she shook her head. "I don't want my own business."

But she wanted something—that was clear from her wistful smile. Candace had once had a crush on her boss, but now she was blissfully happy with her former

nemesis and current husband, Garek Kozminski. What else could she want?

Nikki groaned as she realized what it probably was. "Not you, too."

"What?" Candace asked.

"All the damn babies in this family got to you and now you want one?"

Candace's face flushed bright red.

And Nikki pulled her gloved hands back to her sides. "You're not already…" She hated to think that she'd been sparring with a pregnant woman.

Candace shook her head. "Not yet."

"But you want to try?" Nikki asked. "What about Garek?"

Candace smiled. "He wasn't sure he was ready to be a father yet. But he loves his nephew so much that he can't wait now to have a child of our own."

Nikki shuddered. While she loved her nephews and nieces, she didn't want a baby. She couldn't imagine having one of her own. Since Candace was her friend, though, she summoned a smile and said, "Well, congratulations."

Candace laughed. "You think I'm crazy."

"Only if you expect me to babysit."

Candace laughed harder. "I know better than to ever ask you to watch my kid."

Nikki laughed, too. Maybe she should have been offended, but she was just relieved. Just like she wanted nothing to do with macho men, she wanted nothing to do with babies, either. "Good. Now that we have that cleared up, we can get back to sparring."

Now that she knew she wasn't fighting a pregnant woman.

Candace shook her head. "No, it's not fair. You're so distracted I'm going to knock you out cold."

Nikki grimaced but didn't argue.

"You need to go—talk to Cooper," Candace urged her.

Nikki sighed but again she didn't argue. Then a ringing phone jangled in the quiet of the dimly lit gym. She glanced at her cell sitting on the edge of the boxing ring, under the ropes. The screen lit up with Cooper's name.

"Speak of the devil," she murmured, although Cooper had always been the favorite of her brothers. Until Nick had showed up...

She hadn't been thrilled with his existence at first. But he didn't treat her like the delicate princess her other brothers did. Yeah, it was time to talk to Cooper, time to see if he really intended to give her field work or tie her to the desk like Logan had.

Candace wasn't willing to open her own franchise. But maybe Nick would...

A rush of adrenaline coursed through Cooper. This was it: the first assignment for his franchise of Payne Protection. He was relieved that he finally had his first real job, but he was scared, too. It was all up to him now—up to him and his team to solve the client's problem and protect his interests. But Cooper couldn't help but feel that Myron Webber wasn't being completely honest with him.

He stared across his desk at the dark-haired lawyer and asked again, "You really don't have any idea who might have broken into your estate?"

Myron shrugged. "I'm a wealthy man, Mr. Payne."

"Cooper," he corrected him. The guy was a colleague of Tanya's but Cooper had never met him before.

Myron nodded but he didn't repeat it, like he didn't particularly care what Cooper's first name was. "I assume they were after money," Myron said. "Valuables…"

Cooper glanced down at the notes he'd taken. The lawyer already had a pretty good security system—a high-tech alarm system backed up with armed guards. "They could have picked an easier house to try to get inside if that was the case," he said. "Are you sure you don't have anything of *particular* interest to someone?"

Myron tilted his head at such an angle that Cooper was surprised his toupee didn't slide off. It had to be a wig; it was too thick and dark and perfect to be real. Then the guy narrowed his already small, dark eyes. "I don't think I understand what you're getting at."

Obviously—since he hadn't been forthcoming yet. "I'm just thinking that if it's a certain valuable someone's after that you might be better able to protect it if you were to put it in a safety deposit box in a bank vault."

Myron Webber chuckled. "That would not be possible at all…"

"So you do have some idea what the intruders were after?" And why hadn't he freely admitted it?

The lawyer shrugged his thin shoulders again. "Until the intruders are caught, I have no way of knowing for certain."

Cooper knew better than to argue with an attorney. His best friend was a lawyer, but Steven rarely argued with anyone. He suspected that wasn't the case with Myron Webber. "Do the police have any leads?" he asked the man.

The guy stared blankly at him.

"You have called the police." He made it a statement even though it was clear the guy had not done it. Why not?

Myron sighed. "I am a lawyer," he said, "bound to protect my clients' confidentiality."

"I don't think a police investigation would compromise your ability to do that." But Cooper couldn't be certain. He had never been in law enforcement the way his brothers had been. He could ask one of them, but he really wanted to handle this assignment without their help.

"My clients might not see it that way," Myron said. "That's why I'm hiring you. Not only do I need to make my estate secure from future intrusions, but I also need to find out who's trying to get inside and why."

Of course Cooper's first job wouldn't be a simple one.

"I'll have my computer expert review the surveillance footage you brought me," he said. He had already called Nikki to come to the office to work her magic. "I'll also need to come out to your estate to assess what you'll need to increase protection."

"Everything," Myron said as he stood up. "I need a security team and an alarm system that I can trust."

Cooper stood, too, and extended his hand across his desk. "You can trust Payne Protection."

The guy hesitated a moment before he slid his slightly sweaty palm into Cooper's hand. "I'm counting on that."

Cooper wished he had a client he could trust. He couldn't shake the suspicion that Myron Webber was keeping something more than his clients' confidentiality.

* * *

Lars Ecklund's heart beat fast and hard, and it wasn't just because Nikki Payne was so damn beautiful. It was because she was going to be the one to bust him and Dane for the break-in at Webber's estate. Lars had been eavesdropping outside Coop's office since he'd arrived—even before Webber had shown up for his appointment. Lars knew about the surveillance footage, but he hadn't been able to get to it before Cooper had handed the tapes off to his little sister.

She was little, so very petite that when he stepped into her path as she exited her brother's office, her head barely reached his chest as her body slammed into his. Her breath escaped in a gasp he felt through the thin material of his black T-shirt. Despite how hard she'd hit him, she didn't stumble back or fall, and she certainly hadn't loosened her grasp on the small laptop she held.

Lars had his hand on it, too, but he couldn't tug it from her without her noticing. He couldn't knock it free from her grip, either, to smash it onto the floor like he'd intended. He needed to break the damn laptop, needed to buy him and Dane some time to find out what might be on the footage.

They'd been careful. But had they been careful enough?

She stepped back and glared up at him, her face flushed with anger and her brown eyes narrowed with suspicion. "What the hell are you doing?"

"I didn't see you," he said, his voice gruff with the lie.

She flinched.

"I'm sorry," he said. "Did I hurt you?"

She shook her head.

He didn't think he had physically injured her. But

maybe claiming he hadn't seen her had struck a nerve with her somehow. He couldn't imagine a woman like Nikki Payne ever going unseen. In addition to her beauty, she had a vitality that radiated from her like an energy field that Lars could feel.

His sister, Emilia, never went unnoticed, either. She was so beautiful, with a bright smile and sunny disposition. How had she just disappeared? Where the hell was she? Was she the valuable the lawyer had laughed over trying to fit in a safety deposit box?

"Are you okay?" Nikki asked him as she continued to study his face.

He expelled a ragged breath and fought the temptation to tell her about Emilia. He didn't even know why he was tempted to share with her of all people; he hardly knew her. She would no doubt tell her brother anyway. Hell, she might even tell Myron Webber. Lars didn't know her, so he couldn't trust her. He shouldn't trust any woman.

So many of his buddies had gotten that damn Dear John letter while they'd been deployed. He'd even got one himself, not that he'd been all that serious about the woman. Knowing that he would enlist in the Marines, he'd been careful never to get too serious with anyone. Never to trust any woman.

Even Emilia hadn't done what he'd told her; she hadn't gone to Cooper for help. Instead she'd trusted the wrong person. What had Webber done to her?

Nikki stepped closer to him and peered intently up into his face, and now her brown eyes were warm with concern. "What's wrong?"

Everything. But he couldn't tell her, so he forced a

cocky grin. "Just disappointed...that you're Cooper's sister."

"Join the club," she murmured. But she wasn't flirting back with him. Instead she blinked hard and shoved around him, stomping across the brick and glass reception area to another office.

He followed her and not just in the hope that he could get his hands on that laptop. He wanted to know what had upset her. So before she could slam the door shut behind herself, he caught it and stepped inside with her. Then he closed the door, shutting them both inside the small space. There was only room for a desk, her chair behind it and two small chairs in front of it. The outside walls were brick, the interior ones darkly paneled like the door behind his back.

"What the hell do you want?" she asked.

To find his sister alive and well. To get the damn surveillance footage away from her. And Nikki...

No. He could not *want* her. He barely knew her. And she was Cooper's sister.

"I want to find out why you're so pissed off," he said.

"Some big lunkhead nearly plowed me over," she said as she settled onto the chair behind her desk.

"That big lunkhead apologized," he said. Trying to knock the computer out of her hand had been a stupid move, but then he did stupid things when he was desperate. And he was desperate to find Emilia.

His sister wasn't like Nikki. She was sweet and innocent. Maybe he shouldn't have sheltered her as much as he had. But life had been so tough for her. First their mom had gotten sick—with MS—then their dad had taken off. Lars had had to enlist right out of high school in order to support them. Thankfully, his aunt had

helped take care of Mom and Emilia. And when Mom had died, Emilia had gone off to an all-girls boarding school and then college.

She was completely unaware of the dangers in the world. And that was his fault.

Nikki opened the laptop and pressed a couple of keys.

His heart rate accelerated. What would she see on that surveillance footage? Had he and Dane taken out all of the cameras? Or had they missed some?

"If my apology wasn't enough, I can help you with whatever you're working on," he offered.

She snorted derisively.

"What?" he asked, strangely offended. "You don't think I can help you?"

She shrugged. "You don't look like a computer nerd, but maybe I'm wrong."

"You don't look like a computer nerd, either," he told her. She looked like a doll with her delicate features, perfect curls and slender build.

"I'm not a computer nerd," she said.

"But your brother—"

"Refuses to see that I can do more than computer work," she muttered. "I am not a *secretary*."

He grimaced as regret and embarrassment washed over him again. "I'm really sorry about that. I am a lunkhead."

Her lips twitched as if she was tempted to smile. But she shook her head instead. "And I am a bodyguard. I'm trained and capable of doing the job. I thought Cooper would give me the chance to prove that but then he…"

"He what?" Lars asked when she trailed off.

"He hired all of you."

"I didn't know I was taking your job," Lars said.

"Would it have stopped you from accepting the offer?"

He shook his head. "I need this job." More than she knew. He needed to get inside that estate and look for Emilia. Coop was leaving soon to tour the place. Lars wanted to ask to go with him, but he couldn't be sure that one of the guards couldn't identify him. And what about the surveillance footage…was he on any of that?

She sighed. "So do I…"

"Can I help you?" he asked again, and he edged around the desk to glance at the computer screen. Static played across the screen. "Can you get that any clearer?"

She tapped on the keys, rewinding to the moment the camera lenses shattered. Her breath hissed out between her teeth. "Someone shot it…"

"Can you see who?" he wondered, his heart beating fast. He had shot out two of the cameras while Dane had dealt with the third. That was all he'd noticed while doing recon. But what if there were more?

She tapped buttons, flipping through more footage—more static. Then she rewound farther. "All I see is a big shadow—no discernible image."

She brought up another screen. It must have been her laptop that she'd loaded the footage into because she moved through files, using a special program to enhance the black-and-white video from Webber's surveillance cameras.

"You're really good," he remarked. Too damn good…

She was bound to find something, bound to identify him.

She grimaced. "Yeah, I'm good," she said. "I'm a good bodyguard, too."

He wasn't as convinced of that as her computer skills. She was so small, so delicate. He couldn't imagine her fighting off a man like him, intent on getting inside that estate. He didn't want to imagine how easily she could be hurt.

She narrowed her eyes and peered at that big shadow. She'd lightened the image. But he'd worn a ski mask with the hood of his jacket pulled tightly around it. There was no way to recognize him. Was there? She glanced up at him, as if she'd seen some resemblance.

"The shooter was big," she murmured. "Nearly as big as you..."

He snorted derisively. "Doesn't look that big to me," he said. "And he's not nearly as handsome as I am."

She glanced back at the screen and then at him. And his heart kicked against his ribs. Did she recognize him?

Instead of stepping away, like he probably should have, Lars stepped closer. And he leaned down until his face nearly touched hers. "See? I am much better-looking."

"You're an idiot," she said, and her lips curved into a smile.

"Lunkhead, idiot," he said. "All your compliments are going straight to my head."

She snorted now.

Her compliments weren't getting to him but her closeness was. She was so damn beautiful and when she smiled...

It was like a light had been turned on inside her and glowed out of her skin and her luminous eyes. He told himself that he did it to distract her from the footage.

Or maybe he was trying to distract himself. He leaned a little bit closer and brushed his mouth across hers. Her lips were silky, like her hair was when he cupped her cheek in his palm.

She gasped in shock. And unable to resist the temptation that was the sweetness of her mouth, he deepened the kiss. His heart beat fast and hard—and it had everything to do with Nikki now.

Then his head snapped back, his cheek stinging from a blow he'd never seen coming.

Chapter 3

Nikki's pulse raced as fear coursed through her. Her hand stung from the slap she suspected Lars hadn't even felt. He was so big. But his size wasn't what had scared her. It was her own reaction to his kiss. The fact that she had enjoyed it frightened her most.

"I'm sorry," he said. And he sounded like he really meant it—that he was *very* sorry that he'd kissed her.

His apology didn't appease her. If anything it made her angrier. Hadn't he felt what she had, that spark between them? She had never felt anything like it before. But maybe she'd only imagined it.

"Why the hell did you do that?" she asked.

He shrugged.

"Well, don't do it again."

"Or what?" he challenged her, and he leaned a little closer as if he intended to do it again.

Her pulse leaped, and she nearly licked her lips. But she could taste him already—or still—on the tip of her tongue. He tasted like coffee and dark chocolate and mint and man. But more man than she had ever kissed before.

"Will you tell your brother on me?" he asked.

She shook her head. As her mother could attest, Nikki had never been a tattletale. No matter how hard Penny had tried to get information out of her, Nikki had never ratted her brothers out for their antics. She'd only wanted to be included.

"No," she said. "I'll just slap you again."

He touched his fingers to his cheek—not that she actually believed he'd felt her blow. She could have hit him harder. But then she hadn't really wanted to hurt him. She'd only wanted him to stop—to stop making her feel what she didn't want to feel. Attraction. Temptation. Desire.

But she was still feeling all those things, especially when he touched her, wrapping his fingers around hers.

"Next time," he said, "close your hand."

Her pulse quickened even more. Next time? He intended to kiss her again? And when he did, he wanted her to punch him?

She wasn't sure if she would have actually asked him that because she didn't get the chance before her door opened. Of course her brother wouldn't have bothered to knock. While it was her office, it was his business. Cooper had made that clear to her when he'd assigned her the job of analyzing the surveillance footage.

He was the boss.

"There you are, Lars," Cooper said, his brow furrowed as he stared at his friend standing behind her

desk, holding her hand. That hand got dropped—immediately.

Despite his size, Lars moved quickly getting as far away from her as fast as he could. No. Lars would not be kissing her again. He'd violated the bro code once. She doubted he would risk doing it again.

"You ready to go assess the estate?" Lars eagerly asked.

More furrows formed in Cooper's brow. "How do you…"

Lars shrugged his massive shoulders. "Just figured it would be the next step."

Cooper's brow smoothed, and he nodded in approval. "It is."

"I should go with—" Nikki began.

Just as Lars said, "I'll go along."

Cooper chuckled. "You're both so eager…" He didn't sound nearly as eager as they were.

"You're not?" Nikki asked. This was the first job for Cooper's franchise. Wasn't he excited? Nikki would have been had the business been hers or even if she thought her brother would let her have a significant role in this assignment.

Cooper shrugged now. "It's just…"

"What?" Lars asked. "What's wrong?"

Her brother expelled a ragged breath and shook his head. "Nothing…" He focused on Nikki now. "What did you find on the footage?"

"Nothing."

"I'm sorry," Cooper said. "Of course you need more time."

She shook her head. "I can't find what's not there. They shot out all the cameras."

"They?"

"There are two shadows."

"Two guys?" Cooper nodded. "That's how many Webber's security guards told him there were."

Nikki glanced back down at the screen. "Guys—big women with shoulders pads." She shrugged. "I don't know. They are just shadows."

"Can't you enhance the images?" Cooper asked.

Frustration knotted Nikki's stomach and it wasn't just because she suspected Lars wouldn't kiss her again. It was because her brothers constantly second-guessed her.

"I can't enhance what isn't there," she said. "Even before the cameras got shot out, they sucked. The images are poor."

"You've only been at it a few minutes," Cooper said. "I'm sure you can do better if you give it more time."

She swallowed a sigh. It would do no good to argue with him. She knew that so she simply nodded. "I'll see what I can do. But I should check out the security setup at the estate, too."

Cooper hesitated.

"This system sucks," she said. "The estate needs a better one. I can tell you what it needs."

Cooper knew systems, too. But he hadn't been working in the security business as long as she had. At least not private security. He'd been a Marine—like his friends—and his enlistment hadn't ended that long ago.

He nodded. "Okay."

"She can tell you what you need for an alarm," Lars said. "I can tell you what you'll need in manpower."

Man. Of course. She had no doubt that the lunkhead would recommend only male security guards.

Cooper nodded and turned to leave her office, Lars close behind him. Nikki snapped her laptop shut and stood up to follow them out. It would probably be her only chance to get out from behind the desk.

She had been a fool to think that working for Cooper would be any different than working for Logan. He was going to coddle her just as much as their oldest brother had. She knew that now. She also knew that she didn't need Candace or Nick to open a franchise of Payne Protection. She needed to open her own. It was the only way she would actually be able to work as a bodyguard.

Lars was aware of the danger—all the dangers— not just the one of entering Myron Webber's estate and being recognized as one of the intruders. That was a risk he had to take. It gave him an opportunity to look for Emilia. Kissing Nikki had been a risk he hadn't had to take—one he shouldn't have taken because it put him at risk of getting fired.

Cooper was too protective of his little sister to let her get mixed up with a man like Lars, a flirt who had no intention of ever getting serious with a woman. Cooper knew Lars as well as he knew himself. But despite their friendship, he would fire him. Blood was thicker than water.

Which was why Lars was lying to his friend. Blood was definitely thicker than water. He had to find Emilia.

So why had he given in to temptation to kiss Nikki? Sure, it might have distracted her from that surveillance footage. But that might have been unnecessary if she'd been telling Cooper the truth about being able to learn nothing from it. He wasn't sure she was telling

the truth, though, or if she'd only said that to convince Cooper to let her come along to the estate.

She rode in the backseat of the SUV, behind her brother who drove, while Lars occupied the passenger seat. He couldn't turn around without drawing Cooper's attention and more suspicion, but Lars knew she was watching him. His skin heated from the intensity of her stare. Had she recognized him from that footage and was she just keeping it to herself like she had that kiss?

His lips tingled from the contact with her silky ones. He tasted her, too. The sweetness with just a little hint of bite. She wasn't as delicate as she looked. Her slap had proven that. His skin smarted still where she'd hit him.

"We're here," Cooper said, finally breaking the uncomfortable silence.

The tension remained, gathered low in Lars's guts. How the hell had Nikki gotten to him so quickly? Maybe he was so worried about Emilia that his defenses were down or he was desperate for a distraction. If Nikki knew he was the man on that footage, she probably would have already slapped him again and harder than before.

Coop rolled down his window and reached for the security system next to the slightly crumpled gate.

Lars glanced nervously back at Nikki now. If he passed through those gates with her and Coop and anyone recognized him, the two might not just lose their trust in him but their lives, too, if the guards opened fire like they had the other night. But he wouldn't get through the gates without them.

A voice squeaked from the speaker Cooper had pushed on the security panel. It must have asked for his name because Coop gave it and the gates began to

open. As the SUV moved through them, Lars reached beneath his jacket, ready to draw his weapon if necessary. Cooper was armed, as well, and, Lars knew, quick to draw if he sensed a threat.

"Everyone stay alert," Cooper advised as he stopped the SUV at the front door of the austere brick mansion.

He didn't need the warning.

Nikki snorted. "Of course we will," she said. "We're not idiots. Well, I can only speak for myself."

Lars forced a laugh despite the tight knot of apprehension cramping his guts. "You're going to start that now?" he teased.

She had already called him a lunkhead, but she wasn't wrong. He had been an idiot to risk returning with people who could get hurt in the crossfire.

"Let's not start anything," Cooper said, and he cast a hard glance at Lars. He obviously didn't want his friend anywhere near his little sister.

Lars couldn't blame him. He wouldn't want any of his friends near Emilia once he knew where the hell she was and that she was safe.

"We have a job to do," Cooper continued.

"Of course," Nikki said as she opened the rear door and stepped out onto the brick driveway. She was eager to start.

Lars should have been, too. This was his opportunity to see if Emilia was here or find evidence that she had been. But he had a sick feeling, low in his stomach, that he wouldn't like what he found.

First he had to make certain that he wasn't found out. He'd been heavily disguised the other night, with the ski mask, with the hood. But he wasn't worried about someone recognizing him just from the other night.

He was worried that someone might recognize him as being related to Emilia. They both had pale blond hair and very light blue eyes.

So before he stepped out of the SUV, he pushed his sunglasses farther up his nose and tugged his cap down over his hair. With the wool jacket, he looked like a longshoreman—at least to Nikki. That was what she'd told him when they'd left the office.

He followed Cooper up to the front door, which he hadn't been able to break down the other night. It stood open now, and a grim-faced security guard invited them inside. He barely spared Lars a glance, all his attention focused on Nikki. Apparently he wasn't the only man she distracted with her beauty.

"I'm here to meet with Mr. Webber," Cooper said.

The guard grimaced with resentment. "You're Payne Protection. Mr. Webber is upstairs. He asked that I show you the security room and around the grounds before you join him."

Touring the perimeter of the gated property and scrutinizing the surveillance setup took time—time that had impatience gnawing at Lars like a rat on a corpse. He wouldn't find Emilia this way. She would be inside the mansion, probably upstairs with the slimy lawyer.

He nearly breathed a sigh of relief when finally the guard led them up the wide stairwell to the second floor. They followed the curve of the balcony that overlooked the marble foyer to where a door stood open at the end of the wide hallway.

A soft cry emanated from inside that room, and Lars's heart shifted in his chest. Was she here? Was she hurt? He rushed forward, but Cooper stepped in

front of him, entering the room first. His breath escaped in a soft gasp.

Lars was tall enough to peer over his friend's broad shoulder. The cry had come from an infant, one held in the lawyer's arms.

"You have a child?" Cooper asked with every bit of the surprise Lars was feeling. "I didn't realize you're married."

The lawyer shook his head, and his gaze went to Nikki, who'd stepped around him and Cooper. Interest flared in his dark eyes. "No, I'm not."

"But the baby…"

Lars stared down at the bald-headed infant, who blinked sleepily before opening startling pale blue eyes. And now he knew what trouble Emilia had been in and why she would have sought out an adoption lawyer. She had been pregnant. This child was hers.

He knew it. He felt the bond deep in his madly pounding heart. This was his nephew.

"His mother died in childbirth," the lawyer said.

And Lars's heart stopped beating for a moment. The room, which was already dark thanks to the sunglasses he wore inside, darkened more. His head lightened, and his knees trembled. But he locked his legs; he fought to hold it together—to reveal none of the turmoil he was feeling. He couldn't think about what he'd just learned. He couldn't deal yet with the feelings threatening to overwhelm him.

Instead he focused on the lawyer, who had continued, "He is my sole responsibility now. He is why I need Payne Protection to secure the estate and make sure nobody can get to him."

"Why would someone try to get to him?" Cooper asked.

The lawyer uttered a sigh that sounded long-suffering. "I am a wealthy man."

He was a son of a bitch. And Lars had to curl his fingers into fists so that he wouldn't swing at him.

"You think someone was trying to kidnap him the other night?" Cooper asked.

No. Lars had had no idea the child even existed. Emilia had said nothing before he'd left for his last deployment. Of course she might not have known then. She would have only been a few weeks along. But Lars hadn't even realized she'd been seeing anyone then. Or ever…

The lawyer shrugged his thin shoulders. "I don't know, but I can't take any chances. I have to keep him safe."

No. Lars had to keep him safe. He had already failed the baby's mother. When his and Emilia's mother had passed away from her debilitating MS six years ago, Lars had promised to keep Emilia safe.

He'd broken that promise. The baby's mother had died in childbirth. Pain gripped him, more intense than any he'd physically experienced—even worse than when his mother had died.

She'd been suffering for so long.

But Emilia. She'd been so alive. So vibrant. And now she was gone. He couldn't believe it. No, he just didn't *want* to believe it.

Maybe his pain and tension had shown because soft fingers skimmed over his fist. He glanced down at Nikki's face. She'd stepped close to him, offering support. He'd tried to hide his reaction to what the lawyer

had revealed. He'd tried to hide his pain. But it over-whelmed him.

Emilia was dead.

Emilia Ecklund was dead. She had to be since she'd been living in hell the past few weeks. Hell was sup-posed to be hot, though, and bright with flames. The room where she was being held was cold and dark. Even through the thin mattress on which she lay, Emilia could feel the coldness of the concrete floor beneath her. It seeped through to her bones—to her blood. She was thoroughly chilled. Maybe she would be better off in the real hell than this one.

But the physical discomfort was nothing in compari-son to her emotional pain. She had lost so much more than her freedom. She'd lost her heart when they'd taken away her baby.

Where was the infant? She didn't even know if she'd had a boy or a girl. She'd never had the chance to hold him or her. But she didn't care what she'd had, just that the baby was all right.

She had begun to accept that she would probably never know, though. They wouldn't keep her alive much longer. She knew that. If only she had listened to Lars…

If only she had sought out his friend like he had told her…

She'd intended to when she'd come to River City. She had intended to find Cooper Payne and ask him for help. But then embarrassment had overwhelmed her, and she'd foolishly chickened out. She hadn't wanted Lars to know how badly she'd screwed up—going out with the college guy who had obviously only wanted one thing. After she'd finally had sex with him, he'd

dumped her. So she hadn't told him she was pregnant. But she would have sooner told him than Lars. After all the sacrifices he'd made for her, she hadn't wanted to disappoint her brother.

So in a weak moment she had considered giving up her child. But she never would have gone through with it. Ever. That weak moment had cost her everything. She'd lost her child, her life and her brother.

Lars had to be dead. Or he would have found her by now. She'd written him a letter, just before her meeting with the lawyer, telling him that she'd contacted the man. She hadn't had the guts to tell him why. She had been so scared, and maybe that was why she'd wanted him to know—just in case something happened to her.

Like it had…

She probably should have told his friend instead, the one who'd already retired from active duty. But she hadn't ever considered that Lars might not return from a deployment. He was so big. So strong. So invincible.

Everything Emilia wanted to be. But she was more like their mother, weak and vulnerable. Her disease had only been partially responsible for that. Her bad choices had been equally if not more responsible. Falling for their father had been the worst choice she'd made. The minute she'd gotten sick, he'd abandoned her.

But he hadn't just abandoned her—he'd abandoned his children, too. So when he'd been little more than a boy, Lars had had to take on the responsibilities of a man. That was why he'd joined the Marines out of high school—to support them. He had risked his life to care for them. But even he hadn't been able to save their mother. She'd died six years ago.

Emilia had been sixteen then and Lars, at twenty-

two, had petitioned the court to be her legal guardian. He'd promised then that he would always take care of her, that he would protect her from danger.

"Where are you?" she murmured, her voice a hoarse whisper. From all the screaming she'd done, she must have damaged her vocal cords. But it hadn't mattered. Nobody had heard her cries of pain, her yells for help.

But maybe that was her problem. She'd always relied on Lars to save her. She should have learned to take care of herself. Then she wouldn't be in her predicament. She would have been able to protect herself and her child.

Now the baby was lost to her. And even though she wasn't dead yet, she knew that she would be soon.

Chapter 4

Dane had seen guys blown apart, but he didn't know if any of them had ever been in as much pain as his friend Lars. The guy was doubled over on the leather couch, his big arms wrapped around his torso as if he was trying to hold himself together.

The glass of whiskey Dane had handed him was abandoned on the hardwood floor next to him, untouched. He'd thought the alcohol might numb his pain or at least dull it. But it was almost as if Lars wanted to feel it, like he thought he deserved to feel it.

Dane was in pain, too. His guts knotted with frustration over his helplessness. There was nothing he could do to help. He had no idea what Lars was going through. He'd lost friends over the years, but he'd never lost family, at least not family he'd ever known.

Like Lars's sister, Dane's young mother had aban-

doned him, too. She hadn't died; she'd just left him in a high school bathroom, which had made him a ward of the state. He'd been adopted, but the older couple who'd thought they had wanted a child hadn't really had the time or energy to give him. They'd never acted like his friends' parents.

Dane had always envied the guys with family, the ones who'd received all the letters and packages from home. But now—seeing Lars's pain, feeling some of it himself—he wasn't jealous anymore.

"What can I do?" he asked. It wasn't like he could tie on a tourniquet or apply pressure to this wound. But he wanted—he needed—to help.

Lars released a deep, ragged breath. Then he straightened up. While his face was flushed, his eyes were clear with determination. "You can help me get my nephew."

Dane nodded. "Of course."

But Lars shook his head. "It's breaking and entering. It's kidnapping. You sure you want to be part of this?"

Dane didn't hesitate. He didn't have a choice. While he didn't have any blood relatives, he had family. His unit was family. "Of course," he said again.

"If we get caught…"

They would go to jail. "But you can prove that you're his biological uncle, his next of kin."

"I can't get a judge to order DNA testing on my suspicion," Lars said. "I need to get him first."

"How do we do that?" Dane asked. "What's the plan?" He had no doubt that Lars had one. He looked so determined, so resolute.

But now he flinched as if he felt a moment's regret.

"What?" Dane asked. "What's the problem? Don't you have a plan?"

"I have one," Lars admitted. "But it involves Nikki Payne."

Dane flinched now. He knew as well as Lars did how important family was to Cooper. "Are you sure?"

"I lost my sister," Lars said. "I don't want Cooper to lose his. But it's the only way."

Putting Nikki Payne in danger...

Nikki was seriously in danger—of losing her temper completely. Her brothers could be so damn frustrating. But nobody frustrated her more than Logan. He was the oldest of the Payne siblings by the five minutes he had beaten his twin, Parker, from their mother's womb. He never let any of them forget he was the oldest and the CEO of Payne Protection.

"You let Parker and Cooper start their own franchises," she said. "Why not me?"

He leaned back in the chair behind his massive desk and sighed. "We've been through this before, Nikki. You don't have enough experience."

"I've been working for Payne Protection since you started it." She'd still been in college and had juggled classes and homework, so she'd have time to help Logan with the technical stuff. "I have as much experience as you do."

He chuckled.

"And more than Cooper."

"You know I'm not talking about experience with Payne Protection. I'm talking life experience." He and Parker had come from law enforcement. Cooper from the Marines.

She knew what he meant. "Like any of you would have let me become a cop or a Marine..."

"It would have killed Mom," Logan said.

And that was why she hadn't, even though it was what she'd wanted most: to be like her brothers. But their mother had already been through too much, more even than Nikki had known. "Mom's tough," she said. She'd had to be to survive what she had.

Nikki was tough, too. "I can do this," she said. "I can start my own franchise."

He shook his head. "Not until you get more actual experience."

Frustration overwhelmed her, so Nikki had to bite her lip to hold in the string of curses that sprang to her mind. When she had regained control of her temper, she said, "I'd have that experience if you would have ever let me out from behind the desk."

"I wish you were still there," Logan said. "I wish you hadn't left me."

"Don't worry," she said. "Cooper has no more intention of letting me actually work than you ever did." She felt betrayed all over again, like she had when she'd found out her father had cheated on their mom. She'd felt betrayed then that he hadn't been the hero she'd always thought he was.

Logan grinned. "You couldn't talk him into it like you thought you'd be able to."

A curse slipped out, but instead of being offended, her brother's grin only widened.

"He doesn't need me in the field," she said. All she'd done at Webber's estate had been to suggest a new security system—with upgraded equipment and more cameras. "He hired a bunch of guys from his unit."

Logan nodded. "He told me. Good guys. I've met them before."

"You have?"

"Sure," Logan replied. "Cooper went through basic training with them. They were at the ceremony when we all went out to San Diego."

"Why didn't I meet them then?" Nikki asked. She had gone to that ceremony, too. And she definitely would have remembered Lars Ecklund if they'd ever met before.

Logan shrugged. But she knew her brothers had always worked hard to protect her. That was why she hadn't told Cooper about that kiss. If she'd said anything, he would have fired Lars despite their apparently long friendship.

Maybe that wouldn't necessarily be a bad thing, though. She hadn't been thrilled when he'd hired those guys. But she was realistic enough to know that it didn't matter. Even if he hadn't hired them, he wouldn't have let her do actual field work. Just like Logan, he'd never had any intention of letting her risk her life to protect someone else.

An image of that baby flashed through her mind. He was so small, so vulnerable. If someone was really after him, he needed protection more than anyone else. Usually Nikki shied away from babies. She didn't like the squalling or the smell. She wasn't like Candace; she didn't want any of her own. Ever. She had no maternal instincts at all.

But she had bodyguard instincts, and they had kicked in in that nursery. For some reason—whether it was for ransom like the lawyer thought or something else—someone was after that kid. Nikki just couldn't imagine why.

But she intended to find out.

Logan wasn't going to give her a franchise of her own. Cooper wasn't going to give her field work. So she had to do what she did best. She would investigate. First she'd go over that surveillance footage again. Maybe she could enhance it more and get a better image of the intruders from the other night. Or she could go back farther and determine if anyone had been casing the place.

She could also look into Myron Webber and find out why someone might go to so much trouble to get to him. The guy wasn't being completely honest with them. But then Nikki wasn't surprised. She'd learned that people were rarely ever completely honest.

Like Lars Ecklund…

There was something going on with him, too. He looked like he hadn't slept in weeks. Maybe that was because of PTSD. Then in the nursery, something else had come over him—maybe a flashback or something—because he'd looked devastated. So devastated that she hadn't been able to stop herself from reaching out to him, from offering comfort…

But why had he needed it? What the hell was the deal with Lars Ecklund? Maybe that was another mystery she needed to solve. Maybe she needed to investigate him, too.

"So here's the plan…" Cooper's words echoed the ones Lars had uttered just a short while ago. But the similarities ended there. Cooper laid out a course of action to prevent a kidnapping.

Lars had laid out one to carry out a kidnapping. Unfortunately Cooper's plan was going to make his a hell of a lot harder to pull off.

He exchanged a quick glance with Dane, who sat

across the conference table from him. His friend knew it, too—that they would now have to adjust their plan if they had any hope of carrying it out.

But Lars couldn't fail, not again. He had already lost Emilia. He was damn well not going to lose her son, too.

"The cameras aren't good enough," said the person who had suggested all the extra ones.

Lars's attention moved down the table to Nikki now. He should have been mad at her. She was the one who'd pointed out all the places on the estate that needed more surveillance coverage. When it came to protection, she knew what she was doing.

She was observant. She'd proven that when she'd touched his hand in the nursery. Despite his best effort to hide his feelings, she'd known something was wrong.

Just like now…

She kept staring at him. He felt her gaze boring through him, as if she were trying to see inside his head. Or his soul…

"She's right," Lars forced himself to chime into the discussion. This part of his plan had to work. "You need a guard inside the nursery."

"That—that's what I was going to say," Nikki sputtered.

Lars forced a grin. But the muscles in his face—as tense as he was everywhere—ached as he curved his lips. "Great minds…"

Her mind wasn't the only thing great about Nikki Payne. She had a great body, too—small but curvy. And her lips…

Instead of curving up, hers lowered, and her eyes narrowed as she stared at him. She was definitely trying to figure him out.

He couldn't have that. He couldn't have her figuring out his plan before he had a chance to carry it out.

"Why?" Manny asked the question. "We don't know that someone is really after that kid."

They hadn't been. But they were now since Lars knew his nephew existed.

Manny continued, "Isn't it more likely they're after art or money?"

Cooper shook his head. "Webber doesn't have a whole lot of anything inside that house."

Lars remembered the vast expanses of white walls and marble floors. It had been cold and sterile and almost eerily empty, as if he was ready should he ever need to make a fast getaway.

He glanced at Dane again. They didn't have much time.

Cole chuckled. "Even rich people can be cheap," he said. And he would know. Although nothing about his blue jeans and T-shirt attire suggested it, Cole Bentler came from money. "He's probably got it all stashed in the bank."

"And the only way someone can get to it would be kidnapping his kid," Cooper said.

Lars swallowed his protest. That baby did not belong to Myron Webber. The little boy was an Ecklund, through and through.

"That's why you need a guard with the baby at all times," Nikki said.

Cooper nodded. "True." He glanced around the table at the four huge guys and one woman. "Who wants babysitting duty?"

It had to be obvious to him. But of course he wouldn't have considered it because he didn't want his sister in

danger. Neither did Lars. And he would do his best to protect her. But he needed her. Or his plan was not going to work.

"It has to be Nikki," Lars said.

Down the table Nikki tensed. But she said nothing. He couldn't tell if he'd offended her again or not.

But Cooper laughed. "Just because she's the only woman?"

"It's not like any of us have diaper-changing experience," Lars pointed out. But he would have to learn to take care of his nephew.

Cooper snorted now. "You probably have more than Nikki. None of my brothers or I have been able to convince her to babysit."

"But this isn't actual babysitting," Lars said. And he spoke to Nikki now, meeting her gaze across the conference room table. "Someone else can change the diapers. I'm sure Webber has a nanny." They hadn't seen one in the nursery, but he couldn't imagine the lawyer getting his hands dirty. He was the type to hire other people to do that.

Had Emilia died in childbirth like he'd claimed? Or had he had someone kill her?

Emilia wouldn't have willingly given up her child. Lars knew that. Even though she had set up the meeting with the adoption lawyer, she wouldn't have gone through with it.

"True," Cooper said again. "That's why we need a real bodyguard in the nursery."

Nikki sucked in a breath now, and her face flushed with embarrassment and pain. Her brother might as well have slapped her.

Lars glared at his boss. How could he be so insensitive?

Nikki obviously considered herself a real bodyguard. She wanted the chance to prove herself. Lars intended for her to get that chance even though he was setting her up for failure. He ignored the twinge of guilt he felt. He had to for Emilia's son.

"You want one of us big guys lumbering around the nursery?" Lars asked. "Taking the kid to the park? We're going to stick out like a sore thumb."

"Exactly," Cooper said. "Your presence will dissuade anyone from trying anything. That's how we keep the kid safe."

Nikki shook her head. "A real bodyguard knows that the best way to eliminate a threat is to identify it," she said. "You'll never know who's after the kid unless you give him a chance to try for him."

"You want to use the baby as bait to flush out the kidnappers?" Cooper asked.

"He'll be safe the whole time," Nikki said. "I'll keep him safe."

"Who will keep you safe?" Cooper asked.

"I will," Lars quickly interjected. But it was a lie. He was the one who would hurt her most of all.

Chapter 5

Cooper's heart pounded hard and fast, and sweat slicked his skin. He was going to die...

Of pleasure...

His beautiful wife rested her head on his chest, her brow damp, too. Her heart pounded as frantically as his before returning slowly to a normal rhythm.

Despite the physical release of making love with his gorgeous bride, tension gripped Cooper yet. He couldn't relax, not when he had such an enormous decision to make.

"Wow," Tanya murmured, and her lips skimmed across his chest. "That was amazing."

"It always is." No matter how many times they made love, it was a powerful experience. He'd never known the pleasure—the love—he had with Tanya.

"So why don't you look happier?" she asked, and her fingertips skimmed along the ridge of his jaw, which he was tightly clenching. "What's wrong?"

"I don't know."

"Something's bothering you," she said.

But he couldn't pinpoint it. Was it Webber? Or his own team that was bothering him? The meeting hadn't gone at all well today.

He told Tanya about it, like he told her everything. He loved this time with her—after the baby was in bed, after they'd made love, when they just lay in the dark, holding each other and talking.

Tanya chuckled. "I don't believe it…"

"What?"

"That Nikki wants to be a nanny." The entire family was well aware of Nikki's aversion to babies. She'd rather detonate a bomb than change a diaper.

"Nikki wants to be a bodyguard," he said. "She wants to flush out kidnappers." She intended to use herself as bait every bit as much as the baby.

"You don't know that there really are any kidnappers," Tanya reminded him.

"No," he agreed. "But I couldn't imagine what else they might be after in that house." The cold, stark mansion reminded him of the one where his wife had grown up and where she'd nearly lost her life not too long ago. Despite the sweat on his skin, he shivered.

"I didn't even know that Myron had a child," Tanya said. "I'm sure there aren't too many other people aware of it, either. Of course as an adoption lawyer, he will have babies in his house from time to time but his own…?"

"He claims the kid is his."

"You don't believe him?"

Cooper shook his head. "Not a word that comes out of his mouth."

Tanya sighed. "I'm sorry, sweetheart. I should have

told him you were too busy to take on a new client when he asked me about Payne Protection—"

He pressed a finger across her silky lips. "I had no other clients."

"But your first client shouldn't be someone you can't trust," she said and then sighed. "And nobody really trusts Myron Webber."

"Because he's a lawyer?"

"Because he's Myron Webber," she replied. "There's something just a little…"

"Slimy?" Cooper asked.

She chuckled. "I was going to say *off* about him. But slimy works, too."

"Has he had any formal complaints about him?" Cooper asked. "Anyone who might want revenge on him?"

She shivered and snuggled closer to his chest. He wrapped his arm around her bare shoulders, holding her tightly. His heart swelled with love for her. "He's handled a few adoptions where the birth mothers have changed their minds. They claimed that he coerced them into signing papers they really hadn't intended to sign."

Cooper gasped. "That sounds worse than slimy. It sounds criminal."

Tanya's breath whispered across his skin as she sighed again. "It happens," she said. "The mothers have second thoughts."

"So they get their babies back?"

"Not if it's gone past the waiting period," she said. "And even if it hasn't, a lot of the girls are not able to prove themselves fit to be a parent."

Cooper expelled a breath now as realization dawned. "So one of those girls might feel compelled to take back what he stole from them—a baby."

"He hasn't stolen their babies," Tanya said. "They came to him. They signed the papers. What about the mother of this baby?"

"She's dead." A ghost couldn't steal a child. But another mother could. Nikki was right—damn her—they needed to identify the threat in order to protect that baby.

While Myron wasn't innocent, that tiny infant was. Maybe it was because Cooper had a family of his own that he felt so protective of that child—because keeping his own child safe gave him nightmares. He would do anything for him and for Tanya. And now he would do anything for that infant living on Webber's estate.

Cooper intended to find and eliminate the threat against him, even if that meant putting his sister in danger. Nikki swore she could handle it; maybe it was time he let her prove it.

Floorboards groaned beneath heavy footfalls. Nikki tensed. She had thought she was alone in the building, that everyone else had left after the meeting Cooper had called. She glanced up from her computer. She'd closed her door, but the light that had shone beneath it was gone. Either someone had shut off the light or was blocking it.

Her doorknob rattled as it began to turn. Her hand shaking slightly, she reached for her holster and drew out her gun. As the door creaked open, she pulled her Glock and pointed the barrel at the entrance.

The shadow—the enormous shadow—looming in her doorway, lifted his arms once his shoulders cleared the jamb. "It's me," Lars said. "Don't shoot."

"It's you," Nikki murmured with surprise. The man she usually wound up inadvertently pulling her gun on

was her brother Nick. Of course, he didn't believe it was all that inadvertent.

Maybe it hadn't been in the beginning. But it was now. Nick had become her favorite brother. He was also her best shot at getting field work. He needed to start his own franchise of Payne Protection and soon. Logan wouldn't be able to use the not-enough-experience excuse with Nick. As a former Marine and FBI agent, he had more life experience than Logan.

Of course he was still an FBI agent. He'd given his notice, but he hadn't quite given up his job yet cleaning up corruption in the River City Police Department. He was still running River City PD until his replacement could be found.

Nikki sighed. So her actual best shot at getting field work anytime soon was here—thanks to this man.

"What does that mean?" Lars asked. "That you want to shoot me?"

She slid her gun back in the holster. "No…"

"You don't sound so certain."

"Don't kiss me again," she said.

He chuckled. "That's not why I'm here."

Her stomach clenched with a twinge of disappointment. Not that she'd really wanted him to kiss her again. But it would have been nice if he'd wanted to.

Had that kiss not affected him like it had her? Probably not. He was a flirt. He'd undoubtedly kissed a lot of women—so many that he probably didn't even remember kissing her.

That kiss—and he—had been on her mind entirely too much since it had happened. And that wasn't like her. She wasn't easily distracted.

"Why are you here?" she asked.

He shrugged those impossibly broad shoulders. "I was checking in to see if Cooper has made a decision yet."

"He went home a long time ago," she said.

"Why haven't you?" he asked.

Because, unlike her brothers, she had nobody to go home to. But that was a good thing and it kept her focused.

"I'm working," she said.

"So Cooper did agree to you being the bodyguard nanny?"

"Not yet." But he had to. Right? It was the only way for them to flush out the would-be kidnappers.

"You're welcome, by the way."

She narrowed her eyes. "Why should I be thanking you?" For not kissing her again? She wasn't exactly grateful about that, although she should have been.

"For recommending you for bodyguard duty."

She would appreciate that if she was confident of his motivation. But she'd learned to trust no one. "I was going to suggest the same thing myself."

It had been her plan.

"But Cooper doesn't hear you," Lars said.

And she flinched at the direct hit.

"I'm sorry," he said. "But it's true."

She sighed. "Yes, it is. He's not the only brother who doesn't hear me."

There was no way Logan would ever give her a franchise of her own, no matter how much life experience she managed to rack up.

"It's not that they don't care," Lars said. "They love you and want to—" his deep voice cracked, and he cleared his throat before continuing "—*protect* you."

"Yeah, yeah," she said. "I know the spiel. I've heard the spiel over and over again. They fail to understand

that I can take care of myself. I don't need anyone to *protect* me."

"It's not just a spiel," Lars said. "They mean it. They love you. And they want to protect you. They just don't understand that's not always—" his voice cracked again "—possible."

He looked raw again, exposed, like he had in the nursery, like he was in pain. She asked him now what she'd wanted to ask him then, "What's wrong?"

He shook his head. "Nothing…"

Because she believed in being open and honest, she was blunt. "You look like someone died."

"A lot of people died," he said.

She narrowed her eyes and tried to read his face, but it had gone blank, like he was trying to hide something. Pain?

"In Iraq?" she asked.

Cooper never talked about what he'd seen during his deployments. And Gage Huxton—another bodyguard and Marine—had been through hell. She could only imagine the horrors of war.

But then an image flashed through her mind—of the gun battle in the chapel. Of the young man bleeding out in the aisle, staining the white runner crimson. Of the woman staring up at her with such hatred, the woman she'd killed… No, Nikki hadn't been to war, but she'd survived a battle or two.

But Lars had undoubtedly seen more battles than she had. He didn't have to imagine war. He'd been there. He nodded. "Yeah…"

"I'm sorry," she said, standing up to come around her desk. "You haven't been back very long. Do you need to talk to someone?"

His lips curved up at the corners in a very slight grin. "You?"

"No." She laughed. "Remember. My brothers protect me. I've been through very little." In comparison to war, assaults and hostage situations and shoot-outs were very little. So she said nothing more.

He leaned down, lowering his face toward hers. She drew in a breath, bracing herself for a kiss. But he just stared into her eyes as if trying to read her mind. "Why don't I believe you?" he murmured.

She shrugged. "I don't know. I don't have anything to hide." She suspected that he could not say the same.

"Maybe I made a mistake," he said. "Maybe I shouldn't have recommended you for the bodyguard position."

She sucked in another breath, her lungs swelling with all the air. He glanced down at her breasts pushing against the material of her thin black sweater.

"Your brothers are right to protect you," he said.

From men like him? Yes. But not from doing the job she wanted to do. "They should damn well know by now that I can take care of myself."

He sighed, and he was so close that his warm breath whispered across her face. "I sure hope that you can."

She shivered. "You think I will be in danger if Cooper gives me this assignment?"

She stared up at him, waiting for his reply. But he wasn't certain how to answer her.

Then she laughed—maybe at herself—and said, "I'm sorry I asked that. Of course you don't have any way of knowing if I'm going to be in danger or not. It's not like you're one of the kidnappers."

Not yet. But he would be. He would get his nephew back. It would just be easier to do if Coop agreed to his plan. But would he? Would he put his sister in any danger?

"And you're not like my mom and my brother Nick," she continued.

"What are they like?" he wondered. Coop had talked about his mom before—a lot—during boot camp and past deployments. But he'd never mentioned Nick.

"Mom and Nick—they have this freaky way of just knowing things," she said, and she shivered again despite the sweater she wore.

The material was thin, though. He could catch glimpses of what looked like a red bra beneath the black knit fabric. He would have expected she would wear black underwear under black. But then Nikki Payne was unlikely to do what anyone expected of her.

Should he have suggested her for the nanny position?

He'd done it because he thought he could overpower her and take the baby from her. But she might prove too great a distraction for him to do what he needed to do.

For Emilia...

He owed it to his sister to take care of her son like he'd promised he would take care of her.

"I wish I had that ability," he said. "To just *know* things."

Then he would have known that Emilia would be in trouble before he'd left her. He would have been able to protect her.

"Even they don't know everything, though," she murmured. "They have been surprised."

"Life's full of surprises," Lars agreed, like walking

into that nursery and finding his sister's baby—the one part of her left in this world.

What had Myron done with her body? Would it ever be found? Lars had checked in with the hospitals and morgues in River City, but no Jane Doe matching her description had turned up. And if she'd been identified, the death notification would have been made to him. He was her next of kin. But he wasn't the last Ecklund. Now there was her son.

"Yes..." Nikki murmured, and her gaze slipped to his mouth, skimming across his lips like hers had earlier that day.

He needed to kiss her again. But he didn't trust that she wouldn't pull that gun. And he didn't trust himself to leave it at just a kiss. She affected him too much.

"You're a surprise," she said.

"I am?"

"Yeah, after you mistook me for the receptionist, I figured you were just as sexist as the majority of my brothers."

He chuckled but felt compelled to defend the male Paynes. "I told you, they just love and want to protect you."

"How do you know that?" she asked.

"Because I..." His voice cracked again with the emotion that was still too fresh, too raw, to contain. "I *had* a sister."

"Had?" Her voice cracked as she repeated the word.

"She's gone," he said. And he'd never even had the chance to say goodbye. His eyes burned, and he squeezed them shut. So he never noticed her moving closer until her slender arms slid around him.

He was big—so much bigger than she was—but she

held him. She was strong for him, offering the comfort he hadn't been willing to take from his friend. He hadn't wanted to buckle in front of Dane. When they'd only had each other to rely on in the war zones they'd been in, they had learned to always act tough. But he couldn't summon the energy now to act. He could only feel—his pain—and her.

While her breasts, pressing against him, were soft, the rest of her was harder than he'd expected. Her slender arms were strong, holding him tightly. It had been a long time since anyone had held him.

His arms automatically wound around her, too, and he drew her closer. But she was so small that he couldn't see her face. It was buried against his chest, her breath penetrating the thin material of his T-shirt. He wanted to see her beautiful face, so he lifted her.

But then seeing her wasn't enough. He had to taste her. So he lowered his head to hers. And like he took the comfort she offered, he took her mouth. He kissed her hungrily—with all the emotions pummeling him. He kissed her until his own knees weakened and nearly buckled beneath their combined weight.

Her hands gripped his shoulders. But she didn't push him away. She grasped and tugged him closer. And her legs wrapped around his waist. His erection swelled and pulsed against the heat of her core.

He had never wanted—never *needed*—anyone the way he needed Nikki Payne. Maybe it was because of the rawness of his anguish, because of his loss. Maybe he was only using her to assuage his pain.

Before his knees could fold, he carried her toward her desk. He settled her onto the edge of it and intended

to follow her down onto the surface but a phone rang then vibrated near her hip.

The call was like a bucket of ice water being dumped on him, so he jerked back from her. His body was tense and aching for her.

And she uttered a shaky sigh and reached for her cell. "It's Cooper."

Lars stepped back farther and glanced around the small office. Did her brother have a camera inside? Had he known what they were doing?

Her finger trembling slightly, she pressed the speaker button on her cell screen and said, "Hey, what's up?"

"Where are you?" Cooper asked.

The pressure on Lars's chest eased slightly. At least there wasn't a camera. But maybe Coop possessed that same eerie knowledge Nikki had claimed her mom and other brother had. Maybe he'd just *known* that Lars was doing something he shouldn't be doing with his sister.

"I'm at the office," Nikki said.

"This late?" Coop asked. "What are you doing?"

"I'm reviewing that surveillance footage again."

Lars sucked in a breath. He hadn't realized what she'd been doing.

"I thought you said you couldn't learn anything from it." Coop spoke Lars's thought aloud.

"I'm not just checking that night," Nikki said. "I'm reviewing the couple of weeks before it. These guys obviously cased the place or they wouldn't have known where the cameras were and where the guards would be. They wouldn't have been able to break in like they had without doing some recon."

Lars had done all the recon before he'd even admitted to Dane what was going on. He had disguised himself,

but he worried now that he hadn't done it well enough, that Nikki would recognize him.

"That's a great idea," Cooper said.

"So is my posing as the nanny," Nikki said.

Coop's sigh rattled the phone. "Yes, it is."

She glanced up at Lars, her chocolate-brown eyes wide with hope. "You think it is?"

"Yes," her brother replied albeit with obvious reluctance.

"You're going to let me do it?"

There was such a long pause that she glanced down at the screen of her cell phone as if checking to make sure the call hadn't disconnected.

But then finally Cooper replied, "Yes…"

And Nikki let out a whoop.

"We'll talk more in the morning," Cooper said. "Get some rest."

Unbeknownst to him, his friend had bought Lars some time. She wouldn't look at any more video surveillance tonight. She was too excited, so excited that she threw her arms around his neck and hugged him.

But Lars didn't let himself hug her back. He couldn't let the attraction between them go beyond that—because she would never forgive him when she learned how he'd used her.

And he might never forgive himself for using her.

But hurting Nikki wouldn't be the worst thing on his conscience. It was already weighted down with the worst thing he'd done, which was failing Emilia. He hadn't protected her like he'd promised. But he would protect her son.

Even if he had to hurt Nikki to do it…

Chapter 6

Emilia ached all over from the cold, from the stiffness of not moving much within the small confines of her makeshift prison. Even after all these weeks, she still had no idea where she was. The last thing she remembered was being in the lawyer's office, of telling him she was sorry for wasting his time. There was no way she would give up her baby.

But she'd slurred those words instead of speaking them with the conviction she'd felt. Then everything had gone black, and it had remained that way ever since as no light ever shone inside her cell.

That was what it felt like. It could have been a small room in a warehouse or a shipping container on a boat. She had no idea, no way of knowing where she was. But she had to figure out how to escape.

She couldn't count on Lars to rescue her anymore.

He must have died during that last deployment. Her heart ached with that new loss. It already ached over losing her baby.

Where was the child? Was he or she safe? Healthy?

Every time the door opened she asked, she pleaded, for answers. But there was never a reply to any of her questions. Her captors barely looked at her. Maybe it was guilt that made them unable to meet her gaze.

Or maybe it was disgust.

She was filthy, so filthy that she feared she was getting sick. She wanted to be brave, wanted to fight. But she felt so damn weak, so listless.

If Lars was dead, maybe he could come to her in spirit. Maybe he could loan her some of his indomitable strength. The door rattled as a padlock slid free of a chain.

She was locked up like an animal. And she felt like an animal, an abused one, as she cringed in fear of that door opening. One of these times she knew they wouldn't bring her food or water.

They wouldn't need her anymore.

And they would get rid of her. Permanently.

And her child would never know her, would never know how much Emilia would have loved him or her and that she never would have willingly given away her baby. She never should have considered it. But she'd had a year left of college. And the father had wanted nothing to do with her anymore.

She wasn't sure she could raise a child alone. And she hadn't wanted to put any more responsibility on Lars. Their mother had already asked too much of him.

The door opened slowly, falling back against the outside wall of her prison. Instead of cringing, she should

have been recoiled, ready to strike out and run for freedom. But she could barely roll over on that mattress, barely find the strength to turn toward the door.

When she glanced at the opening, she saw only more darkness, and a huge shadow filled the space. Hope flitted through her heart.

"Lars…" She tried to speak, but her voice came out on an inaudible whisper. Her throat was too dry, too sore.

The man stepped forward, and she could see that he wasn't as big as her brother. Lars had been larger than life. Apparently that had become literal.

She wasn't larger than life, but she had no doubt that it was about to prove too much for her, too. She didn't have time to work on becoming the stronger person she wanted to be, the smarter person. Not if that man was about to take the only thing she had left: her life.

Nikki felt like a *girl*, and she hated it. But she stared down at all the clothes she'd tossed onto her bed, trying to figure out what to wear. She'd almost emptied the walk-in closet off her bedroom, but she still didn't have much to choose from. Her wardrobe was limited while her computer collection and guns and workout equipment filled the other bedroom of her two-bedroom apartment.

"You called me over to help you choose an outfit?" Candace asked. She sounded as horrified as Nikki was. "*We* don't do this."

"I know," Nikki miserably agreed. She couldn't even look at the brunette who stood next to her.

"You call me up to go to the shooting range," Candace said. "You never ask me what to wear there. Or when we go to the ring to spar."

"I know," Nikki said. "But this is different."

"Then you should have called Megan," Candace said, referring to Gage's wife and the woman who was about to become Nikki's stepsister.

"Megan is a librarian." She was also a badass under pressure, like when her wedding had been taken hostage by armed gunmen.

"She's not a bodyguard," Nikki said. "You are. And I need you to tell me what to wear on my first real assignment as a bodyguard."

Candace grabbed Nikki's shoulders and spun her away from the bed. "You what? You have a real job?"

She nodded. But she wasn't as eager as she'd originally been. Maybe because of how Lars had reacted to her reaction to the news. Instead of kissing her again, he'd pulled her arms away from his neck and he'd stepped back.

She hadn't been sure if he'd regretted their earlier kiss or if he'd regretted recommending her for the bodyguard position. She hadn't had time to find out either before he'd run off.

Maybe he was as scared as she was. Not of the job. But of whatever was starting between them. She'd never felt anything like it before.

"Why aren't you happier about this?" Candace asked, her blue eyes warm with concern.

"I should be," Nikki agreed. "I would be..."

If it wasn't for Lars Ecklund messing with her mind or worse yet, her feelings.

She had felt so bad over his losing his sister. She wasn't sure how long ago it had happened, but it was obvious the pain was still fresh for him. Still devastating...

She'd only wanted to comfort him. But then he'd kissed her.

And then she'd just wanted him.

If Cooper hadn't called...

She might have done something stupid. She might have done Lars. Not that she thought he was stupid.

He trusted her to protect the baby. So he was actually smarter than she would have guessed.

"So why aren't you?" Candace persisted. "What's bothering you?"

"A man," a soft voice murmured.

Candace startled and reached automatically for her gun. Nikki hoped she would have reached for hers, had she been wearing her holster. But it was sitting on her bed along with nearly the entire contents of her closet.

She couldn't even see the quilt her mother had given her for the bed, which wasn't so bad. The teal and white bedspread was—predictably for her mother—a wedding ring design. But since it had been a gift, Nikki had felt obliged to use it.

"Mom!" Nikki exclaimed.

She wasn't just embarrassed over her mother sneaking up on her. She was embarrassed that she'd been able to do that because Nikki had been distracted by thoughts of a man. Just as her mother had said. Why the hell did the woman always have to know *everything*?

Penny Payne—soon to be Lynch—smiled like she'd won the lottery. "You're not denying it."

Nikki sighed. There was no fooling her mother, but maybe she could mislead her. "I wouldn't call him a man," she said.

Candace gasped. "I hope you haven't said that to

him!" She was probably imagining her husband's reaction.

But then again, knowing Garek, he'd just laugh. Nikki doubted Lars Ecklund would do the same. He was the macho type who would probably be offended if someone questioned his manhood. That was another reason Nikki avoided men like him.

"The male in question is only a few weeks old," Nikki explained. "I'm going to be his bodyguard nanny."

Candace and Penny exchanged a glance and then burst into laughter. "You're going to be a *nanny*?" Candace asked.

"A bodyguard," she insisted. "I'm just posing as a nanny to flush out would-be kidnappers."

Penny's smile slipped away. "And your brother is allowing that?"

Nikki gritted her teeth to hold back a sharp retort. After mentally counting to ten, she finally managed a curt reply of, "Yes."

Penny shook her head, tousling auburn curls around her face. She looked beautiful—as she always did—and hardly old enough to be Nikki's mother let alone the twins'. "I don't think this is a good idea at all, Nikki."

Of course she wouldn't.

Penny turned toward Candace. "You have more experience and would be better equipped to deal with this sort of assignment."

Nikki flinched, but she couldn't argue that Candace was the more experienced and better bodyguard. "Candace works for Logan, not Cooper," Nikki reminded her mom. "And this is Cooper's job."

His first one for his own agency. Maybe that was what was bothering Nikki; she was afraid of messing

it up for him. It would be his friend Lars's fault if she did, though. He was the one distracting her.

She drew in a deep breath and forced herself to focus. "I can handle this."

Penny looked like she wanted to argue yet. But she turned back toward Candace and studied the statuesque brunette. Her face brightened with a smile again. "Congratulations, honey!" she exclaimed and she pulled Candace into a tight embrace.

Over her head the female bodyguards exchanged a glance, Candace's brow furrowed with confusion. She gently eased back and asked, "Why are you congratulating me?"

Penny waved a hand dismissively. "I didn't figure you'd be superstitious like other first-time mothers. You don't need to wait until the second trimester to make the announcement. You and Garek will have a healthy, beautiful baby."

Candace gasped and pressed her palm over her stomach. "I didn't—I'm only a couple of days late..."

"You didn't know," Penny said. "I'm sorry."

"But how did you know?" Candace asked, her blue eyes wide with shock and wonder.

"You're glowing," Penny said.

Nikki studied her friend's flawless complexion and glistening eyes. She was glowing and beyond thrilled. Nikki hugged her now but felt compelled to tease, "Don't expect me to throw you a baby shower."

Candace giggled. "Could be fun. I'm sure you'd hold it at a shooting range."

Penny grimaced. "Don't worry. I'll take care of it for you."

"Or Stacy will," Nikki said. Stacy had once been

Candace's rival for Logan. But now she was Candace's sister-in-law and very good friend. Nikki often shook her head in wonder over her crazy family.

And no one was crazier than her mother. She probably wasn't clairvoyant—just really observant—but still…

"I have to tell Garek," Candace said. But she paused before rushing off, pointed toward a tan sweater and black pants lying on the bed and said, "That outfit. And good luck."

"I'm going to need it," Nikki muttered after the brunette bodyguard departed.

Penny began, "If you're uncertain—"

"I need the luck with you," Nikki said. "So you won't go behind my back to Cooper and convince him to pull me off the assignment."

Penny's face flushed, probably because she'd considered doing just that. But she denied it. "I'm sure Cooper knows what he's doing. And I know that he hired some former Marine buddies to back you up."

Nikki gritted her teeth again to hold in the hot declaration that she didn't need backup that was burning the back of her throat.

Penny narrowed her eyes. "What do you think of your new coworkers?" the notorious matchmaker asked. "Anyone in particular catch your eye?"

Lars had caught more than her eye, especially when he'd lifted her up in his arms and kissed her so passionately the night before. Nikki's body hummed yet, frustration vibrating through it. If only Cooper hadn't called.

She would have made a horrible mistake. She needed to keep everything professional between them. She couldn't blow her first real assignment.

"Oh..." Penny said as if she'd looked inside Nikki's mind and watched the images replaying there. "It's one of them."

"No." But she couldn't meet her mother's gaze when she said it. Instead she plucked the clothes from the bed that Candace had indicated she should wear. And now she could see that damn quilt again. Wedding rings...

Like she had warned her mother when she'd given her the present, that was the closest Nikki would ever come to wearing wedding rings.

"There's a small child waiting for me to protect him," Nikki said. "I need to get going, Mom."

Penny chuckled. "He's already making you more maternal. You can't wait to hold that baby."

Numbers escaped Nikki. She wouldn't have been able to count high enough to control her temper anyway. It bubbled over and she could only sputter, "I am not maternal—at all! I can't wait to protect that baby."

Penny stepped forward, and all the teasing was gone now. She cupped Nikki's cheek in her palm. "Protect yourself, sweetheart."

For once Nikki didn't shrug off her mom's advice. She knew she would be smart to take it to heart, not just for her assignment but for that man she couldn't get off her mind. She needed to protect herself from Lars Ecklund.

Tension gripped Lars. He hadn't slept at all last night. But then he hadn't slept much since he hadn't been able to find Emilia upon his return from Afghanistan. Now he knew that he would never be able to find her—alive. She was gone, and images of her had kept playing through his head.

But there hadn't been just images of his sister. Nikki had kept him awake, too. He glanced again around the conference table, but she wasn't there.

Had she changed her mind about the assignment Cooper had given her? Had she decided she didn't want it?

Cooper had called this early morning meeting to assign everyone else their positions on the estate. But she hadn't shown up. Maybe it was just because she'd already been given hers. Or maybe it was because she no longer wanted it.

But that was the least of his concerns. While Lars had been given the position he'd wanted—the one he needed to have to carry out his plan—it wouldn't be as easy as he'd thought it would be. He waited until the others left and it was just him and Cooper alone in the conference room before he remarked, "I thought Webber was canning his staff."

Cooper was tense, too, a muscle twitching along his jaw. "That was my recommendation."

"And he didn't follow it?"

"He doesn't think the four of you—"

"Five," Lars corrected him.

Cooper lowered his brows, obviously confused.

"With Nikki," Lars reminded him.

His friend groaned and stroked his hand over his rigid jaw. He didn't look like he'd gotten much more sleep than Lars had. "Don't remind me," he murmured as if he would have preferred to have forgotten all about his sister.

Lars would need no reminders of Emilia. He would never forget her—or how he had failed her. And he would keep her memory alive for her son, too.

But first he had to get to her son. He had to rescue him from the man who was undoubtedly responsible whether directly or indirectly for her death. That would be harder now, though, with Webber's guards still on the estate.

"The five of us—six with you," Lars said, "can easily protect this kid."

"Webber doesn't think so," Cooper said, bitterness making his voice gruff. It was obvious he didn't like his client, which he confirmed when he murmured, "I'm not sure I should have taken this case."

"We can handle it," Lars assured him. He couldn't have Cooper quitting—not yet.

Cooper shuddered as if a chill had raced through him. "I have a bad feeling about this," he said.

Lars chuckled. "What? You psychic now?"

"My mom is," Cooper said. "My brother Nick, too."

"Nikki told me," Lars admitted then wished back the admission when Cooper stared at him through narrowed eyes. "I thought she was just giving me crap."

Cooper chuckled. "That sounds like Nikki. But it's actually true in this case."

"You believe in psychics?" Lars asked with genuine surprise. If only someone could actually predict the future...

He would have never left Emilia if he'd had any idea he might lose her forever.

"I didn't used to believe." Cooper shrugged. "But they're right a lot of the time." Some of his tension eased as he chuckled. "All the time if you ask my mom."

Lars needed to meet Mrs. Payne. He needed her to tell him if he could pull this off, if he could save his nephew. But if she was really the psychic her kids

thought she was, then she would know that he intended to use her daughter.

He thought about last night, about how he'd nearly used her to ease his pain, to fill some of the emptiness stretching inside him now that Emilia was gone. That wasn't his intention. But the attraction between them was more powerful than anything he'd ever felt before, too powerful to resist.

He had to be stronger. Had to stay focused.

Cooper was focused on him, watching him with great consideration, as he said, "And now I got this nagging feeling myself."

"About what?" Lars asked, nerves gripping him.

He knew his friend was smart and intuitive. And maybe that was all Mrs. Payne and Nick were. Had Cooper figured out that Lars had ulterior motives for wanting him to stay on this job?

"I feel like something is going to go horribly wrong with this assignment." Cooper shuddered again. "Like someone is going to get hurt."

"You got someone in mind?" Lars asked, a little uneasy since his friend kept staring at him. Maybe Nikki hadn't gone right home last night; maybe she'd continued to work on that surveillance footage.

But then Cooper wouldn't have assigned him a position right outside the nursery door. He wouldn't have let him anywhere near the estate again.

His blue eyes unblinking, Cooper replied, "Nikki. I think Nikki is going to get hurt."

Damn. Was the whole damn Payne family psychic?

Lars was worried she would be hurt, too. Not physically. He wouldn't let that happen. Emotionally she would be hurt that he only backed her up for the job be-

cause she would be easiest for him to get the baby away from. But then she would actually have to care what he thought of her, and he doubted that she did.

He snorted derisively. "How is she going to get hurt? She's babysitting, Coop. The worst that's going to happen to her is getting spit up on."

Another snort echoed his. And he glanced toward the open door of the conference room. Nikki leaned against the jamb. "Too bad you can't say the same."

He chuckled. "You think I'm going to get hurt?"

Her brown eyes swirled with emotion—anger and something else—a passion that echoed the desire burning in his heart. Damn. She was beautiful. But she wasn't just beautiful. She was smart and strong.

And he knew that she was right. He was going to get hurt. He was already in pain—over losing Emilia—so he wasn't sure how much more he could take, how much more he could survive. But he had no choice. He had to risk the pain.

Chapter 7

"You're not going to spit up on me," Nikki told the baby as she lifted him from his crib. The nanny—the real one—had left him crying in his bed while she went to retrieve his bottle. The woman was older but not very warm or affectionate. She was less maternal than even Nikki was.

Nikki had held enough new babies that she knew to support his neck and cuddle him close to the warmth of her body. He missed his mother. He was so new, just weeks old, but his hands clenched into fists like he was ready to start swinging. Nikki couldn't help but stroke her finger over one of those tiny hands. It unclenched with her touch before he grasped at her finger.

She smiled and murmured, "You are a strong little guy."

He would have to be since he'd already lost so much. Penny often proved to be a pain to Nikki, but she couldn't imagine her world without her mother in it.

"My mom would love you," she said.

"What about me?" a deep voice asked.

She startled, pulled her hand away from the baby and reached for her weapon. The infant was startled, too, and began to cry again.

"Look what you've done!" Nikki said. Despite her uneasiness around babies, she had been doing so well with him—until Lars frightened her. She'd thought he would be the reason for her distraction, not the baby. She was entirely too fascinated with the little guy.

And it seemed as though Lars was, too. He'd stepped forward and stared down at the baby she held. While she wasn't holding him, like she had tried the night before, she could feel the tension in Lars.

"Apparently I'm not the only one afraid of babies," she mused.

"No, no," he weakly protested. "I am not afraid. I can hold him." He reached out, but his hands were almost as big as the baby. He pulled back as if afraid that he might hurt him.

"When they're this tiny, they're hard to just grab," Nikki said. "Hold out your hands."

Lars obeyed, but there was a slight tremor in his fingers. This man had been to war, but he was afraid of a child. Nikki would have laughed if she wasn't able to relate on some level. She wasn't a fan of babies, either. But there was something special about this kid. Maybe it was because he'd lost his mother so young. One of her nephews had, too. But Ethan's nanny had been more a mother to him than his biological one had ever been.

That wouldn't be the case for this little guy, not if Webber kept the same stone-faced woman as his son's

caregiver. Her heart shifted in her chest as she placed the baby in Lars's huge hands.

The switch startled the baby again and made him stop crying. Blinking his wide eyes, he stared up at the man holding him.

And Lars stared down at the baby as if equally enthralled. Nikki was surprised, not just about the expression on Lars's handsome face, but about his eyes. He and the baby had the same very pale blue eyes.

"He could be yours," she murmured, as she noted the uncanny resemblance between the enormous man and the tiny boy.

Lars tensed and glanced over at her. "What?"

"You have the same eyes."

Was that why Lars was so enthralled with the child? Did he know the baby was his? And if that was the case, why hadn't he said anything?

Why would he hide something like that?

Damn it!

Nikki was too observant. He shouldn't have risked coming inside the nursery. He was an interior guard but only inside the stark mansion, not inside the baby's room. That was Nikki's post. But when he'd seen the nanny step out, he hadn't been able to resist the lure of seeing the baby.

And Nikki. They had looked very natural together. Watching them had brought an almost unbearable pressure to his chest. That should be Emilia holding her son. And yet Nikki cuddling with him had been so sweet, so caring.

She acted tough, but she was incredibly sensitive.

She'd tried to comfort him the night before. And now she was comforting his nephew.

She was also astute, so astute that she'd noticed the resemblance between them.

Recalling what he'd learned in his science classes, Lars said, "All babies are born with light eyes. Something about not enough melanin in the womb. But once they're exposed to light, their eyes darken in color."

Nikki tilted her head and studied his face as if trying to determine if he spoke the truth or not. "It's more than the eyes," she said. "The shape of the head, the bone structure…"

"Is hardly developed," Lars said with a laugh he hoped didn't reveal the nerves swimming around his gut. "He's super tiny." He was also super sleepy. The baby couldn't hold his lids open over his pale eyes and closed them. That tightness in Lars's chest increased, as if someone was squeezing his heart.

"I told that nanny he wasn't hungry," Nikki murmured. "He just needed to be held."

"He needs his mother." But since Lars couldn't give him Emilia, he would step into her place. He would be both parents to the little boy just as he'd tried to be for the child's mother.

"Myron says she's dead," Nikki reminded him, and she watched his face as if looking for any reaction.

Lars worked on keeping his expression blank even though the pain nearly overwhelmed him. "Yes." Emilia had to be dead. It was the only reason she wouldn't have been with her son. "That's sad."

"Tragic," Nikki said.

He leaned over the railing of the crib and gently

placed the sleeping baby onto the mattress. "I'm sure he'll be loved." He already was.

The emotion swelled Lars's heart when he looked down at his nephew. Then he turned toward Nikki and the emotion changed. That damn attraction that burned between them ignited. Why did she have to be so incredibly beautiful? Those bottomless, brown eyes with thick black lashes, the delicate facial features, the generous curves...

He cleared the desire from his throat and remarked, "You said your mother would love him."

"She loves babies," Nikki said, and her lips curved into a smile. "Which is a good thing since my brothers and their wives have been having so many."

"You didn't answer my question," Lars said. "Would she like me?" He'd just been kidding when he'd asked, trying to distract himself from how he'd felt watching Nikki hold his nephew. But now he wanted to know. He wondered what the legendary Penny Payne would think of him.

Nikki sighed. "She's a hopeless romantic—even runs a full service wedding planning business out of an old chapel she bought. So she's all about marrying everyone off."

"She wants you married?"

"I think she started planning my wedding the minute I popped out of the womb," Nikki said. "It's probably all in pink."

Lars chuckled at the disgust in her voice. "Pink is pretty." And Nikki was so beautiful, she would look amazing in any color.

"Pink is for princesses," Nikki said with a derisive snort. "I'm no princess."

No. She wasn't. She was tough and no-nonsense.

"And I will never be a bride, either," she continued. "So my mother will just have to get over it."

"What does any of that have to do with what she'll think of me?" Lars asked.

"I don't introduce my mother to anyone I'm seeing because she starts planning the wedding the moment she meets him," Nikki said.

He stepped closer. "Are we seeing each other?" he asked. He was seeing her every time he closed his eyes. And now he couldn't stop looking at her as her face flushed with embarrassment.

She stepped back, but he followed her. "That—that wasn't what I meant," she sputtered. "I know we're not seeing each other."

"I see you," he said. And he did see far more than her brothers did. Or apparently even her psychic mother. He saw a strong, independent woman who didn't want to get married. But more than that he saw a woman who didn't want to get hurt.

And he was afraid that he was about to do just that. But he couldn't resist the temptation to lower his head and kiss her lips. His mouth slid across hers—back and forth—before she kissed him back.

Her hands clutched his shoulders and her lips nibbled on his. Then her tongue slid into his mouth, and he tasted her, the sweetness. She was so damn sweet.

But then her hands shoved against his chest, pushing him back. "No," she said, shaking her head. "You are not going to distract me. I have a job to do." She pointed a trembling finger toward the door. "Get out of here."

He would leave now—because he didn't know yet how he was going to carry out his plan. But once he fig-

ured out how to neutralize Webber's guards, he would be back for his nephew. But when he took the baby, he would lose whatever chance he might have had with Nikki.

A chill chased down Dane's spine and it had nothing to do with the steady drizzle that had been raining down on him as he paced the perimeter of the grounds. It had to do with the way the other perimeter guard kept staring at him.

"You look familiar," the guy said as they met at the front gate of the property, the gate that had nearly trapped him and Lars inside just a few nights ago.

Dane studied the bald-headed, fireplug of a man and shook his head. "You don't look familiar to me."

He hadn't gotten a good look at any of the shooters that night. He'd been too busy trying to get the hell away before he or Lars took a bullet.

"Your buddy—the one inside the house—he looks familiar, too."

Dane shrugged. "I don't know why. We're not from around here."

"Where you from?" the guy asked.

"Chicago."

"I get there sometimes."

"It's a big city," Dane said. "We might have bumped into each other before." He doubted it.

And so did the man who shook his head. "That's not it."

Dane shrugged again and began to pass the guy. But before he could, a big hand wrapped around his arm, drawing him up short. He tried to shake it off, but the guy was strong.

"I'm surprised you haven't asked me about the other night," he said. "Your boss interrogated me for nearly an hour about it."

Cooper. Of course he would be thorough. He would keep investigating until he discovered the truth. Dane understood Lars's reason for not wanting to include him. But still…

Coop would find out eventually and then there would be hell to pay for both of them. But there was no hell like the one Lars was in, having already lost his sister.

No. Dane had no choice. He had to help the friend who needed him the most. And he hoped that when Coop figured it all out he would understand.

"That's why I haven't asked," Dane replied. "The boss asks the questions. I just do my job."

"Isn't that to protect this place?"

"Yeah, and I'll do it," Dane said.

"Then you should be aware that there's a threat out there," the other guard said. "The guys that got in the other night were big like you and your pal there."

"Lot of big guys work security," Dane replied. "You're big, too." He wasn't as tall as he and Lars were, but he was broad and muscular and heavily armed.

Sick of the interrogation, Dane went on the offensive. He stepped forward until he pushed the guy back against the fence behind him. He hoped like hell that it was electrified. He wouldn't mind zapping the guard, especially after all those shots that had nearly hit him the other night.

Lowering his voice to a snarl, he asked, "Are you accusing me of something?"

The guy shrugged. "I'm just saying…"

"A bunch of crap," Dane finished for him. "Why the

hell would my pal and I want to break into some law-yer's pimp shack?"

The guy tilted his bald head and considered. "I don't know."

Maybe he should have been asking questions. So he started now. "I mean really—what's this guy up to that he needs so damn much security?"

The guy shuddered with revulsion. "Nothing good."

And Dane's blood went from chilled to ice-cold. Why the hell hadn't Emilia done as her brother had asked? Why hadn't she gone to Cooper for help?

"And I hope you and your boss know how Webber expects you to protect this place," the guy continued.

"How's that?"

"By eliminating every threat," he replied. "We're told to shoot to kill. If those guys make the mistake of coming back, they won't get out of here alive."

Dane had heard that before—at the start of previ-ous missions. This was the first time he believed that he might not survive.

Chapter 8

Damn him! Lars had been right. The only danger Nikki was in was of being spit up on. At least that was the only danger since she had tossed him out of the nursery. But it wouldn't have mattered if he'd distracted her. No one was going to get onto the estate, let alone into the house and the nursery. She wasn't really a bodyguard.

She was just the nanny.

Especially now that the real nanny had gone, claiming she was sick. The service was supposed to send out another one. Nikki hoped she arrived soon. The baby had begun to cry again. She leaned over to lift him from his crib. And a chill chased down her spine as she felt someone watching her.

Or more specifically staring at her ass. She knew it wasn't Lars. His interest didn't creep her out. Unfortunately, it excited her. She wasn't excited now. She was

frightened. So frightened that she shifted the baby to one arm and reached for her weapon before turning to confront whoever had entered the nursery.

Myron Webber lifted his hands above his head. "Don't shoot."

It wasn't cute when he said it, like it had been cute when Lars had. She hesitated for just a moment before reholstering her weapon. This man, and his beady eyes, made her incredibly uneasy.

"I'm sorry," she said. "I didn't realize you were here." She'd hoped he wouldn't be around very much.

"I left the office early when the nanny service called," he said.

"Yes, the woman who was here got sick," Nikki said. Maybe she got sick of Nikki second-guessing her nurturing skills. "They are supposed to send someone else, though."

He shook his head. "I canceled that."

"Why?"

"Do you think it would be wise to bring in a stranger given that someone is trying to kidnap my son?"

My son. The words echoed hollowly in the room. They just didn't ring true to Nikki. Lars looked more like the baby's father than this man. But Lars was right. She'd looked it up after he'd left. The baby's eyes probably wouldn't remain the same startling pale shade of blue as Lars's. They would darken. His bone structure would change as he grew.

"I would have checked her out," Nikki said, "before I let her anywhere near..." She glanced down at the infant. "What *is* his name?"

The nanny hadn't known, which had been another

mark against her with Nikki. But the man who claimed to be his father hesitated a long moment.

"You haven't given him a name?" she asked.

He sighed. "There wasn't time…with his mother passing away like she had…to decide on what to call him."

"But he's a few weeks old," she murmured. And he deserved a name.

He shrugged now. "I'm not sure I'm going to keep him anyway."

Her arm tightened protectively around the child. He wasn't a puppy. He couldn't be brought to the pound because he wasn't potty training fast enough. "What?"

"I feel like he would be better placed with a family," he said. "So he'd have a father and *mother.*"

Nikki released the breath she hadn't realized she'd been holding. "You're right," she agreed quickly. The baby would be better off with anyone other than this slimy little man. "He deserves a family."

Myron smiled and stepped closer. He gazed down at the child. But he didn't look at him with awe like Lars had. He looked at him with something else, something Nikki couldn't quite name, but it was as if he was admiring a work of art or bar of gold. He wasn't seeing a child. He was seeing money. Whatever family got this baby wouldn't be getting him for free, she suspected.

He held up a bottle. "I brought this up for him."

"You're going to feed him?"

He chuckled. "I'm an adoption lawyer. I've fed babies before."

"Of course."

"And with the nanny being gone…"

"I'll stay," Nikki offered.

He smiled. "Really? You've already worked one shift."

She shrugged. "It wasn't hard work. With the new security force in place, no one can get to him."

Myron's shoulders lowered as if a burden had been lifted from them. "That's good."

"I'm not sure about that," Nikki admitted.

"You want someone to kidnap him?" He sounded horrified.

"I want someone to try," she said. "So we can catch whoever is trying to take him."

The lawyer tilted his head as if considering it. But he shook his head and not one of his perfectly coifed hairs moved. "I wouldn't want to risk his safety." He reached out and stroked his finger along the baby's cheek, which was uncomfortably close to her breast. He glanced up at her face. "Or yours…"

Nikki was beginning to think it was too late for that. She'd already risked her safety by staying in Myron Webber's house. But she didn't care that he was Cooper's first real job. If he tried anything, she would take him down.

Instead she reached out and took the bottle from him. "I'll feed him," she said. "I'm sure you have work to do."

He kept staring at her and must have picked up on the fact that she was trying to get rid of him. Offending him probably wouldn't be the smartest thing for her to do. If he fired Cooper, Cooper might fire her. She didn't have an excuse to be outright rude, unless the guy tried something. Then her brother wouldn't care if she took him down. Knowing her brothers, Cooper would probably do it himself.

She forced a smile and reminded Webber, "You have

a family to find for this little guy…" Taking the baby and the bottle, she stepped back and sat down in the rocking chair near the crib.

"You look like a natural with him," Myron remarked. "Maybe you'd like to apply to be his adoptive parent."

She laughed, albeit uneasily. "Not me…"

"Because you're not married?" He was clearly fishing for information now.

"My boyfriend and I aren't ready to start a family yet," she said, easily uttering the lie. She had no boyfriend. But for some reason she saw Lars's handsome face, the intensity and passion in his pale blue eyes…

And she shivered.

The lawyer nodded. "You're young," he said dismissively.

He probably knew she wouldn't have the kind of money he might ask for this baby. Would he sell his son to the highest bidder?

When he left, she breathed a sigh of relief and murmured, "I hope he's not your father."

Because if he was…the best thing the guy could do for him was to give him up.

"What's your name, sweetheart?" she murmured. "You can't go without a name." Without an identity…

He blinked those blue eyes as he stared up at her as if totally cognizant of what she was saying.

"You remind me of Old Blue Eyes." Her mom had always been such a Sinatra fan. She'd played his albums all the time. "But you're new blue eyes," she said. "A little Frankie…"

He began to scrunch up his face to cry. Maybe he didn't like the name.

"No, you're right," she hurriedly agreed. "You're no Frankie. I'll just call you Blue—short for Blue Eyes."

But the little face stayed scrunched up. Maybe he was just hungry. She touched the bottle. The outside felt hot, so she didn't dare just shove it in his mouth.

Nerves fluttered in her chest. She didn't want to hurt him. The lawyer had been right about that. She couldn't risk his safety, not even to flush out the kidnappers. Maybe she could fool them with a decoy, with a doll like the ones used in movies.

Remembering what she'd seen her mother do when babysitting, Nikki squirted some of the formula on her wrist. It wasn't that hot, which was weird, like the bottle was warmer than its contents. Before it slid off her skin, she lifted her wrist and licked off the formula and grimaced at the flavor. The milk tasted sweet and a little soapy. Maybe the bottle had just come from the dishwasher. But wouldn't the rinse cycle have gotten off all the soap?

She couldn't give him the bottle until she knew it was safe. And she didn't want to call the lawyer back. He obviously didn't know any more about babies than she did despite his claims. So she called the only expert she knew.

"Yes, sweetheart, how did your first day go?" Penny asked.

The pressure in Nikki's chest eased. Her mother drove her crazy but also somehow made her feel safe and secure, too. "It's still going," she said.

"You're still working?"

"Yes, the real nanny left and the client won't bring in a new one."

"So you are babysitting?"

She ignored the amusement in her mother's voice. "Yes."

"I won't tell your brothers that you'll do it for a stranger but not them."

She glanced down at Blue. Despite his scrunched face, he hadn't started crying. He just stared up at her as if waiting for her to take care of him. He didn't feel like a stranger to her. He felt like family. How the hell was she already developing a connection to a baby?

"They wouldn't want me to watch their kids," Nikki said. "I think I'm about to give this baby a bad bottle."

"A bad bottle?"

"Yeah, the bottle's hot but the contents are cold and taste kind of soapy."

Her mom chuckled. "Sounds like someone thawed some frozen breast milk."

"But the mom…"

"What about the mom?" Penny asked.

"She's gone." She'd died in childbirth. She wouldn't have been able to pump breast milk for her son. Unless she wasn't dead…

But why would the lawyer have lied?

His patience expiring, the baby began to cry.

"I have to go," she told Penny. As she fed the infant the bottle, she asked, "Where is your mama?"

What had Myron Webber done to her? If she wasn't dead, where the hell was she?

As Cooper studied the surveillance monitors, his hands curled into fists. He didn't know who he wanted to slug harder—Lars Ecklund or Myron Webber. A hand settled on his shoulder, startling him so much that he turned with that clenched fist and swung.

Nicholas Rus—now Payne—ducked and cursed. "What the hell is it with this family?" he asked. "Usually Nikki pulls a gun on me and now you're swinging."

"Sorry," Cooper said as he expelled a shaky breath. "I thought you were someone else."

Nick glanced at the computer monitor and pointed toward the image of Nikki pushing Lars away from her. "Him?" And his own hands curled into fists. "Who the hell is he?"

"A friend." Or so Cooper had thought. Now he wasn't so sure. He knew Lars was a flirt. Hell, everyone knew Lars was a flirt. But he hadn't thought the man would go after Cooper's sister.

"Is he one of the guys you just hired?"

Cooper nodded. "Yeah. He just got back from my old unit's last deployment. They all did. But Lars seems different..."

"PTSD?" Nick's brother-in-law had come back with it. Gage was doing better now, but he had looked like a ghost of his former self when he'd first returned. Of course he'd been missing in action for six months enduring only the devil knew what tortures.

Cooper shook his head. "I don't think so. The other guys are fine."

"Everybody reacts differently." Nick had been a Marine, too. He understood.

"But he's completely different now," Cooper said. He wasn't the Lars he'd known in boot camp and previous missions. "Like this..." He gestured at the surveillance screen. "He would never go after my sister before."

Nick flinched. While Gage had been missing in action, Nick had gotten his sister pregnant. So again he

understood, probably better than Cooper did. "Close calls can make you want to seize every opportunity."

"He'll have a close call if he tries to seize my sister again," Cooper threatened as the anger coursed through him again.

"Our sister," Nick said. "And if Nikki had truly been upset about that kiss, she would have dropped him."

Cooper turned fully to face his half brother. They were nearly the same age and because of the military background, he had shared an automatic kinship with the man. He respected him. And Nick respected Nikki, so much that he'd asked her to be his best man.

"You really think she can be a bodyguard?"

Nick groaned. "You don't? She came to work for you because she thought you would give her a chance." He shook his head. "Maybe she's right. Maybe I need my own franchise."

"You haven't even quit the Bureau yet," Cooper reminded him. "And I can't have you stealing my most trusted employee." Because he wasn't sure he could trust Lars anymore. And if he couldn't trust Lars, he wasn't sure about the others, either.

"Most valuable employee," Nick said. "She's smart and strong. She saved my life and Annalise's. She knows what she's doing."

Cooper could have wound that tape back, could have showed Nick how their sister had kissed Lars before she'd pushed him away. He wasn't convinced she knew what she was doing.

There was only one thing he was convinced of…and the shiver raced through him again.

"You are really worried," Nick said.

He sighed. "Yeah, I think I've got one of those crazy feelings you and Mom get."

Nick shivered now. "Oh, God...what is it?"

"I can't put my finger on it," he said. "I don't have a vision or—"

"I don't get visions," Nick said. "I just *know...*"

Cooper's stomach lurched with the sickening confirmation. "Oh, no..."

"What do you just know, Coop?"

"That something bad is going to happen."

Nick chuckled. "We're Paynes—seems like something bad always happens around us." He leaned closer to that surveillance screen.

"I'm not talking about the kiss," Cooper said. "I don't know if that's bad or not."

"Turned out well for me and Annalise," Nick said with a grin. Happiness radiated off the guy. "Especially for me." He wasn't the same serious guy who'd showed up in River City to clean up the corruption in the police department.

"You're a lucky..." Cooper bit his tongue. He must have been tired to make such an insensitive slip.

But Nick laughed. "Bastard. Yeah, I am." He was the product of an affair but it clearly didn't bother him like it used to—probably thanks to Cooper's mom. She'd made it clear that her husband's cheating on her had nothing to do with Nick.

Nick was still focused on the surveillance monitor.

"What are you looking at?" Cooper asked. Had he missed something?

"I'm looking at the guy," Nick said. "He's huge."

"Yeah." Lars would make a damn good bodyguard, if Cooper could trust him.

"He's really fair-haired and his eyes…"

"They're a very pale blue," Cooper confirmed.

"That's the description I got from the coroner."

Cooper tensed. "Is he dead?" If Nikki had killed him, she'd overreacted a bit to that kiss.

"It's not the description of a corpse," Nick said. "It's the one he gave me of the guy asking about a female Jane Doe. The guy had come around the morgue, checking to see if a woman—fitting that same description of pale hair and eyes—had turned up dead."

Lars had a sister. He and Cooper had had that in common—worrying about their younger sisters while they'd been deployed. That was why he was so certain that the Lars Ecklund he had known wouldn't have gone after Nikki. But maybe he was less sympathetic because his sister was gone. But if she was, why hadn't he mentioned it to Cooper?

"He hasn't said anything about it to me." And he wondered what else Lars was keeping from him.

Nick must have wondered the same because he squeezed Cooper's shoulder and advised him, "Always listen to that gut feeling."

"I know something bad is going to happen," Cooper said. "But how do I stop it?"

Lars didn't want to leave the estate. But his shift was over. And there was no way he would be able to pull off the abduction tonight, not when the lawyer's limo had dropped Webber off at the house just moments ago.

He couldn't risk it since the other guards were patrolling the estate along with Manny and Cole.

They didn't know what was going on, but he probably needed to bring them in if he was going to be able to

get his nephew back. Not if. When. He had to rescue the infant. Holding him for that little while, Lars had been so scared and humbled. This child was the only part of Emilia left in this world. Lars needed to rescue him.

But he forced himself to walk through the gate that opened for him and head down the street to where he'd parked his truck. In addition to the guards, there were the cameras. He had to make sure they'd seen him leaving.

Damn!

There was a camera in the nursery, too. If anyone saw that footage of him kissing Nikki...

Anyone like his boss—he might get tossed off the assignment. He had to be careful. But maybe he could talk Nikki into deleting the footage. She wouldn't want her brother to see it, either. She wouldn't want Cooper to question her professionalism.

Lars needed to bring it to her attention. So he reached for his phone. He didn't have her number, though. He'd kissed her a few times, but they'd never exchanged phone numbers. Then he'd had no business kissing her. He wasn't free to date anyone, let alone his friend's sister. He had too much going on, too much to work through with his loss and the crime he was planning to commit.

If he was caught...

If he was arrested...

What would happen to the baby then? Where would he wind up? In foster care? Adopted?

Lars had to be careful. He also needed Nikki to delete that footage. He stopped beside his truck, torn between leaving and returning. But Nikki should be leaving soon, too. He didn't like the idea of her being

inside the house with the sleazy lawyer. He'd noticed the way the guy had looked at her—probably like he did—like he wanted to take off her clothes and take her...

Tension hummed throughout his body again, demanding release—in hers. If he turned back and talked to her again, there would be more to delete from that surveillance footage than just a kiss.

No. He needed to leave. But before he could pull his keys from his pocket, everything went black. Something covered his head and wrapped tightly around his arms. He struggled to move, to reach for his holster. But his arms were bound against his sides.

He couldn't see. He couldn't fight. Even his legs were trapped in whatever had been wrapped so tightly around him.

Then he was moving as someone lifted and carried him off. He had been planning an abduction. But he had never imagined he would wind up being the victim of an abduction himself.

Chapter 9

Someone grabbed Nikki, jerking her awake. She reached for her weapon, but it was too late. She'd fallen asleep on the job.

And she groaned when she looked up into the face of the man who'd caught her. Her boss...

He held her arm as if to steady her. She probably had nearly fallen out of the rocking chair in which she'd been asleep. Fortunately she'd put the baby back in his crib before she'd taken her nap, or she might have dropped him.

She wasn't proving to be much of a bodyguard or a nanny at the moment. "I'm sorry, Cooper. I must have just nodded off. Until now I've been alert—"

"You're dead on your feet," he said. "You need to go home."

"The nanny left and Webber wouldn't agree to having a new one come in to the house."

He grunted but nodded. "Probably a wise precaution."

"But I could have vetted her."

"People can get really good fake credentials," he said. "Or even good, innocent people can be corrupted with enough money."

Was that what had happened with the mother? The woman who was nowhere around but pumped breast milk for her baby? She didn't know if that had really been breast milk. She had no proof—yet—to back up her suspicions. So she wouldn't bring them up until she had some evidence that Webber was lying.

Instead she asked, "But would whoever is after the little guy have enough money to bribe someone to help?"

She doubted that a single mother would have that kind of money. But was the mother trying to get her son back or giving him up? Nikki had no idea what was going on, and her head began to pound with her confusion. Or lack of sleep...

Cooper shrugged. "I don't know. I'm just telling you that no one can be trusted."

Somehow she didn't think they were talking about nannies anymore.

"I'm sorry," she said again. "I'll stay awake now."

He shook his head. "No. I'm here to relieve you."

"You're going to babysit?"

"I have a son," he reminded her. "I know how to take care of a baby. But I was actually thinking of bringing in Candace to take over this assignment."

Nikki's breath hissed out. "You're not talking about just tonight, are you? You want to take me off the job

already?" Her eyes stung, and she blinked hard, refusing to give in to tears, even ones of frustration.

"All of the people on Logan's team have more experience," he said.

"So you're throwing in the towel already?" Nikki goaded him.

"What?" Cooper asked.

"That's what Logan will think when you ask for help on your very first job," she pointed out. "He'll think you can't handle it."

"He'll know I'm not properly staffed yet," Cooper said, totally undaunted. Of course he had a better relationship with Logan than she did. He had Logan's respect. "I need more guys."

Guys. Of course. She glared at him.

"Or women—if they're qualified," Cooper said.

"I'm qualified." In addition to the shooting range scores and self-defense maneuvers she'd mastered, she'd proved it under fire—more than once.

"You're exhausted," Cooper said. "You need to go home."

She glared harder.

"You need some rest."

"Then you'll let me come back?"

He hesitated.

That was her greatest fear—that if she left, he wouldn't let her return.

She glanced over at the crib where the baby slept peacefully. She couldn't leave Blue and risk not getting to see him again. But then—when Webber found an adoptive family for his child—the baby would be gone. And Nikki would never be able see him again. How had she gotten attached—especially so quickly—

to a child? That was so not like her. Maybe Cooper had cause for his concern.

"Have I given you any reason to doubt I can handle this assignment?" she asked.

He gestured to a corner of the nursery where a small camera lens poked through the crown molding.

Heat rushed to her face. "I take it you've watched some of the footage?"

His face reddening a little, too, he nodded.

"Why?" she asked, anger pushing her embarrassment aside. "Nothing's happened. Why did you feel the need to check up on me?"

"It's the first job for my agency," he said. "I wanted to make sure everything was going well."

"So you watched footage from all the other surveillance cameras?"

His face reddened more.

"So you trust the others, just not me?"

"Lars is the one I apparently shouldn't have trusted," he said.

Nikki wasn't sure she disagreed but for some reason she felt compelled to defend him. "Because he has kissed me a few times?" She snorted. "You're overreacting."

"A few times?" Now Cooper's face paled.

"Stop it," she said. "Stop acting like I'm some helpless little girl who can't take care of herself. I'm a woman. I date." She couldn't remember when she'd gone out last. So much had been happening with her family for the past couple of years that she hadn't had time to think about herself—about her wants or needs. But thanks to Lars she was suddenly very aware she had denied those needs for too long.

"You're dating Lars?" Cooper asked.

She wasn't sure what the hell they were doing. But she couldn't imagine them doing something as mundane as going out to dinner and a movie. They would both be bored senseless. Then again she couldn't imagine being bored with Lars ever, not with the way he made her heart race, her pulse pound...

"That's not any of your business," she said.

"It is if you both want to keep working for me," Cooper said.

She gasped at the ultimatum. "Really? Not even Logan forbade his employees to date or Candace and Garek wouldn't be married and expecting their first baby."

Cooper's eyes widened with surprise. "Candace is pregnant? She didn't say anything when I called her."

"It's new," Nikki said. "Mom just told her she is."

A laugh sputtered out of Cooper. "Of course Mom did."

"You doubt her?"

"No," he said. And any trace of amusement vanished as his expression became grim again. "I understand her better now..."

Nikki tensed. "What are you saying? You got it, too?" It was bad enough that Nick was that intuitive. But Cooper, as well?

He shrugged. "I don't know. I just have this really bad feeling. That's why I watched that surveillance footage."

"Of just me?"

He nodded, and his handsome face was grim, his jaw rigidly clenched.

She tensed. "Your really bad feeling is about me?"

"Yes," he said. "I have this feeling that something bad's going to happen to you."

She shivered, but then she forced a laugh, albeit an

uneasy one. "You are worse than Logan about sheltering me," she said.

He shook his head. "I don't want anything to happen to you."

"Neither do I."

"You don't care," Cooper said. "You're fearless, Nikki."

"Says the Marine."

"I was afraid," Cooper said. "That fear is what kept me alive. You don't have any fear."

Which just proved again how little her brothers knew her. She was afraid—afraid of falling for someone and being betrayed and hurt like their mother had been. But like Cooper, that fear was keeping her safe. She was in no danger of falling for anyone, let alone Lars.

She wasn't the hopeless romantic her mother was. She would never mistake attraction and desire for love. Even if she had sex with Lars, she wouldn't fall for him. Maybe if she had sex with him, she would be less distracted than she was now.

"You know what," she said. "I'll take you up on that offer for a break."

Cooper looked uneasy. Maybe in addition to his premonitions, he could read minds, too. Maybe he knew what she was going to do: look up Lars Ecklund and scratch the itch he'd started.

Then she would be able to focus again on the case. She'd be able to find out who was after Blue and protect him—with her life if necessary.

"Who the hell are you?" Lars yelled. The blanket covered his head yet, and the fabric was too thick to let any light filter through it. He couldn't see anything.

"What do you want?"

Footsteps scraped across concrete. More than one set. But then it would have taken more than one man to lift and carry him as easily as he'd been lifted and carried. Now the hands—at least two sets—dropped away, and he fell onto the hard surface.

His breath whooshed out on a grunt of discomfort. It wasn't really pain, not compared to what he'd gone through before. While they had put the blanket around him, they hadn't done anything to hurt him. Yet.

"Who are you?"

Was this what had happened to Emilia? Had the same people who'd taken her now taken him?

But why? What did they want? He didn't have the baby, although he had every intention of taking custody of his nephew. Was that why he'd been abducted—because they'd figured out his intentions?

They weren't going to stop him. Nobody could.

He struggled to free his arms, and the blanket finally loosened around him. Fists swinging, he flung off the wool fabric and confronted his kidnappers. He blinked, unable to believe his eyes.

Manny and Cole stood in front of him in what must have been some dark warehouse. It was all metal walls and roof and concrete floor. It was mostly dark, so he didn't immediately notice that another man stood in the shadows—until Dane stepped into the tiny circle of light from the bare bulb swinging overhead.

Shocked, Lars could only murmur, "What the hell…?"

"What the hell—exactly," Manny said. "What the hell are you up to?"

He glanced at Dane whose blank expression gave

away nothing of his thoughts. If only Lars could be as stoic.

Because Manny and Cole must have gotten suspicious of how he'd been acting. He knew Dane wouldn't have betrayed his confidence.

He shrugged off their suspicions. "I don't know what you're talking about."

Manny cursed at him then added, "Don't lie to us! We've been through too much together to keep any secrets."

"What makes you think I'm keeping any secrets?" Lars asked. And he glanced at Dane again. He had to be certain that his best friend hadn't talked, because if he had, it may not have been just Manny and Cole with whom he'd shared Lars's secret.

Cole caught that glance between them and jerked Dane around with a hand on his shoulder. "You said you didn't know what the hell was going on!"

"You lied to us!" Manny exclaimed.

Dane shook his head. "I said I couldn't tell you…"

Cole cursed.

"You just assumed I couldn't tell you because I didn't know," Dane continued.

"Playing semantic games with us?" Cole snorted in disgust. "What the hell happened to us? We had no secrets between us in Iraq or Afghanistan."

Or the other places they'd been that no one could ever know about…

Lars knew everything there was to know about these guys. And above all, he knew that he could trust them. "I intended to bring you in on this."

Because he had no choice.

Dane nodded. "That's why I went along with their plan to abduct you."

Lars glared at him.

And Dane laughed. "And because I thought it was damn funny, too."

Lars glared harder at him.

"You used to love parties," Dane reminded him. "So when they suggested a blanket party…"

"You were all in," Lars said. "You could have just told them."

"It's not my story to tell," Dane said. "And you would have been pissed if I had."

A horrible thought occurred to Lars and he glanced around the warehouse, looking for anyone else who might have been lurking in the shadows. "Did you guys bring Cooper into this?"

"No," Dane said.

"We thought about it," Manny said. "But then decided he has bigger issues right now."

"But you didn't throw a blanket party for him."

Cole chuckled. "He's not keeping any secrets. He's just stressed about starting his own business and taking on his first job. That's why he—and we—need you to be at full capacity. We depend on each other. We can't depend on someone we don't trust."

Lars flinched. It was true, though. Trust was huge in a unit—and, more important, in a friendship. But before he divulged too much, he had to get a promise from them—the same one he'd made Dane grant.

"Coop is stressed and under enormous pressure," he agreed. "So we can't bring him into this."

Manny groaned. "I don't want to keep any secrets, especially not from our new boss." Manny wasn't

known for his ability to stay mum about anything—except their missions.

"It has nothing to do with him being our boss. Coop's our friend," Cole said. "That's why we shouldn't keep any secrets from him. We can trust him, too."

Lars sighed. "I know. But he has too much to lose if this all goes south."

Manny's big body tensed. "What goes south? What the hell's going on?"

"I'm planning to kidnap my nephew."

Cole gasped.

"And I need your help," he continued.

"That little baby at Webber's—he's your sister's kid?" Manny asked, the gears almost visibly turning behind his dark eyes. "What happened to her?"

"She's dead."

Manny and Cole both reached out to him, each grabbing one of his shoulders. "I'm sorry, man," Cole said. "I know she's all the family you had."

Cole had a lot of family himself, but he claimed to not want anything to do with them. Now Lars wondered if that was truly how he felt.

"She's not all the family. She left a son."

"You really intend to kidnap him?" Manny asked.

"I have to get him out of that place," Lars said.

Dane shuddered and nodded in agreement. "It's creepy. And so's the lawyer. Even his own guards don't trust him."

"He has all those guards of his own yet," Manny said. "That's how we were able to slip away tonight to grab you. There are so many of them we won't even be missed. So how are we going to get around them?"

"Same way we got around far more armed men on our other missions," Lars said. "We'll work together."

The two men hesitated. And he couldn't blame them. "I know what I'm asking," he said. "You're risking your lives and your freedom to help me."

Manny snorted. "It's bad when the worst that can happen isn't even getting killed." He was probably thinking about jail. He wouldn't want to wind up in prison; a lot of his family was already there.

"You don't have to help me," Lars said. "Just don't rat me out to Cooper. Or he'll pull me off this assignment before I get a chance to even try for my nephew."

"Cooper is the least of your problems," Dane said.

Lars's phone began to vibrate. He pulled it from his pocket and looked at the screen, which was a text that said: This is Nikki Payne. Call me. His pulse quickened, more adrenaline surging through him now than it had when he'd been abducted.

Dane was close enough that he read the screen, too. "She's your biggest problem," his friend warned him. "I'm not sure how you're going to get around her."

"I have some ideas."

If he could distract her...

"You just lost your sister," Cole said. "Make sure that Cooper doesn't lose his."

"So you're not going to help me?" His heart grew heavy. He had been counting on them. Without them, he didn't know if he and the baby would get out of that estate alive.

Sleep eluded Penny. She lay stiffly in the arms of her fiancé, trying not to keep him awake, as well.

But he was too attuned to her. Her tension was in his body, too. "What's wrong?" he asked.

Her breath slipped out in a sigh that whispered across his bare chest.

"You can't be worried about the wedding," he said. "We have the very best wedding planner, my love."

She tried to smile like she knew he wanted her to, but she was too worried. "I'm not worried about our wedding."

"The marriage, then?"

She'd often remarked how the young couples coming through her chapel needed to focus more on that than the ceremony. The marriage was far more important than the wedding. The wedding was one day. The marriage was supposed to last a lifetime.

She knew that would be the case with her and Woodrow. It wasn't their lifetime she was worried about—it was Nikki's. "I think my daughter is in danger again."

A sigh escaped his lips now. And he asked, "Why?"

"Because she's working as a real bodyguard now."

"I know. I was asking why you would worry about her. That girl has proven over and over again that she can take care of herself," Woodrow said with a father's pride in the young woman who would soon be his stepdaughter.

"I'm not sure that's true this time," Penny said. Because it wasn't just Nikki's life that was in danger but her heart, as well.

One of Cooper's friends meant more to her than she was willing to admit—even to herself. Nikki was so convinced that she would never fall in love that she wouldn't be aware she had until it was too late.

Woodrow stroked his fingers over her bare shoulder,

and as always, her skin tingled with his touch. "You don't have the connection with Nikki that you have with your other kids," he reminded her.

Or that she had with him.

Her daughter had always been more of an enigma to Penny than anyone else. While they looked so much alike, appearance was really all they had in common.

"So don't get worried about something you don't *know* will happen," he advised her. "Nikki will be fine."

Penny wanted to take his advice; she wanted to believe him. But it was just too hard. Maybe she had finally developed that connection with Nikki that they had lacked—because she had no doubt her daughter was in danger.

Real danger.

Chapter 10

When Nikki arrived the next morning to reclaim her post in the nursery, she found strangers inside it. An older couple stood over the crib, staring down at the baby. The lawyer was inside, too, along with an exhausted-looking Cooper. He hadn't called Candace in to take over, at least not yet.

The pressure in Nikki's lungs eased as a small breath of relief escaped her lips. But the tension remained in her body. She hadn't found the release for it that she'd wanted. She'd gone to the trouble of hacking Cooper's phone and retrieving his directory to no avail.

Lars hadn't answered her text. He hadn't called her. He might have been sleeping. From the dark circles, she'd noticed the past few days, beneath his stunningly blue eyes, he didn't appear to have had much rest recently. So maybe his body had finally forced his mind to succumb to exhaustion.

If only she could have done the same…

She'd spent last night awake, worrying. Not just about baby Blue but about her disappointment over Lars not calling her.

Had he been with someone else?

It was a possibility she hadn't considered when she'd decided to text him her number. But now she wondered. Maybe he was seeing someone else already. He was a flirt. He probably flirted with more women than just Nikki.

Nikki had plenty of men who flirted with her, too, or who looked at her like the lawyer had, as if he was undressing her with his eyes. She didn't need Lars to get that release she needed. But there was no way she would ever let someone like Myron Webber touch her.

She shivered over how just his gaze went over her.

"Do you want to pick him up?" the lawyer asked the couple.

The woman nervously shook her head. "No." Apparently she only liked to window-shop. "We've seen enough."

"We'll get back to you," the husband added like he was talking to a salesman on a car lot.

And like that salesman Myron rushed out after them, presumably to show them out. But she suspected he wanted to continue his sales spiel.

Cooper waited until the door closed behind his client before he turned toward her and asked, "What the hell's going on?"

"He didn't tell you?"

"That he was selling his kid?" Cooper shook his head.

"He wants to give him a family," Nikki said. "He's giving him up for adoption."

Cooper ran his hand over his closely cropped hair. He wasn't working as a Marine anymore, but he still looked like one, just like the men he'd hired. "I don't like this case," he said. "At all. I may need to drop this client."

"No!"

Cooper sighed. "There will be other jobs, other opportunities for you to work as a bodyguard."

She wasn't so sure about that, but at the moment she didn't care. "That's not why I want to stay on this job," she said.

"Then why—"

A cry interrupted Cooper. Nikki hurried to the crib and lifted the upset baby into her arms. His blue eyes were squeezed shut with the scrunched-up look on his tiny face, but tears leaked from the corners of his eyes and wet her neck as she snuggled him against her.

"Shhh, Blue," she murmured. "You're all right. I'm here. I'm back. I'll make sure you stay safe."

Cooper stared at her, his eyes wide with astonishment. "He's why you want to stay on the job?"

She nodded. "Yes, he's so alone, so vulnerable."

"He has his father…" Cooper's voice trailed off. "For now…until he gives him up." A father himself, he was obviously appalled at the thought of giving up his child. But then he was married and could give his son a whole family.

"Something's not right about this," Cooper murmured. "About any of this…"

"I know," Nikki readily agreed. "And that's why we have to stay. We have to figure out what the truth is."

"The truth?" a deep voice asked.

Nikki glanced to the open nursery door. The jamb was filled with over six feet eight inches of muscle.

Lars had to duck slightly to enter the room and turn his shoulders a little to the side. He was so big and broad.

Ignoring the quickening of her pulse, she snorted. "Like you would know anything about that."

His brow furrowed. "I'm offended."

Maybe he was, but he wasn't claiming to be an honest man, either. Nikki had a feeling Lars was lying as much as the lawyer was.

"You're late," Cooper said.

Lars shook his head. "No, I'm right on time, boss."

"I texted you a while ago about meeting me here."

So apparently hers weren't the only text messages Lars ignored. He must have been with someone because he still had the dark circles rimming his pale blue eyes. He hadn't been sleeping.

"I'm sorry," Lars said. "I didn't get it."

"Cole's taking your position in the house today," Cooper said. "And you're going back to the office with me."

"Any reason why?" Lars asked.

Nikki pointed toward the camera in the corner of the room and warned him, "*Someone* watched the surveillance footage." Her face heated with embarrassment over what her brother had witnessed. She had been so stupid to not only let Lars kiss her but to also kiss him back, while she'd been on the job.

Lars groaned. "Coop, I can explain—"

"You will," Cooper agreed. "Down at the office." He headed toward the door.

Lars hesitated, his pale-eyed gaze focused on Nikki. He acted like he wanted to say something to her. But when he opened his mouth, Cooper shouted his name.

And the baby began to fuss in her arms. She held

him close for his protection and hers. She didn't want to hear whatever Lars had to say.

Not that she was mad he hadn't called her. She didn't actually care. And really, it had probably been for the best. Having sex with him would not have been a good idea, not when they were working together.

Unless Cooper was bringing him back to the office to fire him...

"Wait," she called out.

And Lars stopped.

"Cooper," she said.

Her brother appeared in the doorway again. "What?"

"Don't overreact," she advised him.

He sighed. Maybe he was irritated with her. Maybe he was just tired after a sleepless night babysitting. He said nothing, just turned and walked away.

Lars paused, staring at her and the baby. He mouthed the words *thank you*.

But she wasn't sure Cooper would listen to her advice. She wasn't sure that she would ever see Lars Eck-lund again.

Ignoring the sharp twinge of disappointment that thought brought on, Nikki focused on the baby. He was so warm, so sweet. She found the bottle the lawyer must have brought up with the prospective adoptive parents.

Like the other one, the bottle felt warmer than the milk. It must have been frozen or chilled. She licked her wrist again and tasted it. It was soapy and sweet.

Could it be breast milk?

But if the mother was really dead, where had the lawyer gotten it? She doubted women sold their breast milk for other babies to consume. Wouldn't they need that for their own babies?

Of course Nikki knew nothing about motherhood, and she had no intention of learning anything. All she wanted was to protect Blue.

She suspected the person from whom he needed the most protection was the one who claimed to be his father. She gazed down at the baby, who stared up at her with those eerily pale blue eyes that so resembled Lars's. Would his irises really darken as he grew older? Or was this the color he'd genetically inherited?

She had another suspicion about Blue's father, about who the man really was. But if she was right, why hadn't that man claimed him?

Careful to avoid the camera seeing what she was doing, Nikki took a saliva swab from the baby and a sample of the breast milk. Then she slid the collection back into the DNA kit she'd picked up on her way over to the estate and tucked it inside her computer bag. She needed to know what the hell was really going on.

"For you," she whispered to the baby as she held him again. "You'll want to know the truth someday." And Nikki wanted to know it now.

Feeling someone's stare, she glanced up and found Myron Webber standing in the nursery doorway. His eyes were dark, so dark that she knew Blue's eyes would never get that color. And they were already bigger in his tiny face than Webber's were in his fleshy one.

"You are very good with him," he told her.

She smiled down at the child. "He's a very good baby."

"That's what I just told that couple," Myron murmured as he stepped closer.

"Are you sure you really want to give him up?" Nikki felt compelled to ask. "If he were mine…"

The lawyer sighed. "He is only mine in the sense that I became his legal guardian when his mother passed away in childbirth."

"Oh," she said. "His mother granted you custody in case she didn't make it? Was it a high-risk pregnancy for her?"

He lifted a slightly shaking hand and ran it through his thick hair. "She was very young. I doubt she had had any prenatal care before she came to me."

Nikki's arms tightened protectively around Blue. "That's so sad. The doctors weren't able to save her?"

His face reddened slightly. "No. No," he stammered. "They couldn't do anything for her."

Nikki didn't have her mom's instincts, but somehow she knew the lawyer was lying. She could have asked him about the breast milk, but she doubted he would give her an honest answer. So there was no sense in asking and alerting him to her suspicions. "What was his mother like?" she asked.

He shrugged. "It doesn't matter."

"Someday he'll want to know about his mother," she persisted. And she wanted to know about her now, like where the hell she was. "He'll want to know about his father, too. Where's he?"

The lawyer shrugged again. "I have no idea. I don't think the mother even knew who he was. And it won't matter to the baby who his biological parents were. He'll have new parents soon. Those are the only people he will need to remember."

"You're sure you don't want to keep him?" she asked.

He laughed. "I'm not father material."

Nikki believed that.

"I prefer the single life." He stepped closer to her. "I

enjoy going to nice restaurants and traveling. What do you enjoy, Ms. Payne?"

The truth. And she doubted she'd get that out of him. She smiled. "My job."

"Your boyfriend must not like how much time you spend at work, though."

She'd forgotten she'd claimed she had a significant other. But she did not want this man's attention. She barely contained a shiver of revulsion over his closeness and the way he kept looking at her.

"My boyfriend appreciates how much my job means to me," she lied.

If she were ever to get involved with anyone, he would have to respect what she did—and not want to protect her like her damn brothers.

Myron looked her up and down and uttered a sigh of resignation. "He's a lucky man."

She waited until he left before giving in to the shiver of revulsion. After eating, the baby fell asleep, so she settled him back into his crib. Then she reached into her bag and, careful to not pull out the DNA kit, she pulled out just her laptop.

She needed to find out everything she could about Myron Webber. But more important, she needed to find out who the baby was—who his mother was.

And who his father was.

She heard a gurgle and walked over to the crib. With something like a toothless grin, the baby stared up at her, his eyes wide and such a pale blue. She had a pretty damn good idea who his father was.

She had a DNA sample from the baby and from the breast milk. Now she needed a sample from that man.

Remembering how he'd reacted the first time he'd

seen Blue and how awed he'd looked when he'd held him, Nikki suspected he cared very much.

So why hadn't he claimed him—like the lawyer had tried?

"What the hell are you up to, Lars Ecklund?" she murmured because she believed he wasn't being any more honest with them than the lawyer was.

Frustration gripped Lars. He couldn't get fired. It would blow what was left of a plan that was quickly falling apart. He wasn't sure what he could say or do to change Cooper's mind, so he held his silence during the drive from Webber's estate to the office.

Cooper said nothing either until he settled wearily into the chair behind his desk. Then finally he spoke, asking, "What the hell are you up to?"

"I'm sorry, Coop," Lars said.

And he was truly sorry that he couldn't be honest with a man who had always been a good friend to him. But it was for Cooper's own good that Lars lied.

It was better that he not know everything that was going on. But there was no denying what he'd seen on that surveillance video.

"I shouldn't have crossed that line with your sister," he said.

Cooper narrowed his eyes as if doubting his sincerity.

Lars was actually being honest about that; he shouldn't have crossed that line because now he couldn't uncross it. He couldn't not want to kiss her again—to touch her again—to hold her...

"What about *your* sister?" Cooper asked.

Lars sucked in a breath as if Coop had punched him. He'd thought he might—physically. Not like this…

"What about her?" he asked.

"I heard you've been looking for her."

"Damn it…" Who had betrayed him? He'd thought he could trust the other guys. He should have known Manny couldn't keep a secret. "Who told you that?"

"My brother Nick," Cooper said. "He told me that someone matching your description was asking at the morgue about Jane Does."

Lars shook his head. He hadn't wanted to outright lie to Cooper. But he had no choice. "He must have gotten it wrong."

"I could have him pull surveillance footage from the morgue."

Lars shrugged. "You really have that kind of time to waste?"

Cooper sighed. "No. I don't. That's why I need you to just be honest with me, man. Tell me what's going on with you."

He shrugged again. "I don't know what you're talking about."

"You've been different ever since you came back."

"A lot of guys are."

"Not Dane. Or Manny. Or Cole. They're the same as they were," Coop insisted. "You're the only one who's different. You've got something weighing on you. You look like you haven't slept in weeks."

Lars gestured toward Cooper, who had dark circles beneath his eyes. "You should talk."

"It's this damn case," Cooper murmured. "Despite what Nikki said, I think I should drop this client."

"Nikki doesn't want you to do that?" He breathed a

sigh of relief and silently thanked Nikki. Hopefully her brother would listen to her this time.

"She's getting attached to the baby," Cooper said. "She wants to make sure nothing happens to him."

Lars had thought Nikki protecting his nephew would make it easier for him to grab the baby. Now he realized that Dane was right; she might be the biggest problem with his plan.

As Dane settled onto the chair in front of Cooper's desk, he felt like he'd been called to the principal's office. It was a feeling he remembered well from his school days. He'd always been getting in trouble.

Back then it had been his fault. Now it was because of the company he kept and the confidences. "Hey, boss, what's up?" he asked.

"You tell me," Cooper said. "What the hell's going on with Lars?"

Dane shrugged. "I couldn't tell you."

Because he had been sworn to silence. But his guts twisted with regret. He hated keeping a secret from a friend, even though it was for another friend.

"He's in trouble," Cooper said.

Lars had already given him a heads-up about the surveillance footage.

"Because he kissed your sister?" Dane asked. "Don't you think you're overreacting a little?"

Cooper glared at him. "Now you sound like my sister."

From what he'd seen of her so far, Nikki was tough and independent. So he wasn't offended. "Maybe you should listen to us."

"I'm not talking about my sister," Coop said. "I think it's Lars's sister we need to talk about."

Dane shook his head. "I've never met her." And now he would never have the chance. His guts twisted with more regret. He had a picture of her on his phone—one Lars had texted to him so that Dane would know what she looked like when they'd been searching for her.

"I think she's missing," Cooper said. "I think Lars needs help."

"If he did, he'd ask for it," Dane said. He hadn't actually asked, though; Dane had given him no choice.

"I thought you knew him best," Coop said. "He's stubborn and proud and he would risk his own damn life before he'd ask for help."

Lars was going to risk his life anyway, and Dane knew there was nothing he could do to stop him. There was no point getting Cooper involved. He had too much to lose. Dane was the one with nothing to lose. And because of that he would do his best to keep Lars alive, even if it meant giving up his own life.

YOUR PARTICIPATION IS REQUESTED!

Dear Reader,

Since you are a lover of our books – we would like to get to know you!

Inside you will find a short Reader's Survey. Sharing your answers with us will help our editorial staff understand who you are and what activities you enjoy.

To thank you for your participation, we would like to send you 2 books and 2 gifts – **ABSOLUTELY FREE!**

Enjoy your gifts with our appreciation,

Pam Powers

SEE INSIDE FOR READER'S SURVEY

For Your Reading Pleasure...

We'll send you 2 books and 2 gifts
ABSOLUTELY FREE
just for completing our Reader's Survey!

YOUR READER'S SURVEY
"THANK YOU" FREE GIFTS INCLUDE:
- ▶ **2 FREE books**
- ▶ **2 lovely surprise gifts**

PLEASE FILL IN THE CIRCLES COMPLETELY TO RESPOND

1) What type of fiction books do you enjoy reading? (Check all that apply)
- ○ Suspense/Thrillers   ○ Action/Adventure   ○ Modern-day Romances
- ○ Historical Romance   ○ Humor   ○ Paranormal Romance

2) What attracted you most to the last fiction book you purchased on impulse?
- ○ The Title   ○ The Cover   ○ The Author   ○ The Story

3) What is usually the greatest influencer when you <u>plan</u> to buy a book?
- ○ Advertising   ○ Referral   ○ Book Review

4) How often do you access the internet?
- ○ Daily   ○ Weekly   ○ Monthly   ○ Rarely or never

5) How many NEW paperback fiction novels have you purchased in the past 3 months?
- ○ 0 - 2   ○ 3 - 6   ○ 7 or more

YES! I have completed the Reader's Survey. Please send me the 2 FREE books and 2 FREE gifts (gifts are worth about $10 retail) for which I qualify. I understand that I am under no obligation to purchase any books, as explained on the back of this card.

240/340 HDL GLN6

FIRST NAME   LAST NAME

ADDRESS

APT.#   CITY

STATE/PROV.   ZIP/POSTAL CODE

RS-217-SUR17

READER SERVICE—Here's how it works:

Chapter 11

The nanny hadn't come back. Either she was still sick or just sick of working for Myron Webber. Nikki couldn't blame her. The man was creepy, and so was the house. The entire estate had an eerie ambiance about it. It was stark and cold.

Nikki shivered as she stepped back from the crib. She missed the warmth and weight of the infant. He had fallen asleep in her arms, and she'd had to force herself to put him in his bed.

Her breath shuddered out as she stared down at him. What if the lawyer gave him away soon? She would miss him. But his getting adopted was the least of her concerns at the moment. She needed to keep him safe.

As night fell, that eerie feeling increased. To keep Blue resting peacefully, she had to turn down the lights, but then the shadows encroached. No light even shone

beneath the door. Had the lights been switched off in the hall?

Someone was supposed to be outside the door, guarding the nursery from outside the room. The day before it had been Lars, but Cooper had brought him back to the office. And as far as she knew, he hadn't returned.

Had he fired him? Just over the kiss?

Or did he believe, like she did, that something else was going on with Lars?

He had been visibly upset—at least to her—when he'd learned the baby's mother was dead. Because he'd been involved with her? He must have gotten her pregnant before he'd deployed. Maybe he hadn't known about the baby. Maybe that was why he'd looked so shocked when he'd seen the infant.

Or had she only imagined his reactions? She wasn't as intuitive as her mom and Nick. She couldn't trust her instincts. She needed facts.

But she hadn't been able to find anything online. Sure, there had been complaints about the lawyer. She'd found those—a lot of those. At least her instincts about him had been right. But none of those complaints had involved Blue. If his mother was alive, she wasn't trying to get him back. Maybe she'd given him up willingly.

A twinge of pain struck Nikki's heart.

Poor little guy...

He deserved to be loved. And protected...

The floor creaked in the hall. Then the doorknob rattled and began to turn.

"Who's there?" she called out as she reached for her holster. But she hesitated before drawing her weapon. She would prefer to not have to fire a gun around the

baby. During her last gun battle, an innocent man had gotten caught in the crossfire.

Woodrow Lynch had nearly died. Nikki shuddered at the thought. Her mother would have been devastated, and she'd already lost too much.

If something happened to Blue, Nikki would be the one devastated. She couldn't risk it. Couldn't risk something happening to the baby. At the very least the noise of the gun firing might shatter his sensitive eardrums. She couldn't risk his safety. She would rather risk her own.

As the door opened, she could see nothing. The faint light she'd had on in the nursery was suddenly extinguished. She saw only an enormous shadow barreling straight toward her.

"Who are you?" she demanded to know again.

And again, there was no reply.

So she drew in a deep breath and recalled everything Candace had taught her. Keeping low, she charged at the shadow. She might wind up getting every bone in her body broken, but she wouldn't go down without a fight.

One hell of a fight...

All the breath escaped Lars's lungs as he flopped—hard—onto his back on the floor. What the hell had hit him?

Before he could regain his feet, a foot struck him right in his most sensitive area. And a groan of pain followed the breath from his lips. Then he cursed.

"Lars!" Nikki exclaimed. She must have recognized his voice because it was still black.

Then the lights flipped on again. He hadn't thought he would need much time to overpower Nikki and grab the baby. Or he would have told Dane to wait longer

before he threw the circuit breaker back on. He hadn't told him long enough. He had underestimated the time he would need to get his nephew, and more important, he'd underestimated Nikki.

She stood over him, her curls glowing in that light. Her breasts heaved as she breathed heavily. She was so damn beautiful.

But her brow furrowed as she glared down at him. "What the hell are you doing?"

Unable to speak yet with the pain in his groin crippling him, he could only shake his head.

Then someone else echoed her question as the door burst open. "What the hell's going on in here?" Cooper demanded.

Lars fought to regain his breath and his voice. He needed to come up with something—some explanation. Or he would be fired right now. Or worse…

He would have killed to protect Emilia if he'd been given the chance. He fully expected Coop to do the same for his sister.

But Nikki answered before he could come up with an excuse. "I was just showing Lars some of the maneuvers Candace taught me."

"Candace is here now," Cooper said. "She's going to relieve you."

Lars wondered if that might not be indefinitely.

Nikki must have thought the same thing because she waved a hand down at Lars lying prone on the floor yet. He would move when all his muscles stopped aching.

"Haven't I proved that I can handle this job?" she asked.

"Yes," her brother assured her. "She's relieving you because you already worked one shift." He glanced down at Lars. "What are you doing here?"

"My perimeter shift just ended," Lars reminded him.

"Exactly. What are you doing in the house?"

"Checking to see if I was done yet," Nikki answered for him.

Cooper tensed now. "What—the two of you have plans?"

"Yes," Nikki answered again.

Maybe she was trying to get him killed. Telling Cooper the truth might have had fewer consequences than telling him they were going on a date.

Trying to play along with the excuse she'd given him, Lars said, "I'm going to show her some more maneuvers."

Like his sister had moments before, Cooper glared down at him.

And heat rushed to Lars's face. "That's not what I meant."

"Since he recommended me for this position, he wanted to make sure I can handle it," Nikki said, jumping in with another explanation.

Cooper gestured at Lars lying on the floor. "Looks like you proved that."

Lars couldn't believe how quickly she'd taken him down. He'd thought he would take her by surprise, get her gun away from her, zip-tie her hands and take the child. But she'd taken him by surprise barreling at him like she had, taking him down at his knees.

"What's going on?" a female voice asked.

"Just showing the boys what you taught me," Nikki said with a chuckle.

The tall brunette must have been the infamous female bodyguard, Candace Baker-Kozminski. She laughed, too. "I see that. Nice job."

Before the discussion could go any further, the baby began to cry. The tussle hadn't awakened him but all the conversation must have. Nikki moved automatically toward the crib and his nephew, lifting him into her arms.

Candace cooed at the baby as she joined her friend.

A hand extended toward Lars. He wasn't sure if it was going to hit him or help him. But he took it, and Cooper tugged him to his feet.

"I'm the boss," Coop said, but then winced and murmured, "Now I sound like my brother Logan."

"You do," Nikki agreed even though she'd been in midconversation with Candace, telling her all about Blue the way a parent would fill in a babysitter.

Lars lost his breath for a moment. That was what he'd called Emilia when she was a baby—Baby Blue because like him, she had the Ecklund pale blue eyes.

Cooper's hand tightened like a vise on his, squeezing painfully until Lars flinched and focused on him again. "I know, I know," he assured his boss. "You're the one in charge."

"Then what the hell were you doing testing *my* employee?"

Lars suspected he wouldn't have minded had Nikki been any employee but his sister. "Helping out a coworker?" he asked the question.

This was Nikki's story, not his. He hadn't planned on failing in his mission. So he hadn't come up with any excuses to use if he was caught.

Damn her. He should have been furious with her.

She was obviously furious with him. Her face was flushed and her usually warm eyes were dark and hard. So why hadn't she given him up to her brother? Why was she making the excuses he was too befuddled to make?

How the hell had she—who was all petite and delicate—easily overpowered him? She'd messed up his plan. Instead of taking his nephew, he could only watch as Candace took the infant from Nikki and snuggled him against her chest. Lars should have been the one cradling him close as he got him the hell off the estate.

Damn Nikki...

Before Cooper could interrogate him any further, she grabbed his arm and tugged him toward the door. "Shift's over," she told her brother. "You don't want us getting overly tired, so that we're not alert for our next shift."

That was why Lars had decided to stage the abduction at the end of her shift. He'd thought she would have been tired. But not Nikki.

It was almost as if she'd expected him, as if she knew what he was up to. Had one of the other guys given him up and warned her about him? Or did she have that thing she claimed only her mother and one brother had?

Had she just *known*?

Teeth chattering, Emilia wrapped her arms around her body, but there was no warmth to hold in. She was chilled to the bone. But maybe it wasn't the cold making her shake. Maybe it was the fear. It was paralyzing her.

She knew she had to rally and fight if she had any hope of surviving. The next time that door opened, she had to be ready to run. She rolled off the damp mattress until her knees scraped over concrete. Then she put her palms on the ground and pushed up. Her legs shook, refusing to hold her weight.

Weeks had passed since she'd had her baby. Why hadn't she regained her strength? Was it because she'd

lost so much blood? Her teeth chattered more, and her trembling increased. She was freezing, but as her arms and legs folded beneath her, her forehead touched the back of her hand and she realized she was burning up. She was sick. She needed help. She tried to scream for it, but only a whimper escaped her lips.

She must have blacked out for a moment because she never heard the door open but someone touched her, dragging her back onto the mattress.

"Wake up!" The words were shouted at her, and a hand grasped her chin, shaking it from side to side until she dragged up her eyelids and focused on the face in front of her.

Dark, soulless eyes stared back at her.

She shivered.

The devil asked, "Who the hell are you?"

"You know who I am."

"Nobody," he said. "I thought you were nobody."

What little she could remember of her meeting with this lawyer had been questions regarding her family, her friends. She'd told him she had nobody because Lars had been gone. And she hadn't wanted him to know how she'd let him down, that she'd gotten pregnant.

"I am," she whispered.

"Then why would somebody be looking for you?"

Her pulse, that had been so thready and weak, quickened. "How do you know?"

"I think he tried calling me," the lawyer admitted. "At least someone did, saying that they had questions about you, but I wouldn't take the call."

Of course he wouldn't want to talk to Lars.

"Apparently that didn't stop him. I have a friend at the morgue."

She shuddered over the reason why he might because he provided bodies to it. He was definitely going to kill her.

"A big guy came by asking about a woman, who would have recently given birth, fitting your description."

A big guy. Could it be…?

"The guy had the same coloring he described—yours. Who the hell is he?"

"My brother," she murmured.

His fingers pinched her chin, squeezing hard. "You told me you had no family."

Tears sprang to her eyes, both of pain and relief. "He's a Marine. I didn't know that he had survived his last deployment."

Especially when he hadn't found her yet.

But he was looking.

"That's too bad," the lawyer remarked, and his fingers slid away from her face.

Her eyes widened in shock. How could he say that was a bad thing? "Why?"

"Because he survived war only to die at home."

"You didn't—you aren't—going to kill him?"

"I can't have anyone asking questions about you," he said. "I can't have anyone getting suspicious of me."

She had been the minute she'd met him. If only she hadn't set up that meeting…

If only she had never considered giving up her baby…

It was all her fault, what had happened to her, what had happened to her child. And now Lars. He had survived war. He could survive anything, couldn't he? She already felt so much guilt over losing her baby. She could not lose her brother, too.

Chapter 12

"I should kill you," Nikki threatened as she slammed the door shut to the home to which Lars had led her. He must have just rented it because it had been like he hadn't known where it was.

He had driven such a circuitous route to it. Or maybe he'd just been trying to lose her. But thanks to Garek Kozminski's tutelage, she'd gotten good at tailing someone—so good that Lars hadn't been able to shake her.

He rubbed his hand around the back of his neck and arched his back until it cracked. Then he ruefully remarked, "I thought you were going to kill me."

"You're lucky I didn't pull my gun and shoot you." If she hadn't been worried about hitting Blue in the crossfire or bursting his little eardrums, she might have killed Lars. She trembled over the realization—

or maybe that was just the adrenaline coursing through her yet.

"I'm lucky you didn't give me up to Cooper," he said as if her shooting him wouldn't have necessarily been a bad thing.

And maybe it wouldn't have been. Of course he didn't know how good a shot she was.

"Why didn't you tell Cooper the truth?" he asked. "Why did you cover for me?"

"Because I'm giving you a chance to explain what the hell you're up to." That was why she had insisted on following him back to his house.

He must have just rented the little bungalow. It was nearly as stark as Webber's mansion, the white walls and wood floors bare. There wasn't even any furniture, only a couple of boxes leaning against one of the living room walls.

He shook his head. "I can't."

She pushed past him in the small foyer and walked over to those boxes. He followed her quickly as if to stop her, but she already saw what she'd expected to see: confirmation of her suspicion.

Her heart pounding, she pointed to the box with a picture of a crib on the outside of it. "I knew it! Blue is yours."

He shook his head again.

The baby was his. Why wouldn't he admit it? And why the hell had he been flirting with her when he had a woman out there, someone who'd given him a baby? Of course he didn't know that she could still be alive.

But he must have cared about her—a lot—since he'd looked so devastated when the lawyer had claimed the baby's mother died in childbirth.

Nikki could have eased some of his pain. But she wouldn't share her information—unless he shared his. Maybe that was spiteful, but that wasn't the only emotion making her feel nausea. She was jealous, too—jealous of the woman with whom he'd made such a beautiful baby, jealous of how much he'd cared about her…

"I gave you a chance to be honest with me," she said. Not that she trusted him to tell her the truth. How could she?

He had obviously been using her, setting her up as the bodyguard because he'd thought he could overpower her. And the kisses, those must have been just to distract her. He was a son of a bitch, and she should have given him up in the nursery. She couldn't even look at him anymore, so she headed back to the foyer and the door.

"Where are you going?" he called after her.

"To tell Cooper everything." And hope he forgave her for not being immediately forthcoming. She had wanted to give Lars a chance to explain first, but he clearly had no intention of doing any such thing.

Maybe it just wasn't in him to be honest. It was a good thing they'd never gone beyond kisses.

She reached for the knob, but before she could turn it to escape, he grabbed her. He had moved quickly and silently; she hadn't even heard his footsteps crossing the wood floor.

Her pulse quickened as adrenaline coursed through her again. She moved to fight him off, like she had in the nursery. But now he anticipated her maneuver and trapped her leg between his thighs. Then he wrapped his arms tightly around her struggling body, holding her against the long, hard length of his.

Through their clothes, she could feel his heat. And his power...

He was so damn big. So damn strong.

She couldn't move. She could only speak, so she said it again, "He's your son, isn't he? How the hell can you keep denying him?"

He just stared down at her, unwilling to share. But he must have been stunned, so stunned that his grasp loosened. She tugged easily free of him and reached for the doorknob again. She didn't hesitate this time; she turned it.

Lars had thought it was over back at the estate, that once Nikki had knocked him down and the lights had come on that he'd lost his chance forever to claim his nephew. He'd thought that at the very least Cooper would fire him; at the most he might have had him arrested. But Nikki had given him time—time to come clean with her.

Maybe he could trust her. The door opened. Hell, he had no choice. He had to trust her. And she was right. He couldn't keep denying his blood—his family. His only family...

"He's my nephew."

She gasped and turned back toward him. "Nephew?" she asked, almost hopefully.

He nodded.

"Is that why you wanted to work for Cooper?"

"I didn't know about Blue," he said, using her nickname for the baby. "I had no idea Emilia was even pregnant when I deployed. I just knew my sister was missing and the last person she had talked to was Myron Webber."

"Son of a bitch," Nikki murmured.

Lars didn't know if she was referring to the lawyer or to him. Did she think he was lying? That he'd made up the story? Or did she believe him?

She reached for the door again. But instead of walking out it, she shut it and turned back toward him.

"Webber is such a sleaze," she said.

He was far worse than that.

"He either killed her or he let her die in childbirth." Pain squeezed Lars's heart. His sister was gone. And Myron Webber needed to be held accountable—but not until Blue was safe.

Nikki tilted her head, and her curls brushed across her cheek. He wanted to push them back, but he'd already touched her too much. He could smell her on his clothes, feel her warmth against his skin. And he wanted to touch her some more...

Maybe he just needed the consolation he'd refused from his friends. Maybe he just needed to feel close to someone. And Nikki was close. But not close enough...

Before he could reach for her again, his phone vibrated in his pocket. He pulled it out and glanced at the screen. "Cooper..."

Nikki snorted. But the second his stopped, her phone began to ring. She didn't even pull it out before murmuring, "Cooper..."

She must have had a special ringtone for him. Or she just *knew*.

"Why haven't you told him?" she asked. "My brother is your friend."

"That's why I haven't told him," Lars replied. "I don't want him getting in trouble with me, jeopardizing his new business and family."

"I don't under—"

"There's no way I can legally compel Webber to hand my nephew over," he explained. "No proof that he's mine."

"DNA—"

"Is inadmissible unless it's court ordered."

She cursed.

And he narrowed his eyes to study her face. "Did you…?"

"Take a sample from Blue along with a sample from you?"

"Yes?"

She shook her head. "I have his. But I needed yours."

He knew how he'd like to give her a sample. But she needed it in a vial—not inside her. He forced his mind from the tension gripping his body—from the attraction that overwhelmed him every time he got too close to Nikki Payne.

He shrugged. "It doesn't matter. Like I said, it's inadmissible. We can't compel him to give up the baby's DNA. I can't even prove that Emilia really met with him. She just told me in her last letter that she was going to."

"She didn't tell you why?" she asked. "Was she going to give up the baby?"

Lars sucked in a breath. "I don't know. I don't think she would have."

"How old is she?" Nikki asked.

Was she…

How old was she? But he didn't correct her. He couldn't bring himself to fully accept that Emilia was gone, either. "Twenty-two." His voice cracked as emotion overwhelmed him. "She should be graduating from college in a couple of months."

Instead she was gone forever.

Nikki stepped closer to him and like she had that day in her office, she wrapped her arms around him, holding him. "I don't think she's dead."

His breath shuddered out in a wistful sigh that stirred Nikki's already tousled curls. "I wish I could believe you, believe in this notion that you think your mom and brother and you just *know* things..."

She chuckled. "I don't have that ability at all," she assured him. "Not like Mom and Nick."

But he wasn't as convinced. She'd been ready for him in the nursery. "Since Nick inherited the ability from your mom, you could have, too."

She snorted. "Nick didn't inherit it from my mom," she said. "He isn't her biological son, although he should be. He is more like her than any of her kids."

"So he's your adopted brother?"

"He's the product of an affair my dad had while he was undercover," she said, and there was resentment in her voice. "He cheated on my mom—while she was pregnant with Cooper. He and Nick are nearly the same age."

"I'm sorry," he said.

She shrugged. "You're not the one who cheated."

But he had kept a secret from her. Would she see that as big a betrayal as what her father had done? She was obviously still upset about what her dad had done. No wonder she said she had no interest in ever getting married. She couldn't trust that it would last.

"But no," she continued as if she hadn't just shared a very big part of herself with him. "I'm not like Mom and Nick. I'm just observant. Webber's been getting breast milk for the baby. Where's that been coming from if Emilia is dead?"

His heart stopped beating for just a second as hope swelled in it. Then it started up again, almost violently hard. "No..." He shook his head. He couldn't allow himself to hope, only to be crushed again. "Are you sure it's breast milk?"

She nodded. "I've sent some of that away to be tested to find out if it belongs to the baby's mother."

"Would another woman sell her breast milk?" Lars asked. "And why would Webber care if Blue was fed breast milk or formula?"

"Health," Nikki said. "A lot of people believe breast-fed babies are healthier and smarter."

"But why..." Then the answer dawned on him.

But Nikki said it anyway. "The healthier the baby, the higher the price."

"He's going to sell my nephew?"

"A couple checked him out this morning."

Lars cringed. "Like they were kicking the tires on a car?"

She sighed and pulled back. "Unfortunately, yes."

"I've already lost her," he said. "I can't lose her baby, too." But he could feel him slipping away from him. Could feel it all slipping away...

Even Nikki since she'd stepped back from him. He felt cold without the warmth of her touch, of her comfort. As if she knew he needed her, she moved toward him again.

"I don't think Emilia is dead," she said. "We will find her."

"I already checked the morgues and hospitals—"

She tensed. "You found her?"

He shook his head. "No..."

"Then she's alive," Nikki insisted, and a smile brightened her face. "Blue's mother is alive."

Lars touched her face, running his fingertip along her smile. Her lips were so silky. She was so damn beautiful. So hopeful...

He couldn't allow himself to hope, though. "She's not like you," he said. "She's not strong. She's used to me taking care of her, handling her problems." When he hadn't been around, she'd turned to the wrong person for help.

"My brothers underestimate me, too," Nikki said as if she'd already formed a kinship with Emilia.

His sister would have been in awe of the little brunette spitfire. And she would have been grateful for how much Nikki had already come to care for Blue.

He was grateful for so much that she'd done. His heart warmed and swelled with it. It wasn't hope. He refused to let himself feel that. So he wasn't sure what it was.

Just that he couldn't fight it anymore.

"You are incredible," he murmured. And he reached for her now, closing his arms around her.

She stared up at him, her eyes wide with surprise. "Wh-why?"

"You should be furious with me—"

"Oh, I am," she assured him.

"But you covered for me with Cooper," he said. "And now you're trying to make me believe Emilia could be alive."

"She could be," Nikki insisted. "She—"

He pressed his fingers over her lips and shook his head. "I need to focus on what I know for certain." At the moment the only thing he knew for certain was that he wanted her, that he had to have her.

So he replaced his fingers with his mouth and kissed her passionately. But his desire was no match for hers. She nipped at his lips with her teeth and clutched his shoulders, bending him even more toward her.

She was so tiny. And he was so big. He had to lift her, which was easy given her slight weight. But despite that, his legs began to shake a little with need. He'd never needed anyone as desperately as he needed Nikki.

She wrapped her legs around his waist, rubbing her core against him. The erection strained against his jeans, making him ache to drive inside her. She pulled away from him slightly, lifting her mouth from his.

Maybe he was going too fast, being too presumptuous. She'd already admitted to being furious with him.

But instead of telling him to go to hell, she asked, "Do you have a bed in this place that's not in a box waiting to be assembled?"

Relief coursed through him along with amusement at her boldness. He chuckled. "I have a mattress upstairs." And he carried her up the creaky wooden steps to show her.

"This is a bad idea," she murmured. But she clutched him tighter instead of struggling to free herself.

He knew it, too, as his phone began to vibrate again. "A very bad idea…"

"Cooper is going to kill you," she said. "Logan and Parker might help him."

"Not Nick?"

"He couldn't be a hypocrite. He got his best friend's sister pregnant." Her face flushed. "Not that…that's not going to…we're not…"

He chuckled as she stammered. Maybe she wasn't as bold as she acted. "We're not going to do this?" he

asked as he stepped into the bedroom where the king-size mattress lay on the floor.

He dropped his arms from around her and she slid down his body, her soft curves brushing against his every tense muscle. He groaned with desire—with need.

"We're going to do this," she said. "We're just not going to make a baby."

Lars pulled a condom from his wallet. "No, we're not." Maybe if he and Emilia hadn't been too embarrassed to discuss it, he could have prepared her more so that she wouldn't have gotten pregnant. But he hadn't wanted to think about that…with her. And now he didn't want to think about her. It hurt too much.

Nikki's fingertips brushed along the rigid line of his tense jaw. "I'm sorry," she murmured.

Had she changed her mind?

But instead of stepping away, she reached for the buckle of his belt. She easily undid it and then her knuckles brushed along his fly, where his erection strained. As her fingers closed over the tab of his zipper, she froze.

And he did, too, every muscle straining, sweat beading on his upper lip. He needed her to release him. But maybe this was her revenge for trying to overpower her. She'd told him she was furious with him.

Then she reached for her gun, and he wondered just how furious…until he heard it, too. First the creak of the front door opening and the creak of the floorboards. They were no longer alone. He had an intruder. Then he heard the front door open again and realized there was more than one.

Had Webber figured out who he was and sent his guards after him?

* * *

He shouldn't have let them leave—separately and definitely not together. Tension pounded behind Cooper's eyes so intensely that he could barely focus on the person who walked into his office.

"Are you okay, honey?" his mother asked.

He wondered why she bothered with the question when she already knew the answer. She must have known before she'd even shown up; it was undoubtedly why she'd come. Because Penny Payne always knew when one of her kids needed her.

He suspected he was not the one who needed her the most. That was Nikki.

Where the hell was she? Why wouldn't she answer her phone? She wasn't the only one ignoring his calls, though. He groaned as he tossed his cell down on his desk.

"No," he needlessly answered his mother.

"Nikki?" she asked.

And again he wondered why she bothered. She knew. But he replied anyway. "Yes. I want to think that she's ignoring my calls because she's just pissed I pulled her off duty."

But she actually hadn't seemed very upset about Candace taking over for her. In fact, she'd been eager to leave—with Lars.

"You think it's something else," Penny said as she settled nervously onto the edge of one of the chairs in front of his desk. She was here because she felt it—that damn feeling he had—that something bad was going to happen.

He should have never let Nikki leave. Instead of hav-

ing Candace protect the baby, he should have had her protect Nikki. She was the one in danger.

And even though she wasn't alone, Lars might prove the greatest threat to her safety.

Chapter 13

Before Nikki could draw her Glock from her holster, a big hand closed over hers.

"If we start shooting, the police will be called," Lars warned her. He'd shoved the condom back into his pocket and buckled his belt again.

"And that would be a bad thing...why?" she asked. She wasn't opposed to the police being called until she remembered that Nick was still running River City PD. So the police wouldn't come alone; they would come with at least one of her brothers.

She dropped her hand away from her holster.

"We can take them without guns," Lars said.

We...

Her pulse quickened with nearly as much excitement as she'd felt when she'd reached for his zipper. He was so damn big—so hard—so hot. She ached inside with

desire, with need. But she would use all that tension to fuel her fight.

Lars stopped talking and gestured toward the open bedroom door. He stood on one side of the jamb while she moved to the other side. Night had fallen some time ago, and they hadn't turned on any lights. Their eyes were accustomed to the darkness. Hopefully the intruders were not.

The first dark shadow walked through the door and right into Lars's strong grip. He pulled the man's arms behind him and flung him against the wall.

The second dark shadow—even bigger than the first—rushed inside to the aid of his partner. And Nikki dropped him with a knee to the groin. He fell to the floor, writhing.

She wasn't prepared for the third. She hadn't heard him. But Lars must have. As the guy reached for her, his strong hands gripping her arms, Lars broke his hold and nearly his neck. Until the guy who'd fallen against the wall flipped on the lights.

Dane gasped for breath and tugged at the forearm Lars had wrapped around his throat. Now that they could see more than shadows of each other, his friend released him, and he dropped onto the floor next to where Manny writhed yet.

"Guess we should've rung the bell instead of breaking in," Cole remarked from where he leaned against the bedroom wall, his hand still on the light switch.

"You think?" Lars asked with a grunt.

"What the hell is wrong with you people?" Nikki asked. Even though she'd grown up with all males but for Penny, she doubted she would ever fully understand them.

"I don't know," Dane replied. "What did you do to Manny? Neuter him?"

"Good thing I don't want to have a family," Manny said between gasps for breath. He kind of sounded like he was having a baby.

Regret flashed through Nikki. But she'd had no way of knowing who they were.

"Why didn't you ring the bell?" she asked. "Or at the very least call out to let us know who you were?"

Cole snorted disparagingly. "What's the fun in that?"

She gestured down at Manny. "Does that look fun to you?"

He shuddered. "No. Guess I'm lucky Lars took me."

"If I'd known it was you, I might have done that," Lars said with a glare. Then he told her, "They had a blanket party for me the other night."

"Blanket party?" Somehow she didn't think he was talking about what he and she had nearly had, if they hadn't been interrupted.

"We wrapped a blanket around his head and abducted him," Cole explained.

"Yeah, but it took all three of them to take me down," Lars said with pride.

She shook her head pityingly. "And today I took you down all by myself."

Manny lifted his hand from where he'd been checking himself—probably to see how much damage she'd done. "I see how you did it."

"We came over here to find out what happened," Cole said. "Why the plan failed…" He turned toward Nikki. "Guess we got our answer."

Anger coursed through Nikki again, that Lars had intended to trick her. And to overpower her.

He very nearly had in this room. His kisses, his touch, had nearly overpowered her common sense. She never should have let him touch her again. Never should have touched and kissed him back…

Her face heated. And she was the one who'd asked about the bed.

Not that she could deny the desire—or the need. It ached inside her yet.

"He underestimated me," she told the others. But she had underestimated him, as well—had underestimated how he could make her feel. So much…

"Did you tell Cooper?" Dane asked.

She shook her head again.

Dane glanced at Lars and then back to her and then down at the mattress on the floor. "Why not?"

"I gave him a chance to explain." She wasn't sure what the hell she'd been doing up here—with him. After what he'd tried, she could never trust him. He'd intended to use her—setting her up as Blue's bodyguard only to betray her.

"Did you?" Dane asked his friend, and he glanced—more pointedly—at the mattress again. Obviously he was worried that Lars had tried to distract her with sex.

Maybe he had—from what she'd been trying to tell him. "I know about Emilia," she said.

"I'm glad he told you," Dane said with a sigh of relief.

"But what are you going to do with that information?" Cole asked as he helped Manny to his feet. "Are you going to tell Cooper?"

He sounded almost hopeful. And she realized it hadn't been easy for any of them to keep a secret from her brother. They loved him like he was their brother, too. But then they'd all been through so much together.

Cooper would want to know what was going on, even if it jeopardized his career.

She glanced at Lars. "Maybe I should tell him." Then she turned back toward the others. "He might listen to me because your lunkhead friend won't."

"What are you telling him?" Dane asked, his voice gruff with frustration. "To tell Cooper? To go to the cops? I've been telling him all that, too."

"Dane's known the longest," Cole explained. "We didn't get the truth out of either of them until that blanket party the other night."

"You had to beat it out of them?" she asked.

Manny finally managed to stand straight. "We would have gotten the information a lot faster if we'd had you there to help."

But they obviously hadn't wanted to involve her. Because she was Cooper's sister? Or because they hadn't trusted her?

"Like I've explained to all of you now," Lars said with a weary sigh. "We have no proof to bring to the police."

"That kid clearly has your DNA," Cole said. "You can prove he's your nephew. Then the slimy lawyer would have to explain what he did to your sister."

Lars shook his head. "I have no way to force him to give up the baby's DNA for a test that would be admissible in court." He glanced at Nikki as he said it.

She knew her test wouldn't serve as evidence for a prosecutor, but she'd needed the proof to support her own suspicions.

"And if we try to ask for the DNA," Lars continued, "Webber will know we're onto him and he'll hide the baby."

"Like he's hidden Emilia," Nikki said.

Lars shook his head again. "I haven't found her body yet." Resignation hung like a heavy burden on his broad shoulders, lowering them. "But I will."

"Emilia is not dead," Nikki insisted. Like Dane, she was frustrated with him, too—frustrated that he refused to listen to her.

Lars touched her cheek, brushing his knuckles almost absently across her skin. "That's sweet…that you want to make me feel better."

His trio of friends stared at them now, their eyes wide with a mixture of surprise and horror. They all knew and respected the bro code that Lars had clearly violated. Or would have had they not interrupted them.

Her face heated, but she refused to give in to embarrassment. Thanks to them she had no reason for it. So she told them what she'd told Lars earlier. "The lawyer's giving the baby breast milk."

They stared at her blankly.

"It's obviously not coming from him," she pointed out.

And Manny chuckled.

"So he's buying it," Cole said with a shrug.

But Dane sucked in a breath and now hope warmed his dark eyes, lightening the color. "Do you think that she's…?"

She nodded. "Emilia's alive."

Dare he hope? Lars hadn't wanted to. That was why he'd refused to listen to Nikki earlier. But what if she was right? What if Emilia was alive?

Several long moments had passed since she'd told his friends her suspicion. They'd come downstairs to

the kitchen where Dane had dropped the take-out food and beer they'd brought.

Manny and Cole scarfed down slices of greasy pizza. The thought of eating made Lars's stomach churn. But then he couldn't think about anything but what Nikki was suggesting.

He shook his head, unable to accept the hope she was trying to give him. Not knowing how much conversation or time had passed since her pronouncement he said, "I don't think that's the case at all."

And they all knew what he was talking about.

"You don't think Emilia is alive?" Dane asked, and his topaz eyes darkened with regret, almost with his own loss.

Maybe because he'd known the longest, he seemed particularly invested in Emilia. Not that the others didn't care because they cared about him. It was almost like Dane cared about Emilia, as well, even though he'd never met her. And despite what Nikki believed, Lars doubted he ever would.

"We've been over the entire estate—every room in the house and on every inch of the grounds." He reminded them of their thorough search. He and Cooper had done it that first day. Cooper had thought they were just thoroughly assessing the security of the estate. Lars had been searching. "We would have found her."

"Yes," Nikki agreed. "We would have…" She'd been part of that search. "If he'd kept her there…"

Dane nodded as he followed where her suggestion was leading. "He has to be keeping her someplace else."

"I have a list of properties he owns," she said.

Of course she would have researched the man. She was intuitive. She would have known something was

up with him just like she'd known something was up with Lars.

"We'll search them all," Dane eagerly offered.

"It's extensive," she said. "We'll need to narrow it down."

Dane nodded. "We may not have much time. Webber's guards are already suspicious of me and Lars."

"And after tonight, they have questions about us," Cole said. "I was in position to take out the one at the gate on your call." He pointed at Lars. "And he had to know something was up."

"The lights going off—it made several of them nervous," Manny added. "They were checking to see who was where…"

Dane sighed. "It doesn't matter that you didn't say anything to Cooper. He might not have to fire us. Webber might…"

She shook her head. "He won't fire *me*."

"Your brother or Webber?" Dane asked.

"Webber," she said.

Lars's guts tightened with dread. He remembered how the man had looked at her—like Lars looked at her—with desire.

"I can buy us some time," she said.

How the hell was she going to do that? Lars's stomach roiled with revulsion over the thought of her flirting with the man. Was it revulsion, though, or simple jealousy?

He didn't want Nikki flirting with anyone but him.

"But we need to get busy on this." She pulled her phone from her pocket and tapped on the screen. "I sent you all the list of properties. And some of the surveillance footage."

"Why the footage?" Dane asked.

"Maybe we can figure out who's been bringing the breast milk to the estate," she said. "Webber must have an errand boy."

"We'll check out some of these properties now," Dane said. "See if any look like places where someone could be held." He stood up, his food untouched. He was as eager to get started as Nikki was.

Lars couldn't move like them, couldn't give in to the hope as easily as Dane had. But he wanted Emilia to be alive, too—too much.

He didn't say anything as they all filed out, couldn't even find the words to thank them until they were gone. But not everyone was gone.

"Why are you still here?" he asked Nikki, staring at her over the empty pizza box and discarded beer cans.

He figured she would have been the first one out the door, leading up the search since she was the most convinced his sister was alive.

Instead she walked up to him and slid her hand into his. Entwining their fingers she tugged him toward her.

She probably wanted him to lead up the search. He would have had he been able to believe that Emilia was alive. Because if she was really alive, she wouldn't be for much longer.

If the guards had alerted Webber that something was going on at the estate, he would make certain to leave no witnesses behind.

He would kill Emilia.

The door rattled. It would open soon. Emilia needed to be ready. But she was still shaking, still alternating

between shivering and sweating. She was sick. Really sick...

But she hadn't bothered to ask Myron Webber for help. He intended to kill her brother. So he was going to undoubtedly kill her, as well.

She hadn't even been able to pump any breast milk for her baby. So her usefulness was over. She was expendable.

In confirmation of her fears, voices drifted through the door that had opened a crack. "We need to get rid of her—*permanently.*"

Chapter 14

"Why are you still here?" Lars repeated the question he'd just asked Nikki.

She hadn't answered him because she wasn't sure why she had stayed, either. But they'd started something earlier, something that she needed to finish. Not to find out where it would lead. She knew it wouldn't lead anywhere because she didn't want it to.

She already knew that he didn't respect her any more than her brothers did. Or he wouldn't have lobbied so hard for her to be the baby's nanny. He'd thought he would be able to handle her easily.

She had given him a fight then. And she would give him a fight now—if he tried to resist her.

"What do you want?" Lars asked almost uneasily, as if he was nervous. Or scared—of her.

"You," she replied succinctly.

He sucked in a breath and shook his head. "Nikki…"

As he tried to pull his hand free, she tightened her grasp on his fingers. "I know it's a bad idea," she said before he could.

"You're mad at me," he reminded her.

"Furious," she said even as she tugged him toward the stairs leading back up to that bedroom, to that mattress on the floor.

"Then why do you want me?"

"Because you drive me crazy," she said. "Because we need to do this. We need to get it over with…"

"You say the sweetest things," he murmured as he followed her.

"We need to get rid of it," she said. Whatever it was… It was too distracting. "Once we scratch this itch, we will be able to focus on what really matters."

"What really matters?" he asked as he reached the top of the stairs with her.

Once she passed through the bedroom doorway, she turned back to him because she knew now this time there would be no turning back.

"Blue—Emilia," she said. "Keeping them safe—that's what really matters. This—" she gestured toward the mattress "—is just sex."

"Just sex," he murmured.

She couldn't tell if he was agreeing with her or doubting her. She refused to acknowledge the doubts. She wouldn't let it become more than sex.

If they kept putting it off…

If the tension kept building…

It might become more than sex. It might seem bigger than it was.

It was just an itch they both needed to scratch. They needed to get this over with. She reached for her holster.

And Lars tensed. "Do you hear something?" He reached for his holster, as well.

She shook her head. "No…"

But if she had, he wouldn't have been able to talk her out of shooting this time. Nobody was going to interrupt them again. She unbuckled her holster and laid it onto the floor next to the mattress. Then she reached for her sweater, tugging that over her head and dropping that onto the floor, as well.

Lars's breath escaped in a gasp.

She followed his gaze over her chest, to where her breasts overflowed the cups of her red satin bra. Smiling at his reaction, she reached for the button of her jeans, undoing it then the zipper to reveal the panties that matched the bra. She kicked off the jeans.

"*Damn*, woman…"

"You're overdressed," she complained. But before she could reach for his belt, he was undoing it.

Despite his earlier protests, he was all in now—and in seconds, he was all naked, his boxers lying on the floor tangled in his jeans.

And she was the one gasping for breath. "Maybe this was a mistake," she murmured.

Because he was so damn big.

Everywhere.

Everything.

His erection was so long, so thick, and it pulsed with a need every bit as great as the need burning inside her.

She wanted him. But she wasn't certain she could handle either him or the desire overwhelming her.

"I'll make sure you're ready," he told her. And his

hands wrapped easily around her waist, his fingers over-lapping. Everything about him was so big.

And made her feel so small and vulnerable.

Usually she resented that feeling. But as he lifted her, she didn't mind the vulnerability. It added an element of excitement that had her pulse racing.

He placed her gently down onto the mattress and he followed her down. He held his weight off her, though, the muscles in his arms bulging. Then he lowered his head and slid his lips across hers, gently brushing back and forth.

She didn't want gentle. She wanted rough and wild and fast. The desire was too great—the need too big to be denied any longer. She nipped at his lips with her teeth, catching the fuller bottom one.

He groaned.

Then she skimmed her short nails down his back. Muscles rippled beneath her touch. She moved her hands farther down—to his butt. And she tugged him toward her.

"You have to be ready," he protested.

"I'm ready," she assured him.

But he kept kissing her, making love to her mouth. And he touched her, skimming his big hands over her shoulders and her breasts. His fingers brushed across her nipples.

And a moan slipped through her lips.

That need—that had already been too great—in-creased to unbearable. She had never wanted anyone like this.

Then he moved his hands lower, over her abdomen down to her core. And his mouth moved, too, follow-ing the path his hands had taken. He kissed her shoul-

ders and then her breasts. His tongue flicked across her sensitive nipples. First one then the other.

And a whimper slipped between her lips. She reached up and clutched his hair. It was like pale gold silk sliding between her fingers. His skin was like that, too—like silk over steel. He was masculine perfection.

And he was driving her crazy.

He plucked at her nipples with his lips before moving his head lower. His tongue traced a path over her stomach down to her core.

She moaned as he teased her with the tip of it. Then he slid a finger inside her—stroking her intimately.

An orgasm gripped her, and her body shuddered with release. But it wasn't enough, not to fill that emptiness inside her that ached for him.

She reached out and stroked her hand down the length of his erection. And he groaned. Then she skimmed her finger across his tip.

"Nikki…" he said, his voice gruff with desire. He pulled away from her touch and fumbled around on the floor. The condom packet rustled in his slightly shaking hand.

So she tore it open for him—with her teeth.

And he whispered again, "Damn, woman…"

When she rolled it onto him, he groaned as if she were torturing him.

She pushed him back onto the mattress and climbed on top of him. Carefully she guided him inside her. She was wet and ready for him. But he was still so big that he stretched her—filled her. She couldn't take all of him.

She braced her hands against his chest, the muscles rippling beneath her touch. And his hands grasped her hips. Together they found a rhythm. It was what she wanted—fast and frantic and powerful.

More powerful than anything she had ever experienced before...

That need she'd felt before was nothing in comparison to what she felt now. Tension gripped her so that she ached and trembled with it. She moved faster.

And faster, desperate for release.

Lars seemed as desperate as she was, groans tearing from his throat as he thrust up. And his hands moved her hips, arching them so that he slid a little deeper with each thrust.

He filled an emptiness she hadn't known she had. Then her muscles clutched at him, and she came. His name escaped her lips on a scream of pleasure more intense than she had ever imagined possible. He kept thrusting, and she came again—the ripples ebbing endlessly through her.

He tensed just before his body began to shudder with release. As he came, he yelled her name.

Limp and satiated, she dropped onto his chest, which rose and fell heavily as he panted for breath. Like she panted. Their hearts raced yet in unison.

This was why she had wanted to have sex with him. So she would know what it was like—what she would be giving up—because she knew that no matter his reasons for keeping secrets from her, she would never be able to trust him.

If she ever was tempted to have a relationship, it would have to be with someone who was completely honest. Always.

Her breath whispered across his skin, and Lars realized she'd fallen asleep on him—while he still panted

for breath. A grin teased at his lips. Wasn't it the man who was supposed to fall asleep after sex?

Of course he had never met a more macho woman than Nikki Payne. Sure, she was beautiful and delicate-looking. But she was one of the strongest people he'd ever met, too. And as a Marine, he'd met some tough sons of bitches.

Like his friends…

They were out there—looking for his sister—because Nikki had given them hope. And she'd tried giving him that hope, too.

But just now she'd given him something else. Something more powerful than hope. And far more powerful than just the sex she'd claimed it would be.

He wrapped his arm around her, holding her close against his side, and stared down at her face. Her thick black lashes lay against her cheeks.

She looked like one of the dolls Emilia used to have. Lars had bought it for her, but she'd never played with it. When he'd asked her why, she'd told him it was too beautiful. She hadn't wanted to risk messing it up.

He understood that now. But Nikki wasn't just beautiful on the outside. She was even more beautiful on the inside. And he'd hurt her.

Not physically. But he'd hurt her because he'd used her. He'd only recommended her for his nephew's bodyguard because he'd thought he could overpower her.

Instead she'd overpowered him. And not just in that nursery. He shouldn't have made love with her. But maybe she'd been using him then—just scratching an itch they'd started together.

But with him it was more than an itch.

He was in danger of falling for her and falling hard.

His breath sighed out now—wistfully. His fingers shook slightly as he reached out to brush a curl back from her cheek.

As he touched her, he froze. Not because he was afraid of awakening her—but because of the noise.

The door creaked open again downstairs—despite his knowing he'd locked it this time. And he heard footsteps crossing the living room floor.

He touched Nikki's shoulder to shake her awake, but when he glanced down, he found her eyes open and staring up at him. They moved like they'd choreographed the routine—dressing, grabbing their weapons…

His friends wouldn't have come back yet and not in silence again. They would have knocked. They'd seen that something was going on between him and Nikki, and they wouldn't have wanted to interrupt.

Cooper might have.

But he knew it wasn't Cooper.

He knew it was danger—even before the shooting began. He'd put Nikki in danger.

He reached out and pulled her back, shoving her behind him. He might not have been able to protect Emilia. But he would protect Nikki—even if he died trying.

Nick was on his way home when he heard the police call. Even though he was still in charge, he could have ignored it. Units were already en route. They would probably beat him there. But for some reason—that sick feeling in the pit of his stomach—he knew he needed to go, too.

He didn't even have to look for the address that had

come along with the call of shots fired. He only had to follow all the flashing lights.

An ambulance was parked in the street with the back doors open. But nobody was inside it, working on the body lying beneath the bloodied sheet.

It was too late.

He glanced toward the house with all the lights blazing and saw a couple paramedics carrying out another gurney. They struggled with the weight of the big body, but there was no urgency in their step, no rush to get this patient to the hospital.

They hadn't been able to help that victim, either.

Nick moved past the ambulance and froze. Parked between it and the curb was a black coupe. It looked like a dozen other cars except for the furry dice dangling from the rearview mirror.

Those dice...

He knew whose car that was. Panic squeezed his heart. "Nikki..."

Cooper had been so worried that something bad was going to happen to her. Nick should have heeded his brother's instincts. He should have done something. He should have helped Cooper protect her.

But he'd thought it was time to let Nikki prove to the others that she could take care of herself. So he hadn't wanted to intervene.

Shaking with fear, Nick turned around and headed back toward the ambulance. It wasn't her body on the gurney; that one was too big.

But the one in the ambulance was smaller, the one lying beneath the bloody sheet.

He had to know...

Had he been too late?

Chapter 15

Pain radiated from Nikki's heart throughout her body. She'd never felt anything quite like this. It was nearly as unbearable as her desire—her need—for Lars had been. She didn't need him anymore. She was furious with him.

What the hell had he been thinking to try to protect her? To shove her behind him?

He'd nearly gotten his head shot off, probably would have if Nikki hadn't dropped him with a kick to the back of his knee. Then she'd taken down the man who'd stepped through the bedroom door firing.

She squeezed her eyes shut, and images jumbled together in her mind—not just of this shooting but of every other shooting in which she'd been involved.

That number was growing. Unfortunately.

She couldn't remember how many had died—not just

tonight but in total. Her body began to shake almost of its own volition. Lars had been shot.

Hadn't he…?

But the image behind her closed lids was of Woodrow lying on the floor, blood pooling beneath him. Then she saw a woman—the one she'd killed—the one who'd nearly killed Woodrow.

"Andrea…"

"Why are you bringing her up?" a soft voice asked. "Are you okay?"

Nikki blinked her eyes open and met her mother's concerned gaze. Usually she would bluff that she was fine, nothing was wrong. But instead she held open her arms for her mother's reassuring hug.

Mom always said everything was fine even when it wasn't. When Nikki's father had died, she'd claimed that she was fine, that they would all be fine. And when Nikki had found out about her father cheating on Penny, she'd claimed then that it was okay—that she had forgiven him years ago.

Nikki didn't care if Penny had. She hadn't. And she wouldn't be able to forgive Lars, either. Not just for using her to try to kidnap his nephew but for protecting her tonight. He hadn't trusted her to protect herself.

But still she couldn't help but ask, "Is he all right?"

Her mother didn't ask who. She just *knew* like she knew so many other things. "Yes, yes," she replied.

But was this like all those other times? Was she claiming everything was all right even when it wasn't?

So many shots had been fired…

At least one of them had to have hit him. There had been so much blood. Nikki glanced down at the streak

that had run down her arm from where a bullet had grazed her shoulder. The trail was dry now, the blood hard.

"What about you?" Penny asked, and her voice quavered slightly as she followed where Nikki had glanced as she saw the blood. "Are you okay?"

Nikki drew in a deep breath and rallied. "Yes, yes," she replied. And for the first time she realized she might be more like her mother than just in appearance because she was claiming everything was all right even when it wasn't.

Even when she knew it would never be all right again. She had done it, the one thing she'd promised herself she would never do. She had let herself get involved with someone. If that wasn't bad enough, the person she cared about had already lied to her, had already used her.

Yes, she was far more like her mother than she'd ever realized—because the first man she was falling for was certain to break her heart.

"Are you trying to get my sister killed, too?" Cooper asked as he pulled the emergency room curtain aside.

Lars looked up from the bandage he'd been studying on his leg. Blood had begun to seep through the gauze. Maybe he shouldn't have refused stitches. But the bullet had just grazed his thigh. He didn't need stitches. He needed his damn jeans and his gun so he could leave.

But first he needed to find Nikki and make sure she was all right. The wound on her shoulder hadn't been more than a shallow scratch. It was the look on her face that had scared him more. She'd looked like she was going into shock.

"Is she okay?" he anxiously asked. "I tried to protect her."

Cooper flinched. "No wonder she looked so pissed when she left with our mom."

"She left?" And she hadn't checked on him? Hadn't she cared?

But if she hadn't cared, why would she have dropped him with that kick? Why would she have made sure he couldn't take a bullet for her?

He'd only gotten hit as the man had gone down as Nikki had taken him down. Lars had shot the next one who'd hit her as he'd gone down. He'd already explained that to the officers at the scene, though. Nikki had talked to another man at the scene, one who'd looked very much like Cooper.

It must have been Nick. He'd never come over to speak to Lars, though. He'd only glared at him the way Cooper was glaring at him now.

"Why didn't you tell me about any of this?" he asked. Nikki must have filled in Cooper. Or maybe she'd told Nick and he had. "I am so sorry about your sister."

"Nikki doesn't think Emilia is dead." Lars wished he could believe that, too. But if she hadn't been dead, she probably was now. Those gunmen had been guards from Webber's estate. He was definitely onto him and tying up loose ends.

Cooper slugged him. Hard. On the shoulder. Fortunately the bullet hadn't grazed him where it had Nikki. "Why the hell did you bring my sister into this mess and not me?" he demanded to know.

"I wanted to give you credible deniability," Lars explained.

"Why?"

"Because I'm going to get my nephew back." And his sister—if by some miracle she was still alive. He

would find Emilia. But he didn't want Nikki helping him. She'd nearly been killed back at his place.

If anything had happened to her...

"You're sure Nikki is all right?" Lars asked again. Even if she was pissed at him, he wished she would have stopped in to talk to him even if just to tell him to go to hell.

Didn't she realize why he'd tried to protect her? Because he cared? Because he was falling for her...

But maybe it was better that she not know that. Because Webber was already trying to get rid of him. If he didn't survive, it was better that Nikki not care about him. It would make it easier for her to forget him.

The door creaked open, spilling faint light across the mattress on which Emilia lay shivering. She tried to rally her strength to fight. This was it.

She'd already heard them talking, so she knew. They had come to get rid of her. But when she turned toward the door, her eyes widened in surprise.

She hadn't expected Myron Webber would return to do his own dirty work. "Don't you want to know why I'm here?" he asked as she stared up at him.

"To kill me..."

He chuckled but didn't correct her. "I found a family for your son."

Son. She'd had a son. She would have named him Lars if she'd had the chance to see him. To hold him...

But she could remember none of that or anything but this room. She did remember how he'd felt inside her, moving and kicking. He was strong. He'd survived.

He was like his uncle.

Lars had to be okay.

But the lawyer chuckled again. "It's all over now," he mused. "I tracked down your brother and eliminated him."

Emilia gasped as pain shot through her. "You had him killed?"

"He killed himself—looking for you—trying to steal your son."

Lars had found out about the baby. Guilt racked her. He should have found out from her. She should have told him before he'd deployed. But she'd been so worried about disappointing him...

Or distracting him while he'd been gone.

She hadn't wanted his worrying about her to keep him from staying focused on survival.

He had survived war. Only to be killed because of her...

"Is he really dead?" she asked, her voice cracking with the emotions churning through her.

Webber nodded. "The news reported no survivors. No witnesses."

He was smug. So damn smug that he wouldn't be caught. That he would never be punished for his crimes.

Anger coursed through Emilia, and for a moment she felt strong. But when she tried to lift her arm to slap him, her muscles were too weak. She could barely raise her hand from the mattress. Tears of frustration and loss burned her eyes, but she was too dehydrated to shed them.

She couldn't even cry for her brother.

Or for herself...

Now that the lawyer had found a family for her son, he didn't need her anymore, either. Just as she'd suspected, he had come back to eliminate her—just as he had eliminated her brother.

Chapter 16

Nikki shoved open the door to the conference room of the original Payne Protection Agency and stalked to the head of the table.

"I don't give a damn who the boss is," she told Logan and Cooper who stood over the chair like they'd been haggling for position. "I called this meeting and I am damn well going to lead it."

She grabbed the chair, but instead of sitting in it, she spun it away from the table. She couldn't sit, not with the urgency coursing through her body. And not with Lars staring at her like he was, as if he had been starving for the sight of her.

She drew in a deep breath and worked at ignoring him as she focused on the others. They were arguing amongst themselves. She could hear Logan and Cooper clearly. They hadn't been arguing over that damn chair. They'd been arguing over her.

"How could you have put her in danger like that?" Logan asked.

"I didn't know that I was," Cooper said.

"What the hell were you thinking to hire guys like this—guys you couldn't trust?" Logan persisted, disparagingly.

"That's ironic, coming from you," Parker tossed in with a chuckle. He enjoyed needling his twin. "You hired the two ex-cons."

His brothers-in-law had gone to prison for a crime they hadn't committed. Of course there had been some that they had.

"I can trust Garek and Milek with my life," Logan said. "Cooper can't trust his team."

"That's my fault." Lars jumped in to defend his friend. "I didn't want to bring him into this mess."

"You shouldn't have," Logan interjected. "And you damn well shouldn't have brought our sister into it, either."

"He was worried about his sister," Dane said. "And with good reason."

The volume rose—more individual arguments breaking out around the table. She put her fingers in her mouth, ready to execute a sharp whistle to draw attention back to the meeting and the person running it.

But someone beat her with the whistle. And Cooper stepped up to her side. "Stop the fighting," he yelled.

All arguing had already ceased. They all stared up at him now.

"Everyone in this room is family," he said with a pointed look at their brother Logan.

A few people were missing. Candace was still working her shift to protect Blue with Milek Kozminski and

Gage Huxton as her backup on the estate. Nick, Mom and Woodrow weren't present, either. But Nikki hadn't wanted any of them there, not when what they had to do was illegal.

"We are bound either by blood or by loyalty," Cooper continued. "I don't question the loyalty of my unit. And I won't tolerate anyone else questioning it, either. They did what they did to protect me. But I'm not the one who needs protecting."

He'd left no doubt who was in charge now. But then he stepped back and turned the meeting over to her. "Listen to Nikki. She called this meeting."

She braced her palms on the edge of the table and leaned forward. Raising her voice so everyone could hear it, she said, "The person who most needs our protection is only a few weeks old."

She had their attention. So she told them the rest of the story, everything she'd learned from Lars. She could have let him tell it, but she hadn't wanted to put him through the emotions that visibly overwhelmed him every time he talked of Emilia and how he felt like he'd let her down. She couldn't comfort him anymore.

"That's why I called everyone here," she said, "because we need to work together to get that baby away from Myron Webber."

"Kidnap him?" Parker asked, his blue eyes widening in surprise. He'd once been a police officer like Logan. Breaking a law would go against all he believed.

"How do we know that baby's really his nephew?" Garek asked the question. A former criminal himself, he was suspicious of everyone. He'd also promised his sister when he'd gone to prison years ago that he would never commit another crime.

"Nick had the FBI lab rush the DNA I took," she said. In addition to what she'd collected in the nursery, Lars had given a sample at the hospital. "It's a familial match between Lars and the baby." She drew in a breath and focused on him now. He hadn't believed her about Emilia. She knew why: he'd been afraid to hope. "And there was a familial match between the baby and the DNA in the breast milk."

A gasp slipped through Lars's lips. "Oh, my God. She is really alive?"

She had been. Nikki had no such confidence that she still was.

"That's why we have to move quickly," she said. "We need to go over all that footage to see if we can pinpoint the go-between for the breast milk and the estate. And we need to check all of the properties Webber owns."

Heads bobbed all around the table; everyone was in agreement with her now. She slapped her hands together. "Let's save that baby and find his mama!" She only hoped for Emilia's sake and Blue's and even Lars's—damn him—that they found her alive.

Lars no longer had any doubts. He still had them about Emilia. She may have been alive and supplying her baby with breast milk, but that didn't mean she was still alive. What he no longer had any doubts about were his feelings for Nikki. He had definitely fallen in love with her.

She was so damn amazing. It didn't matter that she was smaller and younger than everyone in that room. She commanded their respect.

And his love...

But she wouldn't even look at him. To drive her

points home, she'd made eye contact with everyone except him. But then she didn't need to convince him to work with the others. He'd already tried going rogue and failed.

Thanks to her.

And he'd nearly gotten them both killed the night before. He knew he needed help.

More important, he knew he needed her.

But she was clearly furious with him. Was she still angry that he'd set her up as Blue's bodyguard only to try to overpower her? Or that she'd made love or—per her words—had sex with him after that.

Should he have tried to resist her?

It would have been the honorable thing to do. But he'd been past honor at that point. He'd been past common sense or any rational thought at all. He had been desperate with need.

And making love with her had done nothing to lessen that need. Maybe that was why she was mad. Her plan hadn't worked. Maybe she still wanted him as much as he wanted her.

But when he touched her, as she moved to pass him, she tensed. Then she glanced down at his hand like she wanted to burn his touch off her skin.

But he couldn't let her go. Not without saying, "Thank you."

She arched a reddish-brown brow.

"For telling everyone about Emilia." He wouldn't have been able to do it, not like she had. Not without enduring a whole hell of a lot of pain.

She nodded.

And his heart swelled with hope that she'd done it at least partially for him, to spare him some of that pain.

"And thank you for rallying everyone together to help," he said. He wasn't sure that they wouldn't be too late, but he at least knew that they would find his sister.

"I didn't do it for you," she said, her voice cold. "I'm doing it for Emilia. And for Blue." Then she tugged free of his grasp and walked away.

And he knew that even if everything came out as they'd planned, that if they rescued all of his family, he would still have lost.

Nikki...

Cooper had returned from Logan's office to find his occupied. A man had made himself alarmingly comfortable in the chair behind his desk—one he was certain Myron Webber had already searched. Good thing they'd held the meeting at Logan's.

Keeping his voice even, he calmly asked, "Did we have a meeting?"

"No," Myron said. "But we should have."

"I was going to call you with an update," Cooper said. That had been part of Nikki's plan.

The lawyer stood up and slapped a check down on the desktop. "It's not necessary. I no longer require the services of the Payne Protection Agency."

Cooper hadn't wanted this job in the first place—not once he'd met the lawyer and realized how untrustworthy he was. But he'd had no idea of what he was capable.

Nikki had DNA evidence. But still they couldn't call the police. They'd had no court order to get that DNA. It would only get Nikki in trouble for taking it illegally. So they might as well take the child illegally, too. They had to get him away from this monster.

"You can call off the guards you currently have on the estate," the lawyer continued.

Obviously they had refused to listen to him. Like he'd said in the conference room, all of Payne Protection was family—by blood or loyalty.

Cooper didn't even look at the check. "You may want to keep that," he said. "I have some information you're going to want to hear."

"I don't care."

Because he thought his guys had killed Lars?

Or because he'd already killed Emilia?

Cooper suppressed a shudder of revulsion. He didn't even like having the guy in his office. He definitely needed to hire more staff—to get a receptionist in here—someone big and burly who would keep out the unsavory characters like him.

But right now Cooper wanted to keep him from leaving. He didn't possess the finesse of his brothers, though. Logan and Parker would have been able to sweet-talk the guy into staying.

"It's all a moot point," Webber continued. "I found a family for the boy. I won't need any protection at the estate anymore." He headed toward the door but turned back. "I may even sell it and move."

"Where?" Cooper asked.

"Anywhere." The lawyer shrugged. "There's really nothing keeping me in River City anymore."

An arrest warrant would, but first they needed the evidence in order for the prosecutor to issue one. Fortunately she was family, too—Milek Kozminski's wife. So she might overlook how they had obtained some of that evidence.

Unfortunately Myron was a lawyer, too, and while

he didn't abide by the law, he was undoubtedly well-versed in his legal rights. And he would know that the Payne Protection Agency had violated them.

"What's this?" a female voice asked.

He and Webber both turned toward the doorway where Nikki stood. She must have left the meeting right after Cooper had.

"You're leaving town?" Nikki asked the question, and somehow she managed to sound disappointed. But then she would be if the plan she had just spelled out failed.

She cared about Lars's nephew. Sadly she cared about Lars, too.

With a big smile, Myron turned toward Nikki. "Would that bother you?" he asked. "If I left town?"

"Of course," she said. "I'm sure you want to celebrate with us before you do that, though."

"Celebrate?"

She glanced at Cooper, who shook his head. "My brother didn't tell you?"

Because Myron hadn't given him a chance.

"We figured out who was after the baby," she said.

His face paled slightly. "You—you did?"

"Lars Ecklund," she replied. "He was a former Marine."

"What—what would he have wanted with a baby?"

She shrugged. "He's a mercenary. Someone must have hired him to take the child. We haven't figured that out yet. Until we do, we'll need to stick close to the little guy."

"But—but I found him a family…"

Nikki's face paled now, and her body tensed. "Have they taken him already?"

"No," he admitted. "They're coming in from another country."

"And of course the court will have to approve the adoption," Cooper said. "That's what my wife—the social worker—has taught me. But you already know that."

Webber's face flushed now. "Of course."

"So until they can take him," Nikki said, "you will want us to keep him safe, until we can determine who Ecklund was working for…"

"So he's been arrested?"

"He's been killed," Nikki said. "A couple of other men died, as well. But they haven't been identified yet."

"Oh—oh, they haven't?"

She shook her head. "And with the backlog the coroner has…" She shrugged. "We may not know that for a while. I suspect they may have been working with Ecklund."

"Uh, there are a couple of guards who didn't show up today," Myron admitted.

Cooper nodded and reminded him, "I wanted to bring in my own staff because I figured the earlier attempt was an inside job."

"What about this Ecklund?" Webber asked. "Did you know him?"

Cooper sighed. "I knew he was a mess, so I'm not surprised. A lot of former Marines become mercenaries. That's why we worked our plan to flush him out."

"That was your plan?"

Cooper nodded. "Of course…"

"It would have been better if he'd been taken alive," Nikki said. "We might never find out who he was working for."

The lawyer couldn't contain a slight smile.

And Nikki couldn't contain a slight shiver of revulsion.

Cooper wanted to step between her and the sleazy attorney. He wanted to protect her because his instincts were still screaming at him that something bad was going to happen to his sister.

But he didn't even need instincts to know that she was in danger. All he had to see was the way Myron Webber looked at her—the same way Lars Ecklund had.

Whether she would allow it or not, Nikki needed protection. Or that something bad was definitely going to happen to her. Cooper just wasn't sure which man would hurt her worse.

Chapter 17

"You're a dead man, Lars Ecklund," Nikki said as she slid the police report onto the table in front of him.

He jumped as if the sound of her voice had startled him. Hadn't he seen her walk into the room?

His head had been down. Maybe he'd fallen asleep in the silence. Everyone else had left Logan's conference room but Lars. He hadn't been allowed. They hadn't wanted to take the chance that someone might see him. The sun hadn't risen yet when he'd arrived, but it was midmorning now.

He glanced down at the report. "Three casualties," he read. He shuddered as he read his own name. "I bet you liked seeing that."

She hadn't been very nice to him earlier. But she'd been angry—still was—over his protecting her. "I saved you last night," she reminded him.

He sighed. "I know. I should have thanked you for that, too, this morning."

"That's not why I like seeing your name on this report," she said. "Even though I think he bought it, Myron Webber is going to check out what I told him." He was too thorough—and too suspicious—not to pull a copy of the report. So it was a good thing that last night she had convinced Nick to file a fake one.

Lars tensed. "You've seen him?"

"Yes, just a little while ago in Cooper's office," she said. "He was trying to fire us."

He sprang up from his chair then, cursing. And with a slight limp, he headed toward the door.

She easily caught up with him and stepped between him and the door she'd closed when she'd joined him. "I talked him out of it," she assured him. "We have time."

She wasn't so sure about Emilia, though—not after she'd seen that sinister little smile on the lawyer's face when he'd thought Lars was dead and that no one would ever find out about Emilia.

He wouldn't have been as convinced of that if she was still alive. A pang of regret struck Nikki's heart. Maybe she shouldn't have worked so hard to convince Lars that his sister might not be dead.

"I know," he said, and his fingers skimmed across her cheek. "Emilia might not have any time…"

Tears stung her eyes. She had wanted to believe there was a chance. For Blue. And for Lars. She'd wanted him to believe there was a chance. She couldn't imagine losing one of her siblings, even though she had come close so many times.

A couple of those times she had nearly taken out Nick herself.

"I'm sorry," she murmured.

"I'm sorry, too," he said.

Of course he would be but she suspected he wasn't talking about Emilia.

"I'm not even sure which thing I've done that made you most angry," he said.

A smile tugged at her lips. "There have been so many…"

He didn't argue with her, only nodded in agreement. "Which is it, Nikki?" he asked. "Why are you so mad at me?"

She slammed her hand against his shoulder, ignoring the twinge as pain shot down her arm from her wounded shoulder. It was only a scratch, though.

It might have been worse if Lars hadn't shot that second man. And she hadn't thanked him yet. She hadn't even checked on him last night. But she hadn't left the hospital until she'd been assured that he was all right.

"Are you this mad about last night?" he asked.

"Of course…" But even she was beginning to realize she might have been unreasonable.

"Do you regret…what we did?" he asked.

"We?" she repeated. If she hadn't done what she had, he would probably really be dead. Then she realized what he was referring to, and she laughed. "I don't regret *that*…"

She'd never felt so much pleasure—had never had as phenomenal an experience.

"So you got it out of your system now?" he asked. And he stepped closer to her, trapping her between his body and the door at her back. He pressed against her, and she could feel his erection pushing against his fly and her ribs. He was so damn big.

She moved back, but the door stopped her. "I could drop you," she reminded him.

"You could," he readily agreed. "But do you really want to hurt me?"

She shook her head. That was why she hoped she was wrong about Emilia. She hoped she was still alive.

"I don't want to hurt you, either," he said. "I'm sorry if I did."

She blinked again, but that threat of tears wasn't for herself. She must have been thinking about Emilia yet. "You didn't hurt me," she assured him. "You made me mad."

"I pissed you off," he said. "How?"

"Because you tried to protect me."

"I didn't want you to get hurt."

"I won't," she said. "I can take care of myself. I thought you believed that."

He nodded. "I know you can take care of yourself," he agreed. "But that doesn't mean I won't want to take care of you, too."

Something about the way he said it, as he touched her again, skimming his fingers along her jaw, had her thinking he wasn't talking about just protecting her from a barrage of bullets.

He wanted to take care of her another way. Her pulse quickened, and her breathing grew shallow. She wanted him to take care of her, too. *That way...*

His pale eyes darkened as the pupils dilated. And he murmured, "If this wasn't your brother's office..."

"Everyone's gone," she assured him. "You and I are the only ones here."

"You know what I want..."

"What do you want?" she asked.

"You."

She reached up and tugged his head down so that his lips brushed across hers. Then she invited him to, "Take me…"

He lifted his head and tilted it as if listening to make sure they were alone. Then he reached behind her and locked the door. He didn't give her time to undress herself. His hands were everywhere, tugging up her sweater, pushing down her jeans. He touched everything he exposed—her breasts, her hips, her ass…

He slid his hands over her curves before lifting her against him. He'd freed himself from his jeans and sheathed himself in a condom. Then he slid inside her.

A moan slipped from her throat and she tossed her head back, knocking it against the door. They both tensed, waiting for someone to call out. But no one had returned yet. They were still all out searching for Emilia.

It had to be killing him that he couldn't. That he was stuck here. He was probably only killing time with her. And really she was fine with that. She didn't want him to actually care about her.

She just wanted him, almost obsessively. The night before hadn't even taken the edge off the madness that spiraled inside her with the tension. She wanted him more now than she had last night—because now she knew how amazing it was.

She clutched at him, her legs wrapped around his waist and her inner muscles squeezing and holding him deep. He groaned as he moved, thrusting up. And his hands gripped her hips, sliding her up and down the length of his erection.

He moved one hand between them and teased her

nipple to a sensitive point. She bit her lip to hold in a cry. It wouldn't matter how far away her brothers were. If they heard that, they'd come running to help.

She didn't need help.

She just needed Lars.

She grasped his shoulders and slid her hands down his bulging arms. He was magnificent in every way. That tension built even more until she shattered, coming. He thrust again and again so her orgasm went on and on. Then he tensed. And biting his lip, he came, his big body shuddering as his release crashed over him.

His legs trembled a bit beneath both their weights. So she eased up and off him. Her knees barely locked as her feet hit the ground. She might have fallen had he not steadied her with a hand on her shoulder.

But he'd touched the wounded one. And she cried out now—just softly—at the pain.

And Lars cursed with regret over her getting hurt and over hurting her.

She'd gotten mad at him for trying to protect her. But the irony was that he'd failed anyway. He hadn't protected her. She had still been hit. Maybe not as badly as she would have been had he not been there.

But if he hadn't been there, no one would have been firing at her. He pulled his hand away from her wounded shoulder and cursed again. "I'm sorry."

Her eyes narrowed as she stared up at him. "You think this is your fault?"

"Those men were after *me*," he reminded her. "You just got caught in the crossfire."

"No, I didn't," she said, "because you shoved me behind you."

And that was why she was mad. His own frustration bubbled up now. "I wasn't going to let you get shot."

"I took the guy down," she reminded him. "I'm a damn good shot."

She had proven that last night, just like she'd proven she was an amazing lover.

"Do you think last night was the first time I've been shot at?" she asked then snorted at his expression.

He must have looked as appalled as he was. "You've been shot at before?"

She nodded. "Several times. And even without you around, I survived every damn time. You don't have to take care of me."

"I see that..." And if he tried, he would lose her for certain. But these men, these killers Webber had hired to do his dirty work, were especially dangerous. If he didn't protect her, he would probably lose her, too.

Of course she had never really been his to lose.

She released a shaky breath as if they had settled an argument.

But he hadn't made any promises. If they were put in the same situation again, he would do the same thing. He would try to protect her from getting hurt. She would hate him for it. But he couldn't help it. He loved her, and he would give up anything for her—even his life.

His cell rang. But when he reached for it, her hand closed over his. "You can't," she told him. "Dead men don't answer their phones."

He held it out to her. "Then you answer it."

When she took it, she glanced down at the number and gasped. Then she pressed the accept button and addressed the caller by name. "Nick?"

She turned toward him. "Yes, he's here…" And she handed the phone over to him.

"Hello?" He'd seen the man the night before, but they hadn't met. So he didn't address him by name.

"Lars Ecklund?"

"Yes." The man had called him. Of course he knew who he was.

"A few days ago you were asking around the morgue about a body," Nick said. "The coroner just called me. One has shown up that matches the description you gave him."

He sucked in a breath and doubled over as if he'd been struck. And Nikki took the phone from his loose grasp.

"Are you sure?" she asked.

She must have put Nick on speaker now because he could hear her brother's reply. "No. I'm not sure. That's why I need someone to ID the body."

Lars forced himself to straighten up and turned for the door. But Nikki grabbed his arm, holding him back. "You can't leave," she protested. "You can't go down there."

"If she's dead, what the hell does it matter?"

"Blue," she said. "We'll lose our chance to get Blue away from that sleazeball."

Sleazeball was the least of what Webber was. He was a thief and a killer.

"I will pretend I didn't hear that," the FBI agent said. "And because dead men can't ID bodies, I need someone else to do it."

Nikki turned toward Lars. "Do you have a picture of her? I'll do it," she offered.

He shook his head as realization dawned on him.

The timing of the body showing up now seemed a little suspicious. "It could be a trap."

Nick's curse carried loudly through the phone. "He's right."

She nodded in agreement. "I wouldn't put it past Webber. That's why you can't go, Lars," she said. "But it doesn't stop me."

"He'll figure out that you know about Emilia," he pointed out. "Then we'll never get the chance to take Blue."

"Again—not hearing…" The lawman began to hum.

He really wanted to meet Nick now. But he and Nikki were right. Lars couldn't go down to the morgue, not yet. If it was Emilia…

He would have to wait to claim her body until after he'd rescued her son.

"Dane can go," he said. "I sent him a photo of Emilia. He already has it on his phone."

"I'll call him," Nikki offered. She hung up on her brother and dialed Dane.

He didn't want to talk to his friend. He didn't want to talk at all. It had been exhausting sitting here all morning while everyone else went out, searching for his sister. He'd suspected even then that all their searching would be for naught.

He'd gotten exhausted waiting for news and waiting for the time when they could go back to the estate and rescue his nephew.

Nikki's return had brought him back to life, the desire for her giving him energy. But now that was gone…

And he dropped back onto the chair he'd been sitting on at the conference table. Her conversation with Dane

was just a low hum in the background as that exhaustion overwhelmed him.

Slender arms locked around his shoulders, and soft curls brushed his cheek as Nikki hugged him from behind where he sat at the table. She must have concluded her conversation with Dane.

Pressing her lips to his ear, she murmured, "I'm sorry..."

He was, too, because he knew now that there was no way he could risk losing her. Not after he'd already lost Emilia. He would be even more overprotective than her brothers were.

Dane had been to a morgue before. So it shouldn't bother him now. He'd identified friends at makeshift morgues on the battlefield. He'd even identified his adoptive parents after they'd died in a horrible car accident. He had been tense then, nervous of what he might find.

Of what he might see...

Which made sense because he still sometimes saw it—when he closed his eyes. He didn't want that image—of a dead body—to be the one he remembered of Emilia Ecklund.

Standing in the dimly lit hallway outside the door marked *morgue*, he hesitated and looked down at his phone. She stared up at him from the picture Lars had sent him, her light blue eyes sparkling with the smile that curved her lips. Her hair, such a pale blond, streamed behind her as if she were running toward him.

Every time he looked at that photo he imagined that she was. That she was running toward him with her arms outstretched like that scene in every damn roman-

tic movie he'd ever watched with whatever woman he'd been dating at the time. He couldn't remember their faces—like he could Emilia's. He blinked and glanced down and his phone had gone dark, just like that romantic notion.

He snorted disparagingly at himself. Him and romance? That was ridiculous. He didn't want that, didn't want the family entanglements his friends had.

It was better to be like him—to be a loner. Then he would never have to go down to the morgue to identify someone he loved.

Drawing in a deep breath, he pushed open the door and stepped into the morgue. "Special Agent Payne sent me."

The guy just stared at him.

Then he remembered what the lawman had told him—that he'd just changed his name to that of his family. "Rus," Dane said. "Agent Rus."

The older man nodded. "That's right. He's Agent Payne now." He studied Dane for a moment. "You don't look familiar. Are you one of his officers or agents?"

"Does it matter?" Dane asked. "He sent me to identify a body."

"But how can you do that?" the guy asked. "Are you her next of kin?"

Dane snorted. "I have no next of kin."

"Then how do you know her?"

Nick had warned him that this could be a trap—the body turning up to lure Lars down to the morgue. They'd thought that someone could be waiting outside the police department. Now Dane realized that one of them could be inside...

Was that how Webber had known Lars was looking for his sister?

He studied the guy and moved a little closer. The coroner was an older man of smaller stature, much smaller than Dane's. The guy's throat moved as he visibly struggled to swallow.

"Do you even have a body to show me?" Dane asked.

"Of—of course," the doctor nervously stammered.

Dane sighed. "Whatever he's paying you..."

"Wh-who?" His face flushed, and he glanced away from Dane, unable to meet his gaze.

Dane just shook his head. He wasn't a detective. He wasn't going to interrogate the guy. But he would make sure that Nicholas Payne did. He doubted anybody could keep secrets from that man. During their short meeting, he'd felt like the FBI agent had been able to see right to his soul, which had ached with loss.

For his friend. If Emilia was dead, it was Lars's loss, not Dane's. He'd never even met her.

And he might not have the chance. "Show me the body," he said, hoping the entire thing had been just a trap to lure Lars down to the morgue.

Metal whined as the coroner pulled open one of the steel drawers that lined a wall of the tiled room. Even before the doctor pulled back the sheet, Dane saw the pale blond hair streaming out from beneath it. And his guts tightened with dread.

She was dead...

Chapter 18

Knowing how she would have felt—how she *had* felt—every time she had been forced to wait to learn the fate of one of her siblings, Nikki had given Lars something to keep him busy. She'd brought him from the conference room to the video room. But even though he was busy, watching all the surveillance footage from the estate, his mind was no doubt still on his sister—still worrying that it would be Emilia's body Dane identified down at the morgue.

Nikki was worried. She didn't want Lars to lose his sister or for Blue to lose his mother. And selfishly she'd wanted to meet the young woman, too. She had wanted to get to know the woman who'd driven her brother to such lengths to protect her.

To save her...

That he had lied to his friends. That he'd used Nikki.

Because she didn't think he was that kind of man. She believed Cooper, that Lars was loyal. But then Penny had thought her husband was, too. And he'd betrayed her in the worst possible way.

No. No man could be trusted. Nikki had to remember that. And she had to focus on the footage playing out on the wall of monitors.

Logan had a better setup than Cooper had. Of course he'd been in business a lot longer, too. Eventually, after more jobs, Cooper would be able to afford more equipment. Hopefully, all his jobs wouldn't go as horribly as his first one.

"Him," Lars said, pointing to the monitor in front of her. Then he pointed at the one in front of him where he had paused the video. A young man filled both frames, his head down, his shoulders hunched. He was tall and skinny and young, barely out of his teens. "He's the courier."

He certainly was not a guard. "Courier?"

"For the breast milk." Lars pointed toward the cooler the kid carried.

How had she not noticed that? Maybe she'd been more distracted than he was. But then sitting this close to him, with his shoulder brushing hers as he moved, was distracting. Even though she was worried about him and Emilia and Blue, she couldn't help the attraction that came over her again. She'd never known such madness as this never-ending desire for Lars Ecklund.

She leaned closer to the monitors. The kid carried that cooler in every frame. "Yes!" Nikki exclaimed. "That has to be him!"

But Lars didn't share her excitement. He looked at

his phone instead, obviously impatient for Dane to call. Because it wouldn't matter if Emilia was dead.

The courier would only be able to lead them back to where she'd been held, not to where she was. But maybe they would be able to find the evidence they needed to bring down Myron Webber.

Not just for child abduction but for murder.

His breath shuddered out a ragged sigh, and his broad shoulders sagged as if he carried the weight of the world on them.

"This is great," Nikki told him, trying to cheer him up. "You found a lead to her."

He just looked at her, his pale eyes full of misery and guilt. "Too late..."

"We don't know that." Yet. But it was a possibility. "None of this is your fault," she assured him.

"Yes, yes, it is," he insisted. "I promised I would keep her safe—always—and I failed her."

His pain wrenched Nikki's heart. "Lars..."

"When my mom died, I promised her that I would make sure nothing happened to Emilia."

"Your mom died?" She couldn't imagine a world without Penny in it. Her mother was everything to her, though—both her mother and her father. "When was that?"

"Six years ago," he said. "She had been sick a long time with MS."

"What about your dad?" she asked.

He shrugged. "I don't know where he is. He took off when Mom got sick." Since she'd been sick a long time, Lars must have been quite young when his father had taken off, leaving a kid responsible for a sick woman and a young girl.

No wonder Lars looked like he carried the weight of the world on his shoulders. He had carried it—alone— for a long time.

"I'm sorry," she said, and her heart ached more for all he'd already endured.

If Emilia was the body in the morgue…

She wasn't sure Lars would be able to handle the pain and the guilt. Where was Dane? Why hadn't he called yet?

Finally his phone lit up with an incoming call. "It's Dane," he said. But he hesitated before pressing the button to accept the call.

She didn't blame him. In fact, she was glad that he did because she needed a second to prepare for the news, too. She drew in a deep breath, bracing herself. Then she reached for his hand. It was so big—like the rest of him—and so strong.

She had no doubt he could handle most any physical pain. But emotional pain was different. It didn't matter how big or strong a person was; it could cripple him. And if it crippled him, he might not accept comfort. He might not let anyone console him.

He squeezed her fingers before he pressed the button and learned his sister's fate.

Had hers been the body in the morgue?

He didn't put the call on speaker, like she had Nick's. She could only hear his side of the conversation.

"Are you sure?" His jaw was clenched, his handsome face so grim.

But how could he believe anything until he saw for himself? She wouldn't blame him if he insisted on going down to the morgue himself to confirm whatever Dane had told him.

So she wasn't surprised when he clicked off the call, turned to her and said, "I need to leave."

She tightened her grasp on his hand. But she was seeking comfort as much as she was offering it. No...

Emilia couldn't be dead. Blue needed his mother.

Rage surged through Lars. He let it bubble over, let it show in his grasp as he tightened his hands around the man's throat. If he squeezed a little harder, the man wouldn't be able to talk at all—ever again.

Nikki grabbed his arm, pulling him back. But he'd already planned on loosening his grasp. He didn't want to kill the kid. He just wanted to scare the hell out of him.

Of course they had already done that when he'd come home to find them waiting for him inside his studio apartment. Fortunately the video cameras had captured a clear image of his license plate, and Nikki had hacked into the DMV database to find his address. She'd also picked the lock of the apartment door.

The woman had incredible skills and knowledge. So it was no wonder that he'd been unable to resist her. It was no wonder he'd ignored the bro code and crossed the line with her. It was no wonder he'd turned to her to help him deal with his worry and fears over Emilia and Blue.

He'd never known a stronger or more beautiful woman.

She squeezed his arm now, bringing him back to the moment—to their mission. She was both his distraction and his direction.

He blinked and focused again on the young man, whom he'd shoved up against the apartment door. His

hair was greasy and stringy, hanging around a face dotted with acne. He was young. Nikki had learned from his DMV records that Gregory Boone was twenty-one and a community college student. An internet search had revealed his poor choices for what to post on social media and his Craigslist ad offering his delivery services for cash.

"If you don't start talking now, you're going to lose your chance to ever speak again." Lars threatened the kid. For emphasis he tightened his grasp for just a few seconds before releasing him.

The kid gasped for breath and clutched his neck. "I—I don't know what you want."

"Information," Nikki said.

Lars shoved the kid against the door again. "The truth. We want the truth! Did you kill her?"

Gregory gasped again, this time with shock. "I—I would never kill anyone."

Lars believed him. He was too timid. But he had to force him to lose that shyness now. "The woman you've been collecting the breast milk from—she's dead. Did you do it?"

The kid just stared blankly at him. He had no idea what Lars was talking about—had no idea that he was lying. Emilia wasn't dead.

At least she hadn't been the woman in the morgue. He trusted Dane. His friend had been certain; the body wasn't hers. Except for the hair that had been dyed, she'd looked nothing like Emilia.

The coroner was currently being interrogated, as well. He'd been tipping off Webber. But what was their real connection? Had he helped Webber deliver some of the babies he'd offered up for adoption?

Lars doubted Blue had been born in a hospital. Or Emilia wouldn't be missing. Where the hell was she?

Gregory was even more confused than Lars had realized because he murmured, "What woman?"

"You've been picking up breast milk almost daily and delivering it to Myron Webber's estate," Nikki told him.

"Breast milk?" He sounded appalled.

"You don't even know what was in the cooler, do you?" Nikki asked.

Lars shook his head with disgust. "You idiot, you could have been transporting body parts!"

"To a place like that?" the kid scoffed. "The lawyer lives in a mansion."

"Where did you pick up the cooler?" Lars asked. "What was that place like?" Where had his sister been held?

Gregory shuddered. "I'm really happy I don't have to go back there again."

And Lars felt sick. His sister had been kept somewhere the guy had found repulsive. Poor Emilia. But even worse, if the guy didn't need to return, she must already be gone.

The brief relief he'd felt when Dane had assured him his sister wasn't in the morgue left him. Pain squeezed his heart. Lars had been too late to rescue her. But he could get justice for her.

"You're damn well going back there," Lars said, "because you need to show us where it is."

The kid shook his head. "No. No, I can't."

· "You had no problem going back and forth all these weeks when you were getting paid," Lars reminded him.

"But when Webber told me he didn't need me any-

more, he made it clear that I was supposed to forget ever working for him. That I was supposed to say nothing if anyone asked me about it." He trembled in Lars's grasp. "He will kill me if I do."

"And I'll kill you if you don't."

Nikki gasped, and Lars turned to find her brown eyes widened with surprise as if she didn't know whether to believe him or not.

Lars wasn't sure he was just bluffing, either. If there was a chance Emilia was still alive, he would do whatever necessary to find her and save her.

Even kill...

Nick had seen Lars Ecklund, but they had had yet to meet—until now—in his office.

"I'll hold him." He agreed to keep the courier in protective custody until the warehouse could be searched. Of course he hadn't been given much choice.

Nikki had asked, and she'd been fearful that if Nick didn't hold him in a jail cell, Lars might put the guy six feet under. Of course the kid had also admitted that Webber had threatened his life, so holding Gregory Boone wasn't against the rules.

Now holding the coroner...

Nick had had to bend the rules a bit for that. But the prosecutor had given him twenty-four hours. They had twenty-four hours to find evidence for her to make a case against Myron Webber.

Nikki grabbed her vibrating cell and stepped out of the office to take the call. Maybe she'd learned something more. Or maybe she'd just wanted a break from the tension between him and Lars Ecklund.

Instead of sitting in his desk chair, Nick stood. But

even standing, he couldn't meet the blond guy's gaze. He was big. So damn big...

No wonder her other brothers hadn't killed him yet for putting Nikki in danger. They wouldn't have been able to hurt him.

"Are you going to threaten me, too?" Lars asked.

Nick arched a brow. "Too? Logan?"

"All of them," Lars replied. "Even Cooper..." And he flinched.

Nick knew what it was like when a friend felt like he'd been betrayed just because he fell for his sister. Of course it had taken Nick a while—almost too long—to realize that he'd actually fallen for Annalise.

Did Lars know how he felt about Nikki yet?

"I won't threaten you," Nick assured him.

A slight breath of relief slipped between Ecklund's lips. As if he'd been worried about Nick...

"I am going to offer you some advice, though," he warned him.

Lars closed his eyes.

"Praying for patience?" Nick asked him.

Lars's eyes opened again and he stared at him in surprise. "Nikki said that you and your mom just *know* things..."

Nick's mom hadn't known a damn thing. Drugs had destroyed her brain and her sense of decency. Lars was referring to Nikki's mom, though. Nick wished Penny Payne had been his mother, too. But it was enough that he had her now. He'd found his family.

He hoped Lars found his—in the warehouse. They'd had the kid point it out earlier. Nick had officers watching it now. But he would pull those officers once Payne Protection arrived to do the search. The prosecutor had

regretfully informed them they didn't have enough for a legal search warrant.

"I just assumed you were praying for patience," Nick said. Waiting for news of his sister had probably taken whatever he'd already had. "You're going to need it if you want a relationship with Nikki."

Lars shrugged those ridiculously huge shoulders. "I don't think it matters what I want."

"You would let Logan and Cooper scare you off?" Nick asked. Maybe he didn't really care about Nikki. "Parker—you'd just have to buy him a beer." Parker was the easiest going of all the Paynes.

"They're not the ones scaring me off."

Nick gestured at himself.

Lars chuckled now. "None of her brothers is as scary as Nikki. She doesn't want a relationship."

"She might," Nick said. He'd seen how his sister had looked at the big guy. "But more than a relationship, she wants respect. Respect her and her abilities. Don't try to protect her or you'll lose her for certain."

"We're about to storm a warehouse that could be full of gunmen," Lars needlessly reminded him. "If I don't protect her, I'll lose her for certain."

"There's a fine line with Nikki," he advised. "Be careful you don't cross it."

Lars shook his head. "I don't care if she gets mad at me. I don't care if she never wants me to see her again. I'm going to damn well make sure she doesn't get killed. And if I lose her, at least she'll be alive."

Nick grinned. His sister hadn't been looking. She hadn't wanted it, but she'd found the love of her life. Now if only they would both survive to their happy ending.

Chapter 19

Emilia was dead.

She could muster no energy—no will—to fight. Maybe it was the fever that had been raging through her body, making her alternate between freezing and burning alive.

Maybe it was the anticipation. Every time the door had opened over the past few days, she'd suspected that someone was coming to kill her. She knew they intended to. They'd told her, either inadvertently or—in the case of Webber—intentionally that she was no longer of any use.

She was disposable. And soon they would dispose of her. The waiting for the end was the worst. She just wanted it to be over—not her life—but the waiting.

She wanted to live, and yet she was too weak to fight for herself anymore. She was even too weak to fight for her baby boy.

She needed her brother. But Lars was dead, too—because of her.

If only she hadn't screwed up so badly...

This was all her fault. Maybe it was better that she die rather than live with the guilt of what she'd caused.

Sounds echoed within whatever building she was being held. She heard metal creaking. Heard footsteps.

They were coming for her.

The end was now.

This was it.

The unmarked police cars had left a short while ago. Nikki sat in a Payne Protection Agency black SUV with Lars, waiting for the others to arrive.

"They're taking too long to get here," Lars complained, his muscular body tense in the driver's seat. He gripped the steering wheel so tightly that his knuckles had gone white.

She was surprised the plastic hadn't broken into pieces. But she understood his tension. She was on edge, too. But she forced herself to be patient. "They had to come from the estate."

His big body got even more tense, muscles bulging in his arms. "We can't leave the baby unprotected."

"Candace is still there, in the nursery with him, and Milek and Gage are on the estate, too," she assured him. They were pulling double shifts to cover while everyone else got in place for the plan.

"But Webber—"

Her lips twitched, and she gave in to the smile. "He's a little busy down at the bank right now."

"What did you do?" he asked with the same tone her

mother had used when Nikki had ripped her clothes climbing trees or getting into fights on the playground.

Her smile turned into a smirk. "I just messed with his money a little..."

"You hacked into his bank accounts?"

She shook her head then brushed a curl from her eyes. "Of course not. That would be illegal."

"Yes, it would," he agreed, and his voice deepened with concern. "I hope you were careful."

"Nothing can be traced back to me," she assured him. She had made certain of that.

He turned fully toward her, studying her across the narrow space of the console and asked, "Is there anything you don't think of?"

You.

She hadn't thought of him, hadn't thought she would ever meet anyone who would make her question her decision to never risk her heart on love. But he wasn't the chauvinistic lunkhead she'd originally thought he was.

He was a man who took on responsibility for sick women and young girls. He was the kind of man who made promises and strove to keep them—even at the risk of his own life and freedom.

As she stared into his pale blue eyes, something shifted in her chest, her heart lurching as if reaching for him. Like he reached for her...

He lifted his hand and brushed his fingertip along the edge of her jaw. "You are so damn smart," he murmured. "And so damn beautiful..."

Her pulse quickened at his touch—and his compliments. She leaned forward, meeting him as he lowered his head. His lips brushed softly across hers.

It was a gentle kiss. An almost reverent one.

And as he lifted his head from hers, he murmured, "Thank you…"

"For what?" she wondered.

They hadn't accomplished anything yet. They had no reason to even hope anymore that they would find Emilia alive. And getting Blue wasn't a sure thing, either. Webber still had his guys guarding the estate, men who had proven last night that they had no compulsion against killing.

And they couldn't legally force Webber to hand over the baby. There was nothing to link him to Emilia but the letter she'd sent Lars. And they had no way of proving she'd even shown up for that appointment. They needed to find real evidence of their connection. They needed to find evidence to pin a crime on the corrupt lawyer.

So far all he had done was hire a delivery boy. That was no crime. Even the threat was just Gregory's word against his. That was why they hadn't been able to get a search warrant granted for the warehouse.

But they had to search it—and soon. However, they were no longer alone.

A van pulled up to the building that had looked abandoned until now. When the delivery kid had brought them there earlier, they hadn't seen anyone around, and the officers who'd been watching it since then had said that nobody had gone inside yet.

But there was no seeing through the steel walls and roof. There could have been several gunmen in there waiting for them. That was why they had agreed to not to go inside until backup arrived in the form of more Payne Protection bodyguards.

As Lars noticed the van, too, he sucked in a breath. He knew what she did—this didn't look good.

Maybe it was just their transportation. But it was one of those longer, cargo kind of vans used for hauling stuff.

Or disposing of stuff…

Like a body…

Lars closed his eyes, shutting out the sight of the van and the sight of Nikki's beautiful face taut with fear and regret. She knew what the van meant, too.

"She's dead," he murmured.

He'd vacillated between thinking Emilia was alive and dead for weeks now. He had grieved her loss over and over again. So the pain should not have struck him as hard as it did. He should have been used to it. But for a moment it stopped his heart.

"No, no," Nikki said, her voice higher than it usually was. She sounded panicked or scared. "This doesn't mean she's dead yet."

"Stop it!" he yelled at her as his heart began to beat frantically again. "Stop trying to make me hope…"

"Why?" she asked.

"It hurts too much," he said. "It hurts too much to hope for the best and to then be disappointed."

Nikki smacked his shoulder. "Don't give up on her!"

He didn't want to. He wanted to hope. But he had seen too much—far too much devastation—to believe in happily-ever-afters anymore.

"She's not like you," he reminded Nikki.

And that was his fault.

Instead of always trying to take care of Emilia, he should have taught her to take care of herself. He should

have given her the skills that Nikki had: the self-defense moves, the shooting ability, the street sense...

But for as tough and pragmatic as Nikki acted, she was really an optimist. In that way she and Emilia were alike. Emilia had been so sweet and innocent that she'd always seen the best in everyone, that she had believed everyone was a good person.

He should have prepared her for the people like Myron Webber—for the evil men who would prey on innocents like her. But he'd wanted to protect her from that, too.

"We won't know until we go inside if she's alive or dead," Nikki told him. "That's why we have to go in there."

He knew that. He wanted to. But he didn't want Nikki getting hurt. "We should wait."

But even as he said it, he knew he couldn't. He reached for the door handle with one hand and his holster with the other. Nikki followed suit out the passenger side.

It was crazy—the two of them—taking on whatever awaited them in the warehouse. It could have been filled with gunmen already and the van had just brought more...

It could have been wired to explode.

Lars had faced all of those situations before in war. This was war now. And like in most wars, he expected there to be casualties. He just hoped one of those wasn't Nikki. She met him at the back of the SUV, where they had both crouched low so no one would see them. And know they were coming...

She wore a bulletproof vest like the one he wore. Nick had insisted they take them before he had let them

leave his office. But her head was bare, her curls tousled from the breeze blowing around the deserted street. If she got hit in the head...

The warehouse was in the old industrial area of the city—the one devastated when companies had moved most of their manufacturing jobs overseas. It had yet to recover. Lars suspected it never would. And neither would he if something happened to Nikki. Losing his sister would be hard enough.

"We should wait for help," he said.

"There's no time," Nikki replied. "Emilia could still be alive..."

Maybe they had needed the van to move her somewhere else to kill her—to a crime scene that couldn't be traced back to Myron Webber. It made sense.

It gave him hope despite himself.

Nikki gave him hope.

"We need to split up," she said.

A twinge of regret struck his heart. But she wasn't referring to them personally. They had never truly been together in order to break up.

"You take the front," she said. "And I'll move around to the back."

He should have been relieved that she didn't want to storm in the front herself. But she was still going in; she was still risking her life.

"You could wait out here," he told her. "Wait for the others to arrive."

She sighed. "We don't have time for you to act like the macho jerks my brothers are about my safety," she reminded him. "I am a damn good shot. I can take care of myself."

And she could take care of him, as well. She had saved his life once already.

He could return the favor.

But if they separated...

"We should stick together," he insisted. "We need to go in side by side."

Her lips curved into a sad smile. She knew he intended to use his body to shield hers.

"It's the only way I'll do this now," he said. The only way he would risk her life was if he knew he could do his best to save her.

She gave a reluctant nod of agreement. And he leaned forward and kissed her again like he had in the SUV. He kissed her with the emotion that filled his heart with the love he felt for her.

Her breath whispered across his lips as it escaped in a ragged little sigh. She stared up at him, her dark eyes wide as if she were trying to drink in the sight of him.

Or memorize his face...

She was clearly as concerned as he was that they might not survive. Finally she pulled her gaze from his and murmured, "Let's do this..."

Weapons drawn, they headed toward the door to which the van had pulled up. The white cargo vehicle was parked at a dock in front of the building. The sliding door on the side of the van was open, revealing the empty interior. And the overhead door of the dock had been lifted halfway.

They definitely intended to move something.

Or someone...

Emilia...

He ignored the pain lancing his heart and headed for the concrete steps at the side of the dock. He was

so intent on keeping his body between the open door, and whatever dangers lurked inside the warehouse, and Nikki that he hadn't realized she'd slipped away.

Lars didn't know until he heard the gunfire at the back of the building, and he whirled around to see that she was gone.

Damn woman!

Why was she so determined to prove herself all the time? Or was she trying to get killed? Before Lars could move from the stairs to the back of the building, more gunfire rang out.

Closer.

Bullets pinged off the overhead door and the van as gunmen began to shoot at him. He ducked low and returned fire. But the interior of the warehouse was dark. He could see only shadows. While he had extra ammunition, he had to make sure every shot counted. Even with Nikki, he was outnumbered. And if she'd already been hit…

Then he wasn't just outnumbered. He was dead. Because losing her would kill him more effectively than any damn bullet.

Chapter 20

"Damn it! Damn it!" Nick shouted, his voice reverberating off the glass walls of his small office in the River City Police Department.

Penny flinched at the volume and anger but mostly about the fear. She had never heard Nick sound so afraid. And she'd gone through many fears with him.

"Who was it?" she asked even before he clicked off his cell.

His hand shook as he shoved the phone in his pocket. Then he dragged open a desk drawer and pulled out his weapon.

"What is it?" she asked this time.

As if unaware she was even in the room with him, he muttered, "They didn't wait for backup…" He shook his head. "I should have known they wouldn't."

She didn't need to ask whom he was talking about.

She knew. The fear had gripped her all morning. Hell, it had been with her since last night when she'd gone to the hospital to see her wounded daughter.

"Nikki…"

As if she'd asked a question, Nick nodded. "They were sitting on a warehouse where they think Lars's sister is being held."

"And?"

"That was just a report of shots being fired there," Nick said as he headed toward the door. "Nobody else had time to get there yet."

She could have pointed out that he wouldn't, either. Whatever was going to happen was happening now. And there was nothing he could do to stop it.

She reached out for his arm as he tried to pass her. And she held tightly to him. Seeing the guilt in him, along with the fear, she assured him, "Whatever has happened is not your fault, Nicholas Payne."

His eyes widened with surprise as they did every time someone called him Payne. It was his name—the one he would have always had had she and his father known about him.

He shook his head, not in denial of the name because he had finally accepted it. "It is my fault."

She doubted it but asked, "Why? What could you have possibly done?"

"I gave Lars bad advice," Nick said.

Penny tensed. Lars Ecklund. Of course Nikki would have been with him, just as she'd been the night before when she'd gotten shot. The man wasn't good for her.

Why—damn it—why when her daughter had finally fallen in love did it have to be with a man who would probably wind up getting her killed?

Because she was Nikki, of course. She wouldn't fall for a computer nerd or an accountant. As much as she disparaged them, she would fall for a man like her brothers—like her father—one who regularly risked his life. But he hadn't risked just his now; he was risking hers, too.

"What did you tell him?" Penny asked.

Nick shook his head as if disgusted at himself. "I told him not to try to protect her."

Penny sucked in a breath.

"I told him to trust that she can take care of herself. It's why they would have gone inside without backup," Nick explained. He pulled away from Penny—not with urgency but with more guilt. "I need to get there."

It was clear that he knew he would be too late to help. But he had to know just how bad his advice had been.

Was Nikki dead?

Penny couldn't tell. She'd never had the connection with Nikki that she had with the boys, that Nick had with Nikki. From the grim look on his handsome face, she worried that he already knew what he would find when he got to the warehouse.

Nikki's body...

Pain radiated throughout Nikki's chest as she lay flat on her back on the concrete floor. She couldn't get a breath. There was too much pressure on her lungs; her heart beat too fast. Was it pumping blood through her or out of her?

She lifted her hands to her chest. Had the bullet penetrated the vest? No. Her fingertips touched the end of the round. The vest had stopped it. But the impact of the shot against the metal plate had knocked her flat

on her back. If it hadn't, she probably would have gotten hit again because she'd heard another shot after the one that had knocked her down.

Now she heard footsteps scraping across the concrete as someone rushed toward her. Bracing her elbows beneath her, she tried to get up. But she had yet to find her breath. So she could only roll to her side and lift her weapon.

She stared down the barrel into Lars's pale blue eyes. They were wide with fear.

"Are you all right?" he asked as he knelt beside her.

She nodded.

"You got hit…"

"The vest stopped it." But she knew why she hadn't been hit again. The next shot she'd heard hadn't been fired at her. It had been Lars taking out the guy who'd struck her.

"Are you all right?" she asked, and she scanned his face and body for any marks. He didn't have a scratch on him.

"No," he said, his voice low with fury. "You lied to me. You were supposed to stick close to me."

Ignoring the pang of guilt she felt for fooling him, she said dismissively, "That was a stupid plan."

"I am not going to argue with you," he said. "I'm going to get you the hell out of here. There are more gunmen hiding."

She understood why they would hide from him. Their bullets probably wouldn't have stopped Lars even if he hadn't been wearing a vest.

"I'm fine," she insisted even as she struggled yet to breathe deeply. The impact might have broken one of her ribs. Maybe two. But she didn't care about herself

right now. They were too close. So she urged him, "Go. Find. Emilia…"

He shook his head. "No, I can't leave you…"

Another shot rang out, and he flung his body across hers. He jerked as if he'd been struck.

"Are you okay?" she asked.

Nikki saw movement overhead. Lifting her gun, she fired at the man in the rafters. He fell. And while she couldn't see it, she heard him hit the concrete, heard the sickening crunch and crack of bones breaking.

Lars hadn't answered her. So her voice shook when she asked again, "Are you all right?"

He groaned then rolled off her. Reaching behind him, he murmured, "Yeah, the vest stopped that bullet, too."

"And I got the shooter," she pointed out. "Go. Find. Emilia."

He stared at her for a long moment.

"I'm fine," she said, her voice rising with urgency.

Emilia was a witness. If she was alive, these men needed to get rid of her for Webber. The girl probably had a huge price on her head right now.

"Go!" she yelled.

Lars kissed her, just a quick brush of his mouth across hers. "Take cover," he told her.

Finally able to move, Nikki did as he advised. She rolled to the shadows of some boxes stacked along a warehouse wall. "Find her," she urged.

Of course he had no idea where to look. And he had no hope. He wouldn't let himself believe that Emilia might still be alive.

Nikki worried that he was probably right. Webber was too smart to slip up and leave behind someone who could identify him.

* * *

Lars knew where to look for Emilia because he'd seen the direction one of the gunmen headed as he slipped away. The guy Nikki had shot out of the rafters wasn't the one who'd shot Lars in the back. Lars had seen that man moving through the empty crates toward a hallway leading off the main area of the warehouse.

Maybe the rooms along the corridor had once been offices. He couldn't tell. He just glanced quickly through each open door as he moved down the hall.

As shots rang out, he ducked inside one of those rooms just as bullets pinged off the metal jamb near his head. "Son of a bitch…"

More shots rang out in quick succession. Then keys jangled. The guy was trying to unlock something.

The room where Emilia was being held?

A chain rattled.

And Lars's stomach churned as emotions overwhelmed him. Had they chained his sister like a dog?

Fury coursed through him. Unconcerned for his own safety, he rushed back into the hall. The guy turned and fired, but if his bullet struck the vest this time, Lars didn't even feel it. He didn't feel anything. Not even regret as he squeezed the trigger and fired into the assailant.

The guy dropped to his knees and stared up at Lars with a look of surprise. That Lars was alive? Or that Lars had shot him?

The guy fell forward, facedown on the concrete. Lars kicked away his gun before feeling for a pulse.

He was dead.

The chain lay beside him along with a padlock. The key had rolled away.

Whatever had been locked inside that room, they had been determined that it would not escape. Until now...

The door had only opened a crack. Lars couldn't see inside it. But even when he pushed the door open all the way, he couldn't see inside.

There were no windows. No light.

Shadows filled the room. And a sickening stench.

Of must and mold and...

Finally his eyes adjusted and the shadows took shape. Still holding his weapon, he stepped through the doorway. There could have been another gunman inside. He had no idea how many were inside the warehouse.

That was why he hadn't wanted to leave Nikki.

But she'd insisted he look for Emilia. She'd insisted that his sister could still be alive.

She was wrong.

His stomach churning with dread, he walked farther inside the room. Against the far wall, a mattress lay on the floor. Blood had saturated and stained it and part of the concrete around it. That was one of the smells he'd recognized from war: blood.

And fear.

He could smell it inside the room, too.

Emilia must have been so frightened here. Had she been tortured?

Was that why there was so much blood? Or was this where she had given birth to her son?

In a filthy warehouse?

Her body lay, facedown, on that stained mattress, her pale hair spread across her back and the mattress and even the floor. It was so long...

Longer than he remembered. But he had been gone

for so many months. He had been gone too long. And now he had lost her forever.

He moved his hand toward her face, to pull back some of that hair and look at her one last time. But before his fingertips could do more than touch those silken strands, he heard more gunshots.

They rang out inside the warehouse.

There had definitely been more gunmen.

Had Nikki heeded his warning? Had she stayed hidden? Or had she decided to take them all on alone?

She'd already been winded from taking the bullet in her vest. And she'd had to be running low on ammunition. But none of that would stop her.

Damn woman...

He hadn't even had a chance to tell her yet why he'd thanked her in the SUV. He'd wanted to thank her for all she had done to help him.

But most of all he'd wanted to thank her for caring—for caring about his nephew and his sister.

His poor sister...

He hadn't gotten the chance to explain, though. And now he might never have the chance.

Like Emilia, was Nikki dead now, too?

Chapter 21

What the hell was going on? Bullets ricocheted and gunfire reverberated off the warehouse walls. Was this a rescue? Or the end she'd believed it to be?

Emilia had no way of knowing. So she lay tensely on the mattress, playing dead. It wasn't much of a stretch right now. She was weak and tired. But if this was her chance to escape and to see her son again...

She had to take it. So while the gunfire in the warehouse distracted the man who'd come inside the room, she hurled herself at him—pummeling with her fists and her feet.

"Oh, my God," a deep—familiar—voice murmured gruffly.

Emilia froze as she recognized her brother's voice.

"I thought you were dead," they said in unison.

Staring at her in awe—or maybe revulsion—Lars touched her face.

It had to be filthy—like the rest of her.

"You're burning up," he murmured.

Maybe it was the fever that had conjured him up. Maybe he was just a hallucination. She reached out, too, and touched his face. His skin was cool, so much cooler than hers. "Are you real?" she asked.

He nodded, but he looked grim, his jaw tense. Was he mad at her? He had every reason to be. She had been such a fool.

"He told me you were dead," she said.

He didn't ask who. But then he would know; he wouldn't have found her if he hadn't known who had been holding her.

"He thought I was," Lars said. "He thought some of his men killed me."

"But you're okay?"

He nodded. "Thanks to Nikki." He stared out that open door as if looking for the woman he mentioned. "She told me not to give up on you, either. She convinced me that you could still be alive."

Emilia wasn't so certain that Nikki was right. She felt like death. And she definitely wasn't safe yet. None of them was.

More gunfire rang out inside the warehouse.

He flinched with the report of each shot. "I need to go back out there."

But she grabbed his hand before he could slip away. And instead of making her weak, like it had, her fear made her strong enough to hang on to him. "Please... don't leave me..."

She had been alone for so long, too long.

"I need to get you medical help," he said. "You're burning up."

But now she had begun to shiver again, her body trembling with cold. As if to warm her, he wrapped her in his arms and lifted her. Before he could step through the door, a man burst into the room, gun drawn.

A cry of fear slipped through Emilia's cracked lips. They had been so close to escaping.

"Dane," Lars greeted the man.

She remembered his mentioning the name before. Dane Sutton was big like Lars but his hair and eyes were dark.

"Why the hell didn't you wait for us?" the man asked; then his gaze moved to her. "She's alive?"

She moved her lips, trying to speak for herself. But she could form no words. Maybe her attempt to fight earlier had drained the last of her energy. Or maybe it was something about this man that made her speechless.

"She needs medical attention," Lars said.

She was certain Dane could see that for himself. "An ambulance is on its way," he told her brother.

And Lars tensed. "Who was hit?"

Dane said nothing.

"Who was hit!" It wasn't a question this time but a shouted demand for an answer.

"Nikki..."

Lars's breath hissed out between his teeth and he reacted as if he'd been shot.

Nikki—whoever she was—hadn't just saved his life—when Webber's men had tried to kill him. She'd stolen Lars's heart.

There had been so much blood. But then head wounds always bled the worst. Maybe that was why everyone was freaking out so damn badly.

Whatever the reason, Nikki was annoyed. And she was fine. She lifted her hand to the bandage on her temple. The stitches had been a waste of time. She'd probably have a scar anyway. But that was the least of her concerns.

She didn't have time. "Hey!" she called out. "Where are my clothes?"

If someone didn't come back with them soon, she'd leave in the hospital gown. She didn't care. Just as she was sliding off the stretcher, the curtain jerked aside. Maybe that was why she teetered for a moment, unbalanced. It wasn't because her head grew light and stars and flashing lights filled her vision.

She blinked and focused on the worried face of the young physician's assistant. "Did you find my clothes?" she asked.

"You're not clear to leave yet," the PA told her. "You need a CAT scan first."

She snorted. "I'm fine. No blurred vision." Stars and spots didn't count as blurred. "No nausea. No headache. I don't have a concussion."

She'd had enough of them before that she would have recognized the symptoms.

"Ms. Payne—"

"Nikki." She corrected the young man. While Nick had taken their father's name, she had considered getting rid of it. She was still furious with him for betraying their mother. But ultimately she had decided that it was better to keep the name to remind herself that *no* man could ever be trusted.

"You're still not cleared yet to leave—"

"I don't care," she told him. "I'm going." She had to get Blue before Webber heard about the warehouse

shoot-out and took off with him forever. Then she remembered where her clothes had been stashed during her previous ER visits—on a shelf under the stretcher. She leaned over and ignored the wave of nausea that washed over her with the sudden movement.

She did not have a concussion. The bullet had barely grazed her. Everyone had just freaked out over the blood or she wouldn't have even needed medical treatment. She would have stopped bleeding eventually.

The blood loss was what had probably made her dizzy. But she refused to give in to it. She grabbed the plastic bag and pulled it up, dumping her clothes onto the stretcher. "I'm getting dressed," she said. And she reached for the back of the gown.

The young man hesitated a moment before he stepped back and pulled the curtain shut for her.

She released a ragged breath and dropped back onto the edge of the stretcher, muttering, "I thought he would never leave."

She just needed a moment to catch her breath again. And she would get dressed. She'd get the hell out of here. She had a baby to kidnap back from his abductor. But that wasn't even the fight that worried her. The battle that worried her the most was the one she would have convincing her brothers and Lars to let her go back to Webber's estate.

But she had a plan for that…

She just needed the strength to make them listen to her. She drew in a deep breath and stood again. While her head grew light, she didn't get dizzy. Her knees didn't wobble. She could stand.

So she reached for her clothes. As she did, a soft voice called out, "Nikki…?"

Maybe she was imagining things because her name had been little more than a whisper. Her mother had always warned her kids to listen to their conscience. Was that Nikki's trying to talk to her?

But why? She'd done nothing wrong. Sure, she'd lied to Lars about sticking by his side while they went in the front. But it had been more efficient to split up.

And nothing bad had happened.

In fact, he had found Emilia.

Alive.

"Nikki…"

Now she recognized the soft voice even though she'd never heard it before. She pulled back the curtain of the stretcher next to hers. A girl lay on the bed, at least she was so thin and delicate-looking that she looked little more than a girl.

She could have been the twenty-two Lars had said she was. Her face was so pale, her eyes nearly as pale since they were the same eerie light blue of her brother's. And her son's…

But dark circles hollowed out her beautiful eyes, and her thinness made her cheekbones taut beneath her nearly translucent skin. IVs pumped fluids into her and machines monitored her vitals. Despite all the needles protruding from her arm, Emilia lifted her hand and held it out toward her.

"Are you all right?" Nikki asked, her heart aching for the horrors the poor girl had endured. She stepped closer and took the proffered hand.

Weakly squeezing her fingers, Emilia replied, "Yes, thanks to you."

"Thank your brother," Nikki said. "He went crazy trying to find you."

"He said he would have given up if not for you,"
Emilia said. "You convinced him that I could still be
alive."

"Because of Blue."

Emilia's fingers went stiff in her hand. "What?"

Heat rushed to Nikki's face. "That's what I started
calling him—because of his eyes."

"That's what Lars used to call me," Emilia said.
"Baby Blue."

Nikki nodded. She could understand why. They all
had those amazingly pale blue eyes. "Which one of your
parents passed down those genes?"

Emilia shrugged. "Must have been our father, but I
don't remember him. When my mom got sick, he took
off." Betraying the family.

Like Nikki's dad had. She understood how disappointed the young girl must have been to find out her
father hadn't been a man she could count on. But like
Nikki had had her brothers, Emilia had had Lars.

Nikki squeezed her fingers now. "That must have
been rough."

Emilia shook her head. "I had Lars. He took care of
me." She sighed. "That was too much to ask, though.
Too much responsibility."

"His only fear was that he'd failed you," Nikki said.
"That he'd broken the promise he'd made your mother
to always keep you safe."

"Never!" Tears leaked from the corners of Emilia's
beautiful eyes. "*I* failed him. I was so stupid."

Nikki wasn't sure if she was referring to getting pregnant or to meeting with the lawyer. But she squeezed
Emilia's fingers and assured her, "Blue's a beautiful

baby. He's the reason I knew you were still alive because he was being fed breast milk. It's made him so strong."

More tears leaked from the corners of Emilia's eyes. "I want to hold him so badly. I never got to see him, to hold him."

Emilia was stronger than she knew because she gave strength to Nikki. She would do whatever necessary to make sure mother and baby were reunited.

Lars uttered a ragged sigh of relief and let his body relax against the wall of the ER waiting room. The doctor had just assured him that Emilia would be all right. But when he thought of everything she had endured—alone—anger surged through him again. She'd lost a lot of blood during childbirth and had an infection due to poor—if any—postnatal care. She was also dehydrated. The doctor had said Lars had found her just in time.

He already knew that. If he and Nikki hadn't stormed the warehouse when they had, she would have been dead—because Webber's men would have killed her. That was why they had come back with the van. Of course there was only one of them alive to admit it.

And Lars doubted he was going to talk.

But Emilia could. She could tell the prosecutor what hell Webber had put her through. Not that he wanted her to relive that. There had to be another way.

First he had to see her. Her and Nikki…

Both of them would be okay. He had overheard the physician's assistant telling her family that the bullet had just grazed her. None of her brothers had been appeased, though. They'd started walking toward him, stopping only when the doctor came to speak to him.

Now that the MD was gone, they surrounded him

again. When he moved to step forward, Logan shoved him back against the wall.

"Where the hell do you think you're going?"

"Nowhere near Nikki," Parker warned him.

"Back off," Dane said as he shoved between the twins. "His sister is here, too."

Lars stared down the men who all looked eerily similar. Cooper and Nick looked exactly like the twins. "I'm going to see Nikki," he said.

"You're lucky she's alive!" Cooper said. "Or I would forget about all the years we've been friends." His hands tightened into fists. But he held them at his sides.

For the moment.

Lars wouldn't have cared if he'd hit him. "I am lucky she's alive," he wholeheartedly agreed. Because he didn't know what he would do if something had happened to her.

Just considering the loss overwhelmed him. How had she come to mean so much to him so quickly? Because she was Nikki...

She was strong and smart and indomitable.

"You were supposed to wait for us all to get there," Logan said.

"Would you?" Lars asked. "If you thought your sister was about to be killed, would you have stood around waiting for anyone else?"

Logan's cheek twitched above his tightly clenched jaw. "I'm not going to wait for anyone else," he said. "I'm going to stop you before you put Nikki in any more danger."

As he reached for him, Dane stepped between them, trying to protect him. Lars didn't need his protection.

"I have no intention of putting her in danger again," he assured them all.

"He might not," Nikki said as she pushed through the door between the ER and the waiting room. "But I sure as hell do."

Her brothers turned toward her, all uttering some form of protest. Lars knew their words fell on deaf ears. Nikki couldn't hear them. She was too focused. Her gaze cut through the group gathered in the waiting room. She wasn't looking at him. Disappointment flashed through him because of that. He wanted her to look at him the way he looked at her—hungrily. He wanted her, wanted to close his arms around her and never let her go.

Blood had already leaked through the bandage at her temple. A single drop of it had trailed down the side of her face like a crimson tear. But Nikki wasn't a crier. She was too proud for that. Too tough…

"No," he said now, raising his voice above the others. He had her attention now—and her irritation—which hardened her dark eyes and furrowed her brow.

She glared at him.

But he didn't care about her anger. He cared about her life, so he told her, "You are not putting yourself in danger again!"

The glare slipped away, and she smiled at him almost as if she felt sorry for him. "You won't be able to stop me."

Then she gestured at the man she'd been looking at when she'd first walked into the waiting room. And Nick Payne stepped closer.

"Lars Ecklund, you're under arrest," Nick said as he began to read him his rights.

Lars laughed until he felt the cold metal of handcuffs encircle and snap closed around his wrists. He strained against them.

"What the hell!" he protested. "You can't arrest me!"

Chapter 22

"What the hell are you charging me with?" Lars asked Nick as he shoved the larger man ahead of him down the hall toward a holding cell.

He'd passed booking without fingerprinting him or taking his mug shot. And he'd brought him in the back way. As far as most people knew, Lars Ecklund was still a dead man.

Nick couldn't officially arrest him. But he could name some charges that might have stuck. "Manslaughter. Breaking and entering. Obstruction of justice."

"If you were going to charge me with any of those things, you would have to charge Nikki, too," Lars pointed out.

"You want me to?"

"Hell, no." Then Lars paused and glanced back over his shoulder at him. "Actually, it might be a good thing. It would stop her from risking her life again."

"Nothing's going to stop Nikki from doing that," Nick said with resignation. When the call of shots fired at the warehouse had come in, Nick had been blaming himself for giving Lars bad advice. But now he knew even more that his first instinct had been the right one.

His advice had been sound. There was no changing Nikki. And there was no trying to protect her.

"This is what she does," Nick explained to Lars and to himself, "just like you were a soldier and you're now a bodyguard. Nikki's a bodyguard and a damn good one."

She didn't have the gift or curse or whatever Nick and Penny had, but her instincts were infallible. She knew what she was doing. And Nick, more than anyone, never should have doubted her.

That was why he'd agreed to *arrest* Lars at her request. Because he felt guilty...

Lars stared at him as if trying to accept what Nick was telling him. But he struggled with it. "I've never met anyone like her," he said. "My sister is so vulnerable and needs protecting."

"Nikki doesn't need protection," Nick said and ignored the little voice in his head calling him a hypocrite. He tended to forget that himself every once in a while. "She's a Payne—through and through. She's a protector."

"She needs to protect herself," Lars said, and his face paled slightly as if he was reliving her getting shot at.

He probably was.

"She has always protected herself," Nick said. Until now...

Until now she had also protected her heart. She'd worked hard to fall for no one. She'd never even shown

any interest in anyone since she'd found out about her father's betrayal—about *him*.

Until Lars…

She hadn't protected herself from him. It was obvious she cared about him too much.

"And she protected you by having me arrest you," Nick said. "You may not have gotten past Logan and Cooper if I hadn't slapped the cuffs on you. Even Parker was pissed." He chuckled as he remembered how they'd all gathered around Lars in the waiting room, threatening him. He hadn't grown up with his family, so he tended to appreciate them more. He appreciated how they all had each other's backs.

Lars must not have appreciated them, though, because he glared at Nick. "I don't need protection from anyone."

"Liar," Nick said.

Lars tensed so much that Nick was surprised the handcuffs just didn't break and snap off his wrists. But he was glad they held. He really wouldn't want to piss off a man like him, a man this big and muscular.

"You need protection from Nikki," Nick warned him. "She can hurt you more than anyone else can."

Lars didn't argue with him. "She really had you arrest me?"

Nick nodded. "Unfortunately I have a little trouble telling her no." Maybe it was because they hadn't been raised together that he felt that way with her. And because he knew she'd been hurt the worst when she'd learned of her father's betrayal. He felt somehow responsible for her pain and wanted to make it up to her.

"No kidding," Lars remarked. "Talk about abuse of power."

Nick shrugged. "I only have it for a little while longer. Might as well abuse it while I have the chance."

"What?" Lars's brow furrowed with confusion.

Of course he was new to town. He didn't know everything that had happened in River City.

"My old boss is giving up his chief special agent position with the Chicago Bureau and becoming police chief here." Nick smiled at what Woodrow had called his semi-retirement. He would be very busy with the River City PD and with his new bride. "I'll be a fulltime bodyguard soon."

"So arresting me is some kind of last hurrah for you?" Lars asked.

Thinking of all the real criminals he'd taken down over the past several months, Nick chuckled. Viktor Chekov, the notorious crime boss Nick had busted a while ago, would be insulted if Lars Ecklund was Nick's last hurrah.

So he explained, "This is our best chance of getting that baby back for your sister."

Lars stopped struggling against the handcuffs and turned fully around to face him now. "What? How? I'm supposed to be dead."

"Exactly," Nick said. "And dead men can't get in trouble for roughing up another inmate—like one just recently arrested at the scene of a shoot-out in a warehouse."

"The guy who survived?"

Nick nodded. "Just don't kill him, okay? Or I will arrest you for real."

"Is he the one who shot Nikki? I fired at him before he could hit her again, but he ran away. I think he might have been wearing a vest, too."

Thank God Nikki had been wearing one, or she would have been as dead as Nick had feared she was. He'd been an idiot to doubt her, though. Nikki was like a cat, but he suspected she had more than nine lives.

"Is he?" Lars persisted.

Nick refused to tell him that, or he had no doubt Lars would kill the guy. And most people only had one life. "Nikki wants you to get him to make a call to Webber assuring him that the job is done—the girl dead and her body disposed of where she will never be found."

Lars's throat moved as if he was about to choke— probably with emotion at the thought of how close that had come to happening.

"And you're right," Nick said. "Every one of them would have stormed that warehouse, myself included, if we thought our sister was inside and about to be killed."

Lars shook his head. "I still shouldn't have let Nikki go in, too."

Nick snorted. "Like you would have been able to stop her. You would have had to knock her out and tie her up. And her brothers, myself included, would really kill you if you ever laid a hand on her."

"I wouldn't respect you if you didn't," Lars calmly agreed.

And Nick understood why he was Cooper's friend and Nikki's...

Whatever Nikki considered him. He was a good guy. A man of honor and integrity.

"So lock me in that cell and let me get this done," Lars said.

Nick hesitated a moment before undoing the cuffs. He was breaking rules left and right. But with a new baby at home, he understood what Lars's sister must be

going through. He couldn't imagine how crazy he and Annalise would go if someone stole their child. And he knew he would do whatever necessary to bring their baby home.

"Yeah, don't kill him," Nick advised as he finally unlocked the cuffs.

"Dead men can't phone their bosses," Lars reminded him. He was the first man Nick had arrested who seemed eager to get inside a jail cell.

But Nick grabbed his arm, holding him back. "I can't protect you in there," he said.

"I don't need protection."

"Once you go inside you're on your own."

Lars nodded. "I'll be fine."

Nick hoped like hell that was true because he had a feeling Nikki would be devastated if something happened to this man. And because it was her idea, she would never stop blaming herself.

Grasping the steering wheel in stiff hands, Nikki was tense and nervous. She had to force herself not to press too hard on the accelerator. Traffic was heavy downtown. All the cars in front of her car were traveling too slowly, keeping her from the River City Police Department.

Sending Lars to jail had been a horrible idea. Sure, he was big. But there could have been a bigger criminal locked up with him. While he had tried over and over to protect her, Nikki had willfully put him in danger.

Of course he could have refused to go along with her plan. But she doubted that. He would do anything for Emilia—even risk his life.

Or take a life.

If he killed the guard, though, and Webber never got a call, he might try to run—before they had a chance to rescue Blue. Candace would try to stop him, but on the estate, even with Milek and Gage there, they were outnumbered. And now they were tired.

Their shifts had lasted too long. Nikki needed to go to the estate to relieve Candace. She couldn't expect her pregnant friend to risk her life for the little boy who had come to mean so much to Nikki. And Nikki had promised Emilia. She would get to see and hold her son.

She would...

But what about her brother? Would Emilia get to see him again?

"Oh, Lars..." Nikki murmured, her heart beating quickly with fear. What had she done?

The music stopped as a call came in to her Bluetooth. She pressed a button on the steering wheel to accept it.

"Nikki Payne?" a vaguely familiar voice asked.

Then she realized that the caller—who came up on the dash screen as unknown—was Myron Webber. "Yes," she replied. "This is Nikki."

"Ms. Payne—"

"Nikki." She corrected him, forcing a smile into her voice. She wanted him completely unaware that she knew what a bastard he was.

"Nikki," he eagerly repeated her name.

"I was just on my way to the estate," she said.

"Good," he said. "I won't leave until you get here."

"Leave?" Hadn't Lars been able to coerce the man to make the call? Or worse yet, had something happened to him before he had the chance?

"Yes, the adoptive couple would like to take the baby tonight."

"But—but is that legal?" Nikki asked. Like that would matter to a man who had ordered two murders within the past two days.

He chuckled. "As the baby's legal guardian, I can okay their taking him tonight. The official paperwork will take longer to process. But this way they can start bonding with the baby right away."

The baby needed to bond with his mother. Maybe, through her breast milk, he had been able to do that. Maybe he would recognize her if he ever got the chance to be in her arms.

"Of course it all has to be official," Nikki said. She hoped like hell it wasn't that cold couple who wouldn't even hold the baby. But it didn't matter...

It wasn't as if the adoption was actually going to go through. They would never get Blue. She would make sure of that—no matter what she had to do.

"There's plenty of time for the adoption process to go through," Webber said as if he didn't have a care in the world.

And she knew that the call had been made. Webber thought there was no way he could be caught—that both Emilia and Lars were dead.

She couldn't wait to see his face when he learned the truth. Maybe she should have gone into law enforcement instead of protection—because she would have loved to slap the cuffs on him herself.

"I need to stop by the office," Nikki said, "to get an SUV to use as the transport vehicle."

"We will be using my car and driver, of course," the lawyer insisted.

"Our company SUV has bulletproof glass," she said.

"I hardly think that will be necessary now." Now that he thought Lars was dead.

"It's company protocol," she fibbed. Fortunately she had been so close to Cooper's office that she pulled into the parking lot as they spoke.

Webber had one more request for her. "Wear something dressy, and I'll take you out to celebrate after we drop off the baby."

She shivered at the thought of going out with him. "Celebrate?"

"Yes, we can celebrate the little guy getting a new family." He was probably going to celebrate the murders of Blue's real family, though.

Nikki couldn't wait to see his face when he realized how they had tricked him.

"Sounds great," she said as she imagined her celebration. "I will be there soon."

And hopefully soon she would be able to put Blue in his mother's arms and the lawyer behind bars instead of Lars. For Webber's sake, she hoped Lars had not been released because she was sure the Marine would rip the lawyer apart for the pain and misery he'd put his sister through.

Lars might have been safer in jail than he was stepping into the Payne Protection Agency. Not only did Nikki's brothers want to kill him but now it sounded as if they all wanted to kill each other, too. The minute he pushed open the door he heard voices raised in anger. He couldn't tell who was whom; just as they all looked alike, they all sounded alike, as well.

"That's crazy!"

"It's not going to happen!"

"It's out of the question!"

Maybe they were discussing his murder and how to dispose of his body. After the way they had acted in the hospital, he wouldn't have put it past them.

Then he heard a female voice rise sharply above the others. "Stop being idiots!"

That was *his* Nikki. His heart stopped beating for just a moment as he considered what he'd thought—what he felt. He had never been possessive of anyone before—had never thought he would want to be. But Nikki...

She was so tough—so independent. She would never want to be anyone's—let alone his.

"I know what I'm doing," she continued. "Haven't I proved that to you all over and over again the past couple of years?"

"But Nikki, this is too dangerous. You can't be alone with Webber."

"I won't be alone," she said. "You'll all be there in case I need backup." Her voice rose again but with a singsong note to it as she goaded, "But I won't..."

"You won't because you're not going." That was Cooper. Even if Lars hadn't pushed open the conference room door, he would have recognized that tone of his friend's—the no-argument tone.

Obviously Nikki hadn't heard it before because she just laughed at him. "Of course I'm going."

They had formed a protective circle around her, but she pushed through them and headed toward the door—toward Lars. When she noticed him, she stopped. And he stopped breathing for a moment.

She wore a black dress and high heels. While she was beautiful in jeans and a sweater, she was stunning in that dress.

And he was stunned into silence.

"You got out of jail!" she exclaimed as she wound her arms around his neck for a quick hug.

He lifted his arms to hold on to her, but she quickly stepped back.

"Oh, no!" she exclaimed. "You're here to try to stop me, too."

He would have had he not been locked up long enough to think about everything Nick had told him about her. She was a bodyguard; it was as much who she was as what she did. And because he loved her, he needed to accept and respect that.

"Of course he doesn't want to stop you," Logan said. "You're risking your life for him."

"For my nephew," Lars corrected him. "And she would do the same for any other client—if you dumbasses would let her do her job."

"Who the hell do you think you are?" Logan said. As he started forward with hands fisted, Cooper pulled him back.

Lars was the man who was in love with her. But he couldn't say that in front of her brothers until he'd told her privately—because he was pretty sure she wouldn't want his love. She'd made it clear that she never intended to fall in love herself. She didn't want romance and marriage. She just wanted to do her job.

So all Lars could say was, "I'm the man whose life she has saved. I'm the man whose sister's life she saved. I respect that she can take care of herself and others."

She stepped closer again, wound her arms around his neck and pulled his head down for her kiss. Her lips skimmed across his.

Heat flashed through his body. Maybe that was just

because the temperature was rising in the room as her brothers' blood boiled with anger. Was that why she was suddenly being so demonstrative? Just to make them crazy? He didn't care what they thought, though. He only cared what he felt—for her. He wanted to wind his arms around her and hold her close. But she was already pulling away from him. Maybe it had just been for her brothers' benefits.

Of course she'd kissed him and more when it had been just the two of them. He wanted that chance again—to be just the two of them. To be that close to her, to be part of her.

"I have to leave now," she said almost regretfully. "He's waiting for me."

"Blue?"

"Webber," Cooper answered for her.

And knots of fear formed in Lars's stomach. But he had trust that she could and would take care of herself. Yet he found himself saying, "I'll go as backup."

"Absolutely not," Logan said.

"If he sees you, it would blow the entire operation," Cooper said, and his voice had softened with understanding. Had he realized how much Lars cared about her? "Your presence would put her in the most danger."

A feeling of helplessness paralyzed Lars. He felt like he had when he couldn't find Emilia. He hated this feeling, hated not being able to help the woman he loved. If he tried to protect Nikki, he would wind up getting her killed.

So he had to step back and let her leave. And with all her brothers watching, he couldn't even tell her how he felt, that he had fallen for her—harder than when she'd dropped him on that nursery floor a couple nights ago.

Maybe that was when he'd fallen for her. Or hell, maybe it was the first time he'd seen her. She was so damn beautiful. She had to make it back to him…

She had to—so he could tell her he loved her.

Chapter 23

The crying was so soft at first that she had to strain her ears to hear it. What was it? An animal?

Then the crying grew louder, filled with pain and fear. It tore at Emilia's heart and her womb. And she jerked awake with a cry of her own and tears streaming down her face.

"Shh… You're okay. You're safe." And big arms wrapped around her, holding her closely.

She rested her cheek against the man's strong shoulder, but as she did, she realized this wasn't her brother holding her. Lars was bigger than this man, if only slightly. And he didn't make her feel like this.

Her pulse quickened—just with fear—and she jerked away from him.

"Who—who are you?" Emilia asked, her voice quavering. Had one of Webber's hired gunmen found her at that hospital? Lars had promised she would be safe;

he'd said he would have someone guarding her room. "What do you want?"

Had he come to kill her? But he'd been holding her as if he was comforting her. But it wasn't comfort she'd felt. It had almost felt like excitement. The man eased off the edge of her bed and stood up. His dark eyes intense, he looked as unsettled as she was.

"This is Dane," Lars answered for his friend as he walked into the room. "Since we got back, he's been helping me look for you."

"Thank you," Emilia said. But it wasn't enough to express the gratitude she felt. Or the regret and embarrassment. "I'm sorry." Tears stung her eyes and she squeezed them shut.

But this time when strong arms closed around her, she knew it was Lars holding her. She settled her head onto his shoulder as she had so many times before. He had always been her comforter, her protector.

There was a tension in his body that suggested he might need some solace, too.

"Nikki is working on getting Blue back," Lars said, his voice gruff with emotion.

She opened her eyes and glanced over his shoulder. But Dane was gone. Only she and her brother were in the hospital room now. She felt a twinge of something that she refused to acknowledge as disappointment. It was probably relief. The man had to think she was a hot mess. Not that she cared what he thought. All her concern was for her brother.

She stared up into Lars's face. His jaw was rigid, his brow furrowed. He was worried.

"You don't think she'll be able to?"

His breath shuddered out. "No, I don't think there's

anything Nikki Payne can't do," he said. "I won't make the mistake of underestimating her again."

He sounded awed. And from what little Emilia knew of the young female bodyguard, she was awed, too. If only she had been as smart and strong as Nikki.

"I'm sorry," she said again. But she knew it wasn't enough. "I should have done what you told me to do if I ever got in trouble. I should have gone to Cooper."

"You were scared," he said.

She'd had no idea what fear was until she'd woken up all alone in that cold, dark room—her womb empty and no memory of how that had happened.

"I was stupid," she said. "All of this is my fault."

He shook his head. "No, it's Myron Webber's fault. He's a baby thief and a killer. You had no way of knowing how treacherous he is." His breath shuddered out in a ragged sigh. "And that's my fault. I always tried to shield you from the real world—from danger."

Emilia tightened her arms around him. "And you did a great job."

"Too good," he said. "Maybe if you'd known the dangers out there…"

"I would have been smart enough to avoid them." But Blue's father hadn't seemed like a danger. He'd been a sweet-talker, a charmer. But he'd only wanted one thing. And she'd been stupid enough to give it to him.

Now Webber, she'd realized right away that something wasn't right about him. He'd been too determined to talk her into giving up her baby, even after she'd told him she'd changed her mind. That she never should have wasted his time.

"Nikki knows about all the dangers," he said, "but instead of avoiding them, she runs right toward them."

"She's doing that to get Blue back." It was clear to her, though, that Lars wasn't worried about his nephew. He was worried about the woman trying to rescue him.

Lars sighed again. "I know. But…"

"You love her."

He nodded. "I hope I get the chance to tell her that."

"What are you doing here?" Emilia asked. "Why aren't you—wherever Nikki is?"

"If Webber sees me, he'll realize that I'm not dead and that probably neither are you."

And that would put Nikki's life in even more danger. That was a risk Lars obviously wasn't willing to take.

"So make sure he doesn't see you," she said. She understood that Lars needed to be close to Nikki, needed to be there if something happened.

She hoped nothing did; she hoped that Nikki made it safely back with Blue. But she—better than anyone else—knew how dangerous Myron Webber was. If he knew what Nikki was up to, he wouldn't hesitate to kill her.

"I'm sorry I have to do this," Myron Webber said. "But with everything that has happened lately, I've learned to take no chances anymore." He reached out toward her.

And Nikki tried not to flinch as his hands ran down her sides then around her back. He was checking her for a wire. She held her breath as his fingers moved along the bottom of her bra beneath the thin material of her dress. Her lungs ached with the breath she held, hurting her already injured ribs. Maybe she should have let them X-ray her back at the hospital. She probably had some broken bones. There wasn't much they could do

to treat broken ribs except wrap them. And then Myron would have thought for certain that she was wired.

With her wearing heels, she could see directly into his eyes, which darkened with desire as he touched her. She struggled to hang on to her breath until his fingers moved away. Then she let out a shaky sigh, which stirred the hair she'd curled over her forehead and temple to hide the stitches from the bullet that had grazed her. She'd already ripped off the bandage, like she'd ripped the one off her shoulder, too. She'd suspected Myron might search her.

"Sorry," he said as he stepped back slightly. "But I had to be certain." They stood on the driveway just inside the gates of his estate.

She shrugged. "I understand."

"I need to keep this, too," he said as he held on to the holster with her gun.

She shook her head. "I need that to protect Blue."

"I am having some problems with trust right now," he said.

"Why?" Hadn't he believed the guard who'd called him from jail? Had the guy snuck in some secret message for him?

"Your brother was friends with that Ecklund character," Webber said.

"He knew him," Nikki said. "They weren't friends." They were even closer than that after what they'd been through—boot camp and war.

"I'm not sure I should have trusted him," Webber continued as if she hadn't spoken.

"Cooper?" She tensed. "He's the most honorable man I know." But as she said it, an image of Lars popped into her head. He was honorable, too.

Sure, he had lied to her but his reasons had been altru-

istic. Just like hers for lying now. She was wired with a transmitter far too small for even someone tech savvy to find. Webber hadn't had a chance. She couldn't even feel it; it was sewn into the cup of her bra like an underwire.

Just so he wouldn't touch her again, Nikki reached for the baby, whom she'd had to put down for Myron's search. But Candace had already strapped him into the car seat before she'd left with Milek and Gage. They'd all acted very casual, as if nothing unusual was going on. But Candace had squeezed Nikki's hand before passing her the baby carrier.

All Nikki needed to do was fasten Blue's seat into the back of the SUV. As she leaned over to do that, she felt Webber watching her. And a chill of revulsion chased down her spine.

One of his guards patted down the driver of the Payne Protection SUV. "If this is for my benefit, move your hand a little higher and to the left," Garek Kozminski quipped.

The guard was not amused. He moved his hand, and Garek flinched in pain.

"He's clean," the guard told Webber. "No wire." And no gun. He'd taken Garek's weapon, too.

Garek shuddered at the thought. "You don't have to worry about a wire with me."

"Kozminski, right?" Webber said.

"Yes, sir," Garek said.

"You're a bodyguard now?" the lawyer asked as if doubting him. He was aware of the ex-con's reputation; everyone knew of the Kozminskis.

But they were reformed—after a fashion. If they broke or bent a law, it was for a damn good reason. Garek nodded. "Sure am. Are we ready to leave now?"

Webber looked at him and then at Nikki. "I thought it would just be you," he said.

Garek chuckled. "She's a good driver, sir. But she's not me."

Nobody at Payne Protection could drive like Garek. Only his brother Milek came close because he'd been studying under him the longest. Garek had only started training Nikki a few months ago.

"I need to ride in the back with the baby," Nikki said. "To keep him safe—though that's going to be a little harder to do without a gun."

Webber hesitated for a long moment before nodding. Nikki quickly slid into the backseat between the door and the baby carrier. So Webber had to take the seat on the other side while his guard climbed into the front passenger seat.

"Where to?" Garek asked as he slid behind the steering wheel. The gates opened as if Webber had pressed a button inside the vehicle. Garek drove through them and paused at the end of the driveway.

Nikki glanced around the street, but she could see none of the Payne Protection Agency SUVs. She knew they were nearby, though. But they were so good that they were invisible.

"Where to?" Garek asked again.

Webber named the most expensive hotel in the city. Only the very rich stayed there and most of those were international visitors.

"It's not a local family?" Nikki asked.

Webber glanced down at the sleeping baby and smirked. "Local families couldn't afford this little guy. He's the perfect specimen."

"So this couple is going to stay here until the official paperwork processes?" Nikki asked.

He smirked again. "Official paperwork can be bought."

"They bought the baby?" she asked, and her stomach lurched.

His smirk widened.

With a sick realization, she asked, "You took money from all of them, didn't you?"

"I had to," he said with a suddenly heavy-sounding sigh. "I think my time in River City has run out."

Nikki gasped.

He knew they were onto him. The fake police report, the call from jail—none of it had fooled him. But if he'd had a coroner on his payroll, he could have someone else, someone in the police department.

"And if *you're* up to anything," he warned her, "your time will have run out, too."

He pointed the barrel of a gun—her Glock—across the baby carrier at her. She met Garek's gaze in the rearview mirror. He widened his eyes, indicating she should give the signal for their backup to rush in. But she was too aware of that gun barrel being held right over the sleeping baby.

If the gun went off, the noise would be too close to the infant, close enough to blow his eardrums. And if the vehicle moved at all and jarred the barrel, a bullet could hit the baby. She couldn't risk it. She had to find another way to get Webber to put down the gun.

But she was quickly running out of options.

Lars was too late. He knew it when he saw the faces of the Payne brothers. They had gone pale with fear, their blue eyes wide.

"He's onto them," Cooper said as Lars hurried up to where they were climbing into SUVs on the street outside the gates of Myron Webber's estate. He didn't protest Lars jumping into the vehicle with him.

"Where are they?" Lars asked. He assumed they weren't on the estate or the Paynes would have crashed through the gates already. "Are we close enough to get to them?"

"We're not far behind them," Cooper said as he pulled the vehicle onto the street and accelerated. "We'll get there in time. Nikki hasn't even given the signal yet."

"What's the signal?" Lars asked.

"Blue," Cooper replied.

If she said the baby's name, she needed help. Of course she would have been more concerned about the infant than her own safety.

The speaker in the SUV crackled. "We're being followed," a deep voice murmured.

Lars recognized the voice from the meeting in the conference room what seemed like a lifetime ago. "What the hell is Kozminski doing?" Why would he let Webber know they were behind them?

Webber's chuckle radiated from the speaker. "I know. Let's say I've lost my trust in Payne Protection. Those are my men. I had to hire some more of them, though. I seem to have lost quite a few lately."

Thanks to him and Nikki. Lars cursed. "They're surrounded."

"Garek can lose them," Cooper said.

Nikki's voice rang out, the clearest of all of them. "You can't trust hired hitmen. Their only allegiance is to money."

"Nothing wrong with money," Garek remarked. "Now that gun in my side...there's something wrong with that."

"Myron, why are you doing this?" Nikki asked, her voice coming steadily and clearly through the speaker. She knew no fear. Then her voice changed, became almost flirty as she continued, "There is no reason for these guns. We're going to bring the baby to the hotel with you. And then I thought we were going out to celebrate."

Webber chuckled. "You're good. Even now I have no idea what to believe..."

"Believe me," she urged him.

But then the lawyer cursed and yelled, "We're being followed!"

"Yeah, your guys are following us," Garek replied resentfully.

"No!"

And then Lars heard it—a shot ringing out. It didn't come through the speaker. It came from beside them. He turned just in time to see the gun pointing out of the driver's window of the vehicle next to them.

"Duck!" he yelled at Cooper as the glass shattered.

Bullets pinged off the metal.

"We need to take them now!" The order came through the speaker.

It was Logan giving the order. "We're going in..."

They were already in. Lars drew his gun and returned fire. "We need to catch up to Nikki."

First they had to pass the truck trying to take them out, though. Lars fired again and again until the driver slumped over the steering wheel and the truck swerved off the road.

"Faster," he urged Cooper. "Try to catch them."

But they were too late. He heard the noises crackling through the speaker before the vehicle even came into view. He heard the squeal of tires. The screams.

Nikki's.

The lawyer's.

Cooper pressed harder on the accelerator, pushing his vehicle forward. They rounded a corner.

And then Lars saw it—the Payne Protection black SUV with Nikki and his nephew inside. Like the truck, the vehicle swerved back and forth across the road. While the tires squealed, the brakes made no noise, left no black marks on the pavement. Instead of slowing, it sped up, as it continued its manic back and forth.

Then the tires dropped off the shoulder of the road, and the SUV tipped onto its side. But it didn't stop there. The high rate of speed at which it had been traveling gave it momentum, and it kept rolling—over and over—with Nikki and his nephew inside.

Had he just lost them both?

Chapter 24

Anger coursed through Nikki, numbing her pain. Why the hell hadn't her brothers stayed back? Why hadn't they waited for her signal? If they had, they might not have forced hers and Garek's hands. He'd purposely rolled the SUV, knocking the gun from the hand of his now unconscious passenger.

Unfortunately Garek was unconscious, too, his blond head in the airbag that had sprung from the steering wheel he was pinned beneath. He didn't move.

But he had to be okay. He and Candace had a baby on the way. She refused to believe that he was hurt. He was too good a driver. He'd purposely orchestrated the crash, so he would know how to survive it. He'd meant to take out the passenger's side of the vehicle. It was a maneuver he'd taught her.

Nikki turned toward the crying baby. The crash had

startled Blue awake. He screamed, but his little voice was loud and strong. His carrier had protected him from injury.

Nikki wasn't so sure about herself. She'd struck the back of her head and her arm against the door. She reached out for the carrier to release Blue. But before she could find the clasp, the door creaked open behind her.

Maybe it was one of her brothers. But none of them would have shoved the gun into her side. She glanced around the interior. Webber had already scrambled out on his side. And now he dragged her from the back with his hand in her hair while the other held her gun on her.

He wasn't that big. But he was strong with the kind of strength born of desperation. He knew it was all over now. Gunfire rang out from the street above where Garek had rolled the SUV.

She hadn't been a soldier like Cooper or Lars. But she imagined war would have been a little like what she was experiencing now. She couldn't pull her gun; he'd taken that when he'd searched her.

She had no way to protect herself. If she tried to struggle or fight with Myron, he might just pull the trigger. So she moved with him as he pulled her toward the cover of the woods on the other side of the battered SUV. Her heels sank into the soft ground, though, and she nearly stumbled.

Tears sprang to her eyes as he tugged harder on her hair. "You said I could trust you," he said. "You said you were honorable."

"I am," she said. "The honorable thing is to bring that baby back to his real mother."

He laughed. "She's dead."

Nikki had wanted this—so badly—to see his face when he learned the truth. If it was the last thing she saw, it might be worth it. Despite his hand in her hair, she twisted around so she could see his face as she told him.

"Emilia is alive," she said. "We found her in the warehouse."

His small eyes widened now, going wild with that desperation as his fleshy face paled. "No..."

"She's already given her statement to the authorities." And now sirens cut through the gunfire. Maybe they were only responding because someone had reported the crash and the shooting. Or maybe Emilia had given the prosecutor enough evidence for Amber Talsma-Kozminski to issue the warrant for Webber's arrest.

Myron shook his head, and now his perfectly coifed hair moved, sliding slightly off his head. "No, no, that's not possible. She's dead, just like her brother."

A man scrambled down the bank from the street. He wasn't an officer; the police wouldn't have arrived already. And it wasn't one of her brothers. This man limped slightly from the bullet that had grazed his thigh the other night. The setting sun glinted off his pale blond hair.

He looked like an avenging angel. And he had every reason to want vengeance against the man who'd tried to kill his sister—after treating her so inhumanely for weeks.

"He's not dead, either," Nikki said as she gestured at Lars. He looked so damn handsome and strong.

His eyes—those beautiful pale eyes—met hers briefly before he focused on the lawyer. He held a gun,

the barrel directed at Webber. Through gritted teeth, he advised the lawyer to, "Let her go."

"No, no, it's not over," Webber said. But there was finality in his voice. He knew it was over. And he moved the gun barrel to Nikki's head.

If he fired, this bullet wouldn't just graze her temple like the one in the warehouse. It would go right through her skull.

She stared at Lars, hoping to catch his attention again—hoping to let him know...

What? That she loved him? She was more afraid to admit that than she was of the bullet going through her brain. The bullet might hurt less.

"It's not over!" Webber shouted as he cocked the trigger.

Nikki squeezed her eyes shut just as the gun fired.

Lars couldn't quite steady his hands, not yet. He couldn't believe what he had done. The risk he'd taken...

Emilia held out her arms for the baby he passed to her. Her pale blue eyes filled with tears as she stared down at her son. "He's so beautiful," she murmured. "So beautiful..."

Just like she was. She had never looked as lovely as she did smiling down at her son.

"Do you think he knows me?" she asked hopefully.

"He finally stopped crying," he said. Ever since the crash, he'd been crying nonstop. The doctor had assured them that there was nothing wrong with him, though. The carrier had protected him.

If only Nikki had been strapped into one, as well.

Lars had thought he'd fired too late. That Webber had gotten off a shot because the minute he'd pulled his

trigger, Nikki had dropped. She'd insisted that she'd meant to so that Webber wouldn't hit her.

But then she hadn't been able to stand up again. She was hurt. And he had no idea how badly yet.

She was still with the doctor, but she'd insisted that he waste no time in reuniting mother and son. She should have been the one to do the honors, though.

She was the one who'd taken all the risks to rescue the baby. If Webber had pulled that trigger any faster...

She would have died. He shuddered as he considered the horror of that—of a world without Nikki Payne in it.

"Lars?" Emilia called to him.

"Nikki said he would know you," Lars said, "because of the breast milk." She'd told him that before the ambulance had taken her away. She'd made him promise to remind Emilia of that—that she already shared a bond with the infant.

The baby snuggled against his mother; he did know her.

The tears spilled over Emilia's eyes, running down her beautiful face. "Oh, Blue, my baby Blue..." She tensed and glanced up at Lars. "Where is Nikki?"

Lars couldn't speak for a moment as emotion overwhelmed him.

She gasped. "Oh, no—she's not—she's okay, isn't she? She has to be okay."

He shook his head. "I don't know..."

She must have hit her head during the crash like Garek had. He'd regained consciousness, though, and had walked himself to the ambulance.

Lars had had to carry Nikki. He hadn't wanted to let her go. Even now his arms ached to hold her...

But she needed an MRI. Something was wrong with

her—something that had weakened his usually indomitable Nikki Payne. It had to be something serious.

"Go to her," Emilia urged him. "Make sure she's okay."

But Lars was too late. By the time he got back to the ER, Nikki was gone.

Penny's heart ached with the loss of her daughter, of the fearless tomboy she had known.

"Who are you?" she asked the woman who sat in the passenger seat, her bare shoulders slumped. She wore a cocktail dress and heels. "And what have you done with my Nikki?"

"Funny," Nikki muttered. And her voice sounded funny, almost as if she was on the verge of tears.

Nikki never cried. No matter how badly she got hurt. She had always fought tears—every bit as fiercely as she'd fought her brothers.

She was tough.

"Why did you want *me* to bring you home?" Penny asked.

"Because I'm fine."

That wasn't what she'd been asking, though. Why her mother? Why not Lars Ecklund? Or Nick?

Nikki usually never called her. She hated it when Penny mothered her. Yet she'd sought her out—twice now having her mother drive her home from the hospital.

"You have two broken ribs and a concussion," Penny reminded her. But she knew the physical pain wasn't bothering Nikki at all.

Nikki shrugged. "The doctor released me."

Because Nikki had given him no choice. She'd been

going to leave no matter what. She'd been in a hell of a hurry to get out of the hospital.

"Why did you want to leave so quickly?" Penny asked.

"You know I hate being fussed over."

A chuckle slipped through her lips. She knew that too well. "If that were true, why did you want *me* to bring you home?" she asked again.

Nikki's breath escaped in a shaky sigh. "Because I needed my mother."

And Penny's heart contracted with love. "Oh, sweetheart... What's the matter?"

"I'm scared."

That was the first time Nikki Payne had ever uttered those words.

"You've been in too many gun fights for me to count," Penny said. "And you're afraid now?"

Nikki could only nod.

"Of what?"

Nikki said nothing.

But when Penny turned to her, she knew. She had recently been that afraid herself, when she'd nearly lost the man she hadn't even realized yet that she'd fallen for. "You're afraid of love."

"No, no," Nikki murmured, but it was a weak protest. "That's not it at all. I just didn't want to intrude."

"Intrude on what?" Penny asked.

"Lars with his sister," she said. "And the baby. They're a family. They should all be together."

"I doubt they would have thought you were intruding," Penny said. "Especially since they're all together again because of you."

Pride welled in her heart. She had spent so much time

worrying about her daughter that she had never realized just how amazing she was. She reached across the console and squeezed her hand. "I am so proud of you."

Nikki glanced across at her, and tears glistened in her eyes. She blinked hard, though, fighting them as she always did. "Why?"

"You are so strong and, except for this moment, always so fearless," Penny said.

Nikki's lips curved into a slight smile. "I thought that's what you didn't like about me."

Penny squeezed Nikki's fingers a little too tightly and admitted, "Sometimes...but now I miss that courage."

Nikki's shoulders straightened and she lifted her chin. "What do you mean?"

"You're being a chicken."

"How?"

"You're afraid of Lars."

She snorted. "I can take him."

"Then do it," Penny challenged. "Take him, Nikki. Take what you want."

"I want to be a bodyguard," she said. "I want my brothers to take me seriously. I don't want *anything* else."

Penny sighed.

"I'm not you, Mom," Nikki said. "I don't need the fairy tale. I don't need the happily-ever-after."

Penny had never thought she would have one of her own. That was why she'd spent the past several years focusing on giving that fairy tale to other brides. But ever since Nikki had been born, Penny had been anticipating the day that her daughter would find her true love.

"I know," Penny said. "You don't need a man. You

don't need love. You're strong and self-sufficient. But you've found it now."

"I don't know what it is," Nikki said. "And I don't believe anything is ever happily-ever-after."

"You don't think your brothers have found love?" Penny asked. "You don't think I have?"

Nikki's face flushed. "No, I know you have. Woodrow is amazing. And all my sisters-in-law are, too."

"So you're not as smart as your brothers are?" Penny asked. "You think you haven't chosen as wisely as they have?"

"I haven't *chosen* at all," Nikki said. "Because I didn't want to fall for anyone—ever—but most especially not some macho, overprotective type like my brothers."

Oh, her poor baby...

She had it bad.

"I don't want this," Nikki persisted. "I don't want to *feel* this way."

"Why not?" Penny asked.

"Because I'm more like you than I thought I was," Nikki said. "And maybe Lars is like my dad. Maybe he'll break my heart like Dad broke yours."

Penny couldn't argue with her. She could only shrug. "And what if he does?"

Nikki gasped with shock.

Maybe Penny had sounded callous. That wasn't what she'd intended. "I survived getting my heart broken," she said. "You would, too."

Nikki shook her head. "I'm not as convinced of that as you are. And maybe I'm not as brave as you are. Instead of surviving, I would just rather not risk the pain at all."

Penny knew very well how stubborn her daughter could be. No matter what she said, she knew she wouldn't be able to change her mind.

Just like she and the boys hadn't convinced Nikki to not want to be a bodyguard. Penny knew she wouldn't be able to convince Nikki to risk her heart on love.

But Penny also knew how precious true love was and how difficult to find. If Nikki didn't take the chance now, she might never find it again.

Chapter 25

Pain pounding inside her head, Nikki closed her eyes and tried to will it away. It wasn't the concussion. The effects of that had worn off a week ago just shortly after she had rushed out of the hospital that night. Her head pounded now because of the nonstop ringing of the phones.

Payne Protection had made national media again for taking down the adoption lawyer who'd stolen babies from scared single mothers. But instead of Logan's face being plastered all over the news, it was Cooper's. He hated it. He'd tried to pass off the interviews to her but Nikki had refused. Cooper was the boss.

It was enough that he had let her do her job. She didn't need the recognition. A knock at her office door drew a weary sigh from her. Cooper had finally hired a receptionist, but the young guy kept asking Nikki where

everything was and how to run the computer program. It probably would have been less work had she been doing the job herself.

But keeping busy wasn't a bad thing. It kept her mind off the fact that work was all she had. Of course it was all she'd ever wanted, though.

So she should have been happy. Her brothers finally respected her now and appreciated that she had more abilities than computer hacking.

But something was missing…

Lars had been off the past week. He'd been helping take care of Blue while Emilia had been in the hospital, recovering from her infection and blood loss.

She couldn't be missing him. He hadn't been around long enough for her to miss. She missed Blue, though— she missed him so much that she almost thought she heard his cry.

It was probably just the phones. Or maybe the receptionist…

The guy was some big bodybuilder type that Cooper had hired to keep out unwanted guests—like Webber showing up in his office that day. But he was afraid to answer the phone let alone deal with visitors.

"Come in," she called out, wondering what question he would have for her now.

But the person who'd knocked wasn't the dark-haired male receptionist. Her visitor was a female with pale blond hair who swung a baby carrier at her side that looked nearly as heavy as her slight build.

"Emilia…" She rushed around her desk to reach for the baby—not just to help the young mother but because she had missed Blue so much. She put the carrier on her desk, so she could gaze down into his amazing

eyes. But when she found him sleeping, disappointment flashed through her.

"I hope I'm not bothering you," Emilia said. "I tried to call ahead, but I only got voice mail. And when I walked in, the receptionist just waved me back. If you're busy, I can come back another time."

"No," Nikki said. She didn't want them to leave. But she found herself peering around them to the open door. "I'm glad you came by. I would have gone to the hospital to see you."

"But you didn't want to run into my brother?" Emilia asked.

Heat rushed to Nikki's face, but she shook her head. "No, not at all..."

"So you haven't been avoiding me?" Lars asked.

She jumped and turned back to the open door. He hadn't been there a second ago. So she hadn't expected him to show up. And she hadn't expected her reaction to seeing him again. Her heart stopped beating for a moment before resuming at a frantic pace. She pressed a hand to her chest as if that might slow the rhythm.

"Of course not," she said. "I've been working."

"And he's been taking care of Blue for me," Emilia said with an adoring smile at her brother. "I'm sorry I've caused so much trouble."

Nikki reached out and squeezed her hand. "It wasn't you at all," she told her. "It was the lawyer."

Emilia shuddered. "I never thought I'd be happy someone was dead." She reached out and ran a fingertip over the sleeping baby's dimpled chin. "But now he can't hurt us anymore."

"Nobody will," Lars assured her. "I won't let anything happen to the two of you."

Nikki's heart ached for the guilt she heard yet in his voice. But before she could say anything, Emilia punched his arm.

"It's not your responsibility to take care of us," she said. "It's mine." She lifted her chin, and pride burned in her pale eyes. "I'm going to take care of my son and myself."

She turned to Nikki now. "Will you help me?" she asked.

A smile tugged at Nikki's lips. So much for self-sufficiency. "I'd love to help you—with Blue—with whatever you need."

"Teach me how to be like you," Emilia implored her.

"Like me?"

"You're tough and independent," Emilia said. "You don't need anyone."

That was what Nikki had thought. It was what she'd believed—until now. She looked at Lars, and she couldn't look away. It was more than how damn handsome he was; it was who he was. Honorable. Responsible. Loyal. Loving.

"That's not true," Nikki said. "If it wasn't for your brother, I would be dead." And instead of thanking him, she had run away from him. No wonder her mom had been so disgusted with her that she had teased about not even recognizing her. "He saved my life."

He closed his eyes and flinched as if reliving that moment.

Nikki had thought the gun that had gone off was the one pressed to her head. She'd thought she was going to die.

Lars shuddered. "That was too close," he said. "But you were already dropping like dead weight away from

the barrel of his gun—away from him. Even if I hadn't shown up, you would have survived."

Nikki had claimed she'd purposely intended to fall, but she figured it might have had more to do with the concussion she'd sustained in the crash. And with the sick realization that she might have been about to die.

"Will you teach me?" Emilia asked her. "Will you teach me how to be a survivor?"

"You already are," Nikki assured her. "I don't think too many people could have survived what you have. You're amazing."

Tears glistened in Emilia's eyes. Then she turned toward Lars and said, "I see why you fell for her."

Her heart skipped a beat again. Did he really care about her? Did she want him to? She wanted him—even more now than she had before.

It had been a long week without seeing him. And she knew now it was him that she had been missing. She did need Lars. But with his sister and Blue present, she could say nothing. It wasn't until after they'd left that she realized it might have been her only chance to tell him how she felt.

For the receptionist asked her, "The guy that just left, he must be the one quitting, right?"

"Someone's quitting?" Nikki asked.

The young man nodded. "Yeah, I'm pretty sure he's the one I overheard telling Cooper that he had to go, that he doesn't want anything to do with family and falling in love."

So maybe Lars had fallen for her, just as she had fallen for him. But like her, he didn't want anything to do with those feelings. Or her.

To the point that he was leaving...

* * *

Lars opened his door to a petite, curly-haired woman and for a moment, his breath caught in his lungs. But desire didn't overwhelm him as it had earlier when he'd joined Emilia in Nikki's office. No, this woman—while eerily similar to Nikki in appearance—was older but no less beautiful.

Or bold. She looked him up and down and then nodded. "Of course…"

"Excuse me? Have we met?"

"I'm Penny Payne—soon to be Lynch." She introduced herself.

"You're Nikki's mother." The one who just knew things. Did she know how he felt about her daughter? After Emilia's slip earlier, Nikki knew. But she hadn't reacted at all. She hadn't cared.

Penny stretched up on tiptoe, reached out and patted his cheek. "I see it."

He gasped. Was she a mind reader, too? "What?"

"I'm here for your sister and the baby," she said.

And still dumbfounded, he idiotically repeated, "What?"

"I thought I heard the car," Emilia said as she pushed past Lars in the doorway. The baby carrier struck the back of his knee, nearly making it buckle from where Nikki had kicked him the night she'd saved his life from the gunmen who'd stormed this house. "Thank you for coming to get me, Penny."

The two women embraced as if they were old friends. And without another word to him, they headed off to the SUV Penny had parked at his curb. The older woman cooed over the baby as she helped Emilia secure his carrier into the backseat.

"What the hell…?" he murmured. He stared after them for a few moments before he stepped back into the house and closed the door.

"What the hell?" A female voice repeated his words, but there was anger in her tone rather than confusion. "You're quitting? I guess I shouldn't be surprised. You were ready to quit on Emilia."

Had he entered some kind of weird female twilight zone? First Penny Payne showed up and whisked Emilia away as if the strangers were the best of friends. And now Nikki Payne appeared out of nowhere like an apparition in his living room.

"I thought Emilia was dead." But still he shouldn't have given up on her.

"What about me?"

His heart hurt. "For a moment—back when I shot Webber—I thought you were dead, too."

"Is that why you're quitting?"

"Quitting what?" he asked, still totally confused. "Do you think I'm giving up on you?"

"Aren't you?"

He closed the distance between them in two long strides. But before he could reach for her, she stepped back. He moved forward again—as if they were dancing. And maybe they had been since they'd met—circling each other, stepping forward and back.

But Lars had never been much of a dancer. He was too big and uncoordinated to handle intricate footwork. He was best at simply hanging on and swaying to the music, so he took her in his arms and pulled her against him.

Her curves soft against him, she was so petite and delicate and female. But she held herself stiffly in his

arms. She was mad at him. And he was used to that but this time he didn't understand why.

"Why would you care if I quit?" he asked.

She wouldn't look up at him. So he reached down and with a finger under her chin, lifted it. But she still wouldn't meet his gaze; she stared at his shoulder instead of his face.

"You've made it clear that you have no interest in a relationship," he reminded her. "That you don't need anyone."

Finally she met his gaze, her dark eyes bright with unshed tears. She blinked, fighting against them, fighting against what she was feeling for him. Her breath shuddered out in a ragged sigh, and sounding miserable about it, she admitted, "I need you."

Even while his heart swelled with hope, he felt a twinge of regret. "I hate that it makes you unhappy."

She shook her head. "Not unhappy. Scared."

His always fearless Nikki afraid? He tightened his arms around her. "I will never hurt you," he promised.

"My mom thought my dad would never hurt her," she said. "But he did—in the worst possible way a man can betray a woman, he betrayed my mother."

Now his pride stung. "I am not your father. I would never break my vows."

"Vows?" she asked, her voice tremulous.

"Yes," he said. "I know we haven't known each other very long. But I already know I want to spend the rest of my life with you."

Her face grew pale with fear. Marriage did scare her. Maybe too much. Maybe he needed to back off, at least about marrying her, for a while.

Loving her—he couldn't back off that. Even if she

never got over her fear of marriage, he would continue to love her.

"Then why are you quitting?" she asked.

"I'm not."

"But the new receptionist said he overheard you telling Cooper that you were resigning," she said, and her voice cracked with emotion, "that you didn't want any part of all this family, falling in love business."

Lars shook his head. "That wasn't me. I love all this family and falling in love business," he assured her. "I love you."

She blinked again, clearing the tears from her eyes, and smiled. "I love you, too."

And finally she sounded happy about it.

She wound her arms around his neck as he lifted her off her feet and swung her around. She giggled as she spun.

He lowered his head and kissed her smiling lips. And as always, passion overwhelmed them. He carried her up the stairs to the mattress still lying on the floor.

It had been a week since they'd seen each other—a week since they'd made love. But it felt like a lifetime since he'd kissed her, since he'd touched her...

It was all new again. He undressed her slowly, marveling in every curve he uncovered, touching and kissing every inch of silky skin.

She moaned and shifted beneath him. But Nikki was never passive. She unbuckled his belt and unzipped his pants. Her fingers stroked over his erection as she freed him.

And desire tested his control and won. He pulled off the rest of his clothes and fumbled around for a condom. He had to be inside her, had to be part of her again.

She was just as desperate for him. She grabbed the condom from him and tore open the packet with her teeth. Then she rolled the latex onto him.

He groaned. But before he thrust inside her, he made sure she was ready for him. He stroked his fingers inside her. Then he moved down her gorgeous body and he lapped at her with his tongue.

She moaned and clutched at his shoulders, pulling him up. He moved between her legs, which she locked around his waist. Her lips brushed against his chest. She was so much smaller than he was that he had to be careful not to crush her.

Because he didn't trust himself, he rose up on his knees—holding her on him. Then he clutched her hips and helped her ride him. She slid up and down, and as she did, she bit her lip to hold in a cry of pleasure.

He wanted her to scream. So he teased her nipples with his thumbs. Then he moved his hand lower and pressed his thumb against the most sensitive part of her.

She locked her legs around his waist as her inner muscles clutched his erection. And she came, screaming his name.

And the tension that had wound tightly inside him became unbearable. He thrust in and out of her until he joined her in ecstasy, his body shuddering with the power of his release. He'd never known pleasure like he'd found with her.

Spent, they lay back on the mattress, panting for breath. He rolled onto his side and, as he wound his arm around her, his knuckles hit the floor.

"I better get some furniture," he said, "since I'm staying."

"You are." It wasn't a question now. She believed him.

"I have no intention of leaving," he assured her. "Ever."

She smiled—almost shyly and said, "I have furniture."

While she might not be open to a proposal of marriage yet, she was open to living together. For now—that would do—so Lars could prove to her that he would always be faithful, that he would always keep his word and that he would love her forever.

Epilogue

Dane glanced down at the picture on his phone—the one of a smiling Emilia. She was found. He didn't need the photograph anymore. He would know her anywhere.

But he'd made a concerted effort not to see her since that day in the hospital. He would not be tempted into making the plunges his friends had; he would not be falling for anyone.

Ever.

Just like he'd told Cooper, he wanted no part of all this family and falling in love business. He just wanted to be a bodyguard.

Cooper had laughed off his concerns and assured him that was all he expected of him. "I'm not my mom," he'd said. "I'm no matchmaker."

"But Lars and Nikki—"

"You think I wanted that to happen?" Cooper had

shaken his head, but he'd been smiling. He was happy that his friend and sister were together—or would be once they both stopped avoiding each other and what they felt.

Lars and Nikki hadn't wanted it to happen, either. But it had.

Dane touched the trash can icon on his phone. He needed to send Emilia's picture there. Needed to leave River City and forget all about her and her son.

He was not a family man. He'd never had one and he never wanted one.

Maybe he would reenlist. Getting deployed again to a war zone would be safer than staying here. He would rather risk his life than his heart any day.

* * * * *

Look for Dane and Emilia's story, the next thrilling installment in the
BACHELOR BODYGUARDS *series,*
coming fall 2017!

Don't forget the previous titles in the series:

BEAUTY AND THE BODYGUARD
BODYGUARD'S BABY SURPRISE
BODYGUARD DADDY
HIS CHRISTMAS ASSIGNMENT

And if you love Lisa Childs, be sure to pick up her other stories:

RED HOT
TAMING THE SHIFTER
THE AGENT'S REDEMPTION
AGENT TO THE RESCUE
AGENT UNDERCOVER
THE PREGNANT WITNESS
CURSED
BRIDEGROOM BODYGUARD

Available now from Harlequin!

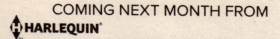
#1939 COLTON UNDERCOVER

The Coltons of Shadow Creek • by Marie Ferrarella

Betrayed by her ex-lover, Leonor Colton, the daughter of a notorious escaped serial killer, returns home to Shadow Creek to lick her wounds. She catches the eye of Josh Howard, an undercover FBI agent investigating her mother's jailbreak by keeping tabs on her children. But a hit man may force Josh to reveal himself—if Leonor doesn't end up a victim first!

#1940 THE TEXAN'S RETURN

by Karen Whiddon

Mac Morrison returns to his small hometown in Texas determined to clear his ill father's name of murder and reconnect with Hailey Green, his high school sweetheart. When evidence begins to implicate him, will he be able to save the woman he loves from a vicious killer *and* convince her they belong together?

#1941 SECRET AGENT UNDER FIRE

Silver Valley P.D. • by Geri Krotow

The True Believers are still wreaking havoc in Silver Valley when a string of fires are found to be linked to the cult. Fire chief Keith Paruso is mesmerized by Trail Hiker secret agent Abi Redland, but with an arsonist on the loose and Abi's own secrets between them, their love might turn to ash before it can even catch fire...

#1942 COVERT KISSES

Sons of Stillwater • by Jane Godman

Undercover cop Laurie Carter discovers two things when she starts investigating Cameron Delaney: that he is *very* attractive and that his girlfriend was murdered—by a serial killer! Cut off from the FBI, Laurie must turn to Cameron—a man she's not sure she can trust—to uncover the killer before he makes her his next victim.

HRSCNM0317

SPECIAL EXCERPT FROM

HARLEQUIN®

ROMANTIC suspense

*Undercover FBI agent Josh Howard is supposed to be
investigating Leonor Colton's involvement in her mother's
jailbreak, but a hitman may force him to reveal his identity
to save her life!*

*Read on for a sneak preview of
COLTON UNDERCOVER, the next book in the
THE COLTONS OF SHADOW CREEK continuity
by USA TODAY bestselling author Marie Ferrarella.*

"Back at the club, when we were dancing, you told me that I
was too perfect." *If you only knew*, he couldn't help thinking.
"But I'm not. I'm not perfect at all."

So far she hadn't seen anything to contradict her
impression. "Let me guess, you use the wrong fork when
you eat salad."

"I'm serious," Josh told her, pulling his vehicle into the
parking lot.

"Okay, I'll bite. How are you not perfect?" Leonor asked,
turning to look at him as she got out.

"Sometimes," Josh said as they walked into the B and B,
"I find that my courage fails me."

She strongly doubted that, but maybe they weren't talking
about the same thing, Leonor thought.

"You're going to have to give me more of an explanation
than that," she told him.

Making their way through the lobby, they went straight
to the elevator.

The car was waiting for them, opening its doors the
second he pressed the up button.

He'd already said too much and he knew that the more he talked, the greater the likelihood that he would say something to give himself away. But knowing he had to say something, he kept it vague.

"Let's just say that I don't always follow through and do what I really want to do," Josh said vaguely.

That didn't sound like much of a flaw to her, Leonor thought.

After getting off the elevator, they walked to her suite. She used her key and opened her door, then turned toward him.

Her heart was hammering so hard in her throat, she found it difficult to talk.

"And just what is it that you really want to do—but don't?" she asked him in a voice that had mysteriously gone down to just above a whisper.

As it was, her voice sounded very close to husky—and he found it hopelessly seductive.

Standing just inside her suite, Leonor waited for him to answer while her heart continued to imitate the rhythm of a spontaneous drumroll that only grew louder by the moment.

Josh weighed his options for a moment. Damned if he did and damned if he didn't, he couldn't help thinking. And then he answered her.

"Kiss you," he told Leonor, saying the words softly, his breath caressing her face.

She felt her stomach muscles quickening.

"Maybe you should go ahead and do that," she told him. "I promise I won't stop you."

Don't miss
COLTON'S UNDERCOVER by Marie Ferrarella,
available April 2017 wherever
Harlequin® Romantic Suspense books
and ebooks are sold.

www.Harlequin.com

Turn your love of reading into rewards you'll love with
Harlequin My Rewards

**Join for FREE today at
www.HarlequinMyRewards.com**

Earn **FREE BOOKS** of your choice.

Experience **EXCLUSIVE OFFERS** and contests.

Enjoy **BOOK RECOMMENDATIONS**
selected just for you.

PLUS! Sign up now
and get **500** points
right away!

Earn
FREE
REWARDS
HarlequinMyRewards.com
Join
Today!

MYR16R

THE WORLD IS BETTER WITH

Romance

Harlequin has everything from contemporary, passionate and heartwarming to suspenseful and inspirational stories.

Whatever your mood, we have a romance just for you!

Connect with us to find your next great read, special offers and more.

f /HarlequinBooks

🐦 @HarlequinBooks

www.HarlequinBlog.com

www.Harlequin.com/Newsletters